The Darkness at Decker Lake

A novel by

Martin H. Zuckerman

This book is a work of fiction. Places, Events and Situations in this story are purely fictional. Any resemblance to actual persons, living or dead, is coincidental.

To all those hapless homeowners who decided to live in communities run by Home Owners Associations

PROLOGUE

New York State near the Canadian border has the most fabulous and pristine forests, streams and brooks and rivers. In addition, there is an abundance of wildlife; an assortment of the most beautiful birds, deer, bears, small and large animals. The land and its natural beauty can overwhelm the senses for those that love to look at the splendor of nature, listen to the sounds of the forest and the rushing waters.

The many small towns that dot the landscape are unremarkable but have residents that form the substance of American life. They typically go about their business and enjoy less material items than those that live in the large cities and urban areas, yet they have lives that are equally if not more satisfying.

Certainly they are generally free, for the most part, of certain stresses that drive others and may not have or want the mental or physical challenges of being more successful than their neighbors.

Small town life demonstrates that it's true we can enjoy our lives without the pressure of having to work harder and longer just to earn more so we can have that large automobile, or fancy truck or super large television or the latest in technology.

At least it's true for some and in many small towns you notice the lack of these things.

This is a story about a lake community, just north of a small unremarkable town in a New York State rural area near the Canadian border.

It is a special community in that it is set in a place where senior citizens might decide to retire. The housing is reasonable, the food natural and less costly and external entertainment is rare.

The people of this community are loners, meaning that they have little need for social interaction, have few if any relatives and like it that way. Isolation is a distinct part of their emotional makeup.

It is in that setting that this story takes place and it is in that setting that may make you wonder if isolation is all that it is supposed to be or does it sometimes take a sinister form.

For the residents of Decker Lake, it is a story that they will never forget.

CHAPTER 1

It's a cold and damp evening at the shore of the Lake. Late fall typically came with many inches of snow, but here it is, the evening of Dec 2 and the weather is still just cool and damp, no signs of the winter happening. Even though it's only 4 o'clock, the dusk is beginning to roll in like a cold fog off the ocean to a warm beach. But, unlike a fog, the dusk has an eerie sound to it, an undercurrent whisper of longing and failure, hardly heard yet somehow felt deep within the soul. Something is being said, yet it is indistinguishable from actual words. It's a sort of whisper, hinting of an impending doom.

This late fall event and feeling of despair has not changed from day to day. Everyone feels it but no one talks about it at any length, as if not speaking will ward off the evil. It's been years since this Lake has had any happiness associated with it. No one can afford to leave and no one can afford to stay. It's being trapped by the unseen; the unheard; the unknown. It's the moving shadow caught at the corner of the eye. When you turn your head, no matter how quickly, there is nothing there. Yes, no one stays out after dusk, here at Decker Lake, because the Darkness is about to come in.

Goosebumps rise on the bare skin of George's arms, yet he doesn't understand why. He always dresses warm enough wearing a down vest over his short sleeve shirt and has never felt the cold before. Maybe it's his age, now that he has turned fifty-five. He has been taking his usual late afternoon walk on Decker Path, the compact dirt pathway that runs along the shore, three quarters of the way around the lake. The part of the lake not included in the path is the North section and is heavily wooded. Periodically a few quads could be heard running slowly in the wooded area, but most of the woods is so dense, and there is so much tree fall, that it is mostly impassable. Very few venture into this area. George's house is near one end of the path and the walk to the far end and back is about four miles, and if he keeps a brisk pace, it takes him about ninety minutes, He decides to turn back and quickly makes his way to his home at the west edge of the lake.

Everyone knows that it's not a good idea to be caught outside, particularly since Evelyn Jones disappeared; and without a trace, no less. No one is sure whether she was on the path or it happened elsewhere, only that she was gone. The only information that the authorities offered was that her car, clothes, jewelry and other personal belongings were also gone. So she might have moved or ran off in the middle of the night.

The woods and her home were thoroughly searched for any sign of foul play but nothing was evident. The lake, being one of the deepest in the county, was not searched. The case would remain open but unofficially it was closed. Evelyn Jones was just an 'officially missing person'. She had neither any known relatives nor any significant other. No one was pushing and no one was looking, so the case went nowhere.

George thinks to himself but is speaking out loud to keep himself company.

"When I get back home, I'll build a fire". He feels more comfortable with the .45 on his hip.

George is walking up the path to his front door and looks at the nicely appointed log cabin. The front door is set right in the center of the cabin with the two bedrooms to the right and the common area, the dining room, kitchen and living room to the left.

He opens the door with his key, a key that was hardly used as the door in a previous life was always unlocked. He steps into the small foyer, takes off his down vest and hangs it on the hook attached to the closet on the left.

He turns absentmindedly and locks the front door and recalls that before Mary left to Mildred's and before the anxiety, the door was always just left open.

The fireplace was positioned perfectly to add extra warmth and light to his living room. Mary loved the fireplace and the seasonal fires that George built. She would stare at the fire each night and watch the dancing flames. George could see her eyes moving back and forth across the logs as the flames either grew or dimmed or moved from left to right. She was so beautiful, dark hair, full and flowing, tall and slim. She had the body and agility of a gymnast and at 5'8"and140lbs, and trained in the martial arts, she could handle herself against the toughest opponent.

George realized that he was referring to Mary in the past tense and was shocked at the revelation. He decided then that he must ignore basic human nature and even his innermost feelings and deliberately think of her as alive, just not here right now and wait for her return. He would not allow or host any other thoughts.

Above the fireplace were a shotgun and a rifle. Although George did not believe in hunting, he knew enough to have some protection in the home. Both were loaded. George also carried a .45 Cal. Colt, particularly when he knew he might not be home as daylight fell.

George has, between jobs, been living at the lake for five years. Mary left him about a year ago, shortly after an incident at the lake shore that she could not or would not fully explain; just about seeing things.

He recalls that she told him, "George, I believe we need to leave this place and find something that we can enjoy somewhere else. Even though we love our evenings together and the comforts of our cabin, what was once beautiful and serene seems to be something else. Anyway, I must go to see my cousin Mildred who is having some difficulties. You understand." And of course he did.

He remembered how she expressed her reservations about the lake to him. "Something is going on here, seeing things that aren't there and hearing things that aren't being said and although I must leave in a couple of days, in the meantime you could look into finding us another place. Whatever is going on is not something we need to be involved with. I know how hard it is for you to avoid involvement when you suspect something out of the ordinary is happening."

He told her that it's important that they sell the house before they leave, that selling it while it's empty would never bring back their investment. He understood that she must go to Mildred's and he would find a way, but it might take some time. He told her to "be careful and don't forget to contact me when you get to Mildred's."

What Mary would not say in detail had to do with her experience in the forest and the shadowy figures she had seen stalking through the woods as they passed by the Hendersons' home. There were two of them, large and bulky figures. She could not determine whether they were men, but they were larger than anyone she knew. After the figures had moved on, she went to the area where they had been and found no sign of them ever having been there; no footprints, no broken twigs, nothing. She began to doubt her own senses. "Did she actually see something or did she imagine it?"

The only thing she was certain of was the silence that had been invoked by their presence and the return of the forest noises upon their departure. This and the whispering in her ear when she sat by the lake shore, demanding that she leave or suffer the consequences. When she turned her head to see who was speaking, there was no one there, but the whispering returned when she faced the lake. It was all too eerie. She and George did not come here to be subjected to terror. It was a 'retirement' and was to be their 'Happy Place'.

She could never tell George about this. He might think something was wrong with her, and then again it might drive him to begin an investigation, but she also knew she had to leave in two days.

She didn't know that George was experiencing much of the same feelings and creepiness that she felt.

She also couldn't openly mention that the Agency contacted her for a 'project' because you never knew if they were listening in to conversations. Hence the code word 'Mildred'. Coincidental or not, between the Agency and the anxiety, she knew she must leave. She wanted George to leave as well, even though they both knew that when they did, she would still be going on her own. George would know, if not exactly, why she had to go off, just not where.

A third reason she could not tell George was due to the short conversation she had with Harvey. Harvey liked their lake front house and expressed his desire to purchase the property. Harvey's expression made her afraid, not of the request, but of the look in Harvey's eye. He told her that she and George could move to the senior citizen home in Florida and they would be happier, happier than staying at the lake. Harvey's request felt more like a threat than just a friendly conversation.

No one knew about George, or what he retired from or what his 'jobs' were. She didn't want George to revert to his baser self and she knew if he believed Harvey had threatened her in any way, Harvey would be gone. And gone in such a way that no one would ever find him. No, it was better to just entice George to move on, as they had done so many times before. She knew that George was tired of all the interruptions in their lives because of his profession but also knew that once more wouldn't hurt.

George agreed to leave, but explained that he needed to wait until he sold the lake front house. Mary, just as she previously explained, packed her things, took the old Volkswagen and left two days later, telling George again that she would be staying at her cousin Mildred's.

George was waiting for the next message that she "found the ear rings" which meant she arrived safely. He might not know where she was but he would know she was safely in place.

Just because he didn't receive the arrival message didn't actually mean that something had befallen her, but he was concerned. George did not and could not notify the FBI or any police agency due to the special circumstances regarding Mary so he decided to make a general inquiry through normal procedures.

No accidents were reported. Hospitals were checked as well as motels on the route. Eventually he realized that Mary was gone, gone to Mildred's. Since there wasn't a real Mildred, he understood somewhat of her situation, but not exactly. Whatever the circumstance, if she wasn't meant to be found, she wouldn't and if something happened, well, he'd rather not think about that. It's just that she didn't send the 'found the ear rings' message. She might be in a situation where she couldn't.

Evelyn Jones disappeared a little less than three months later.

He had worked with the sheriff during the search for the Jones woman and in his mind, while he was working his way through the thick underbrush of the woods; he was also looking for Mary.

His attempt to sell the house failed. The real estate people came in for a look early in the day, but never came back with any prospective buyers. The lake Board of Directors and Harvey said they would purchase the house, but their offer was less than what he originally purchased the house for and it was too great a loss. So he stayed and hoped that Mary would contact him. He refused to believe that she was gone – permanently.

After his refusal to sell the house to the Board, he began to feel a subtle animosity from the Board members, particularly from Harvey, the President. They wanted his house and they wanted it cheap. He believed that eventually, Harvey would not take 'no' for an answer.

George would cross that bridge when it came. He certainly was not afraid of Harvey.

Decker Lake

Decker Lake is a mid-size lake community twenty miles northwest of the tiny Village of Deckersburg. The community is isolated from the village and is mostly self-sufficient. A small general store and delivery service to that store provide all the goods that seem to be needed. The lake community is said to have about 600 families, few of which are ever seen in the town. No one except for the Board of Directors and their billing agent actually know how many or who were actually living at the lake. The large majority of the residents are retired and only a few have any visitors. A small number of the homes are summer retreats for people from the city, Albany or New York and only used for a few months of the year. Some are summer rentals.

Retiring to a community so far off the beaten path is typical for those without family ties or children and most have little expectation of anyone coming in for a visit. The social activity is limited to neighbors getting together for a BBQ, which is also a rare occasion; or perhaps having a meal at Jesse's Tavern.

The entrance to Decker Lake is a one mile stretch of chip and tar road, barely able to support two cars side by side. The only sign acknowledging the way to the lake says "Decker Lake This Way". On the maps, the road is called Decker Street and comes in south of the lake. At the lake end of Decker Street is a split crossroads that leads to the center of Decker Path. The split crossroads is called Decker Lane East and Decker Lane West. You can travel about a mile down each fork of Decker Lane before you arrive at Decker Path. A number of roads split off from Decker Lane, east and west so the residents can drive to their homes. Decker Path itself is a walking path and runs east and west and completes a three quarters walk by the lake shore. Lake front homes are located and attached to Decker Path.

The property lines from the lake front homes extend from the lake side of Decker Path to the lake itself. Most lake front homes have a small dock and every three hundred feet or so, there is an easement for others at the lake to gain access. Each easement ends in a small beach and landing area for canoes and rowboats. Powered boats are not allowed at Decker Lake.

Bleeker Road is about 200 feet on the woods side of Decker Path. The lake front homes can be accessed by car from Bleeker Road.

Jesse's Tavern is at the Left Crossroads of Decker Street and the beginning of Decker Lane.

On the opposite side of the crossroads is the Decker Lake clubhouse. This is a commonplace brick building containing a small office, a kitchen area used for those times when there might be a meeting or an occasion and a single large open space with a number of round wooden tables. Chairs are place here and there but for the most part are leaning against a wall, since there have been few events and virtually no meetings for a number of years. The whole clubhouse is no more than two thousand square feet.

Only a few people ever stop in at the clubhouse and typically when they do, they travel just across the road to Jesse's for what could be arguably the best burger in the county.

Jesse's Tavern is owned and run by Harvey Paul, who purchased the place from Jesse maybe two or two and a half years earlier. Ever since Harvey took over the Tavern, the food has become intriguing, better quality and better tasting, even though he only offers a limited menu. Many of the residents enjoy the lunch and dinner offerings. (Breakfast is not served at the Tavern.)

The original owner, Jesse, told everyone he was a retired firefighter. He had no family to speak of like everyone else at the lake, other than a son, Billy, whom he called periodically just to make sure he was okay. He missed Billy but couldn't bring himself to sell the tavern and move.

"What if it didn't work out?" was his main concern.

He enjoyed running the tavern and conversing with the lake residents. George and Mary ate at the tavern regularly when Jesse ran the place, but since Harvey took over, neither ever went back. The friendly feelings that Jesse projected quickly left when Harvey began running the place. And a number of months later, there was something else, impossible to describe, since it was only a feeling. You know it when you feel it; a cold skin crawling feeling; akin to when a child is crying when he believes there is a monster in the closet or something unknown staring at him from the ceiling. No, George and Mary had this feeling and they would not frequent the tavern again. Many of the neighbors felt the same way, but others did not, or just didn't talk about it, particularly since Harvey was such a good cook and the menu offerings were delicious.

Jesse sold the tavern to Harvey and moved away. He left no forwarding address and didn't give anyone any contact information. Some of the older residents said that Jesse left the same way he came, without notice or fanfare. Yes, it was true that Jesse was in his seventies and maybe it was about time for him to leave, but he acted like a much younger man, really enjoyed the camaraderie of the tavern and no one ever considered that he would ever sell, leave or otherwise.

Human nature being what it is, Jesse was missed for a short time, but Harvey took his place and Jesse was soon just a fading memory.

Harvey was typical of a forty-three year old man, living alone. In fact, Harvey was so typical, that in order to describe him, the best description would be inconspicuous. He looked like anyone, everyone; white, brown hair, brown eyes, medium height and medium voice and in fact, medium everything. He was rarely seen outside of the tavern. He spent his time in the living area behind the tavern that Jesse had built so he could be close to his place.

Jesse loved his quarters. The living room was large enough to have a central fireplace surrounded by a two section couch and a recliner. A large 65 inch flat screen TV decorated the wall at just the right viewing height so all seated could easily watch. A few bookshelves, tables and end pieces finished the decoration. Jesse kept the place neat and Harvey liked it that way. No lady friends ever came by and he did not have any other guests. Everyone thought it was a bit peculiar but most minded their own business and didn't spread unfounded rumors.

But Harvey cooked a great steak and offered an assortment of special dinners, which is rare in a small community.

What could be considered as interesting for someone who seemed to be an entrepreneur, Harvey did not advertise his establishment and was satisfied just serving the Decker Lake community. He hired a handyman, waiter, cleanup person to help with the everyday tasks at Jesse's. This was Barry. Barry was a very large man and looked like he could be an offensive lineman for a football team. He always dressed in all white; pants and V-neck T-shirt with sleeves, almost like a uniform. He was quite hairy, at least with the parts in obvious view, arms and chest, with the exception of his head, which had typical male pattern baldness. Barry kept his thinning hair closely cut, almost shaven. He probably only shaved his face twice a week and had that unshaven look that many believe is a fashion statement but others believe it makes you look like a thug. With the exception of this employment, no one had ever spotted Barry before so it would seem that Harvey knew him prior to moving to the lake.

Harvey also took advantage of the lack of energy by the retired residents and became the President of the Board of Directors. Everyone believed that Harvey, being younger, would have the energy and ability to ensure that the lake was clean, roads well cared for and the community served as it should be. Serving the community was Harvey's prime consideration and that's exactly what he said when introducing himself for the Board of Directors position as President. With no opposition, he was elected unanimously.

Prior to running for the office, Harvey wanted to see how difficult the position might be, so he reviewed engineering reports about the lake and found that the lake was a natural body of water, was fed from a number of streams and had the proper water replacement factor to maintain the lake's clarity.

The roads were chip and tar and did not require a lot of maintenance. Plowing throughout the winter was a rather simple task, and he outsourced this to a local company, which came in after each snow storm and quickly cleaned the community's roads. No one cared about events, so he didn't have to provide any.

He was able to concentrate on the two major tasks that he needed to do to maintain the reason behind all his efforts; making money the easy way and furthering the scheme he was putting in motion.

Serving the community as the President of the Board and serving the community as the owner of Jesse's Tavern would give him the position he needed. Harvey loved serving the community. Harvey loved making money. Above all, Harvey loved a good scheme.

Shortly after Harvey purchased Jesse's Tavern and became the President of the Homeowner's Association, a second couple, Phil and May Gruenweld, moved in, also younger, more near Harvey's age, not typical of who normally purchased and moved to Decker Lake.

The lake owned a number of properties purchased from those who either passed on and were buried in the small cemetery just behind the town, or left and moved into nursing facilities in Utica, New York. Recently and coincidentally, shortly after Harvey purchased Jesse's Tavern, those who decided they needed to move on to a senior citizen facility began choosing one outside of Pensacola Florida.

Harvey was very familiar with the general managers of the home in Florida, who were looking for more residents. The home was accredited and cost considerably less than the one in New York. The weather was better and transportation to the home was included in the upfront fees. It was a package that the older residents found hard to resist. The Mallorys, whose home was purchased by Phil and May, were the first elderly couple to move to the Sunshine Forever Home in Florida. A postcard sent back to Jesse's Tavern addressed to Harvey, expressed their happiness with the great choice and hoped that others would follow. There was no better place than the Sunshine Forever Home.

Harvey posted the card on the bulletin board in the clubhouse.

The particular property purchased by Phil and May was just off the right fork as you left Jesse's Tavern. It was in a central location built on the side of a hill and had a view of the lake, just a mile down the road.

Phil was a strongly built man, a bit taller than George, which meant he was more than 6'3" in height. He had a strange look about him. Whenever he said hello to a neighbor, he made deep eye contact. He smiled a tight lipped toothless smile which looked predatory; sort of what a wolf or coyote might demonstrate when looking at prey.

The narrow nose, ridged eyebrows and long chin added to the aggressive look and most could not look directly at him for too long a time.

His wife didn't work or express any desire to talk to the neighbors. She kept to herself and rarely was seen outside of the home, except when she and Phil ate in Jesse's Tavern.

Phil was appointed by Harvey to the lake Board of Directors to fill an empty spot and May was appointed and acted as the secretary and treasurer until they could find someone to fill the position. The by-laws allowed the appointment and even though it was improper for a husband and wife to fill two or more positions, no one complained or raised the issue.

It seemed that George was the only concerned resident but he was too pre-occupied and later on, with the disappearance of Mary, he certainly had no time to worry about this. The annual dues had not gone up for years and the rare annual meeting issued the same budgets over and over. In fact, he could not remember when they last had an annual meeting and the only election was the one initiated by Harvey.

To the left of the clubhouse is a small general store owned by the community and run by Micah Townsend, a family fixture in the area. The Townsends have lived in the area pretty much forever. They traced their family to the some of the first European immigrants. Hard working people, their descendants had worked farms, stores and land in this area for generations and Micah may be the last of the direct line as he had never married, never had children and no other relatives were ever mentioned. Micah had a long term no cost lease to run the store with annual renewals. He did a good job and the community was never without anything they needed. Any items that were not stocked were ordered quickly and readied for pickup by the residents.

The nearby village of Deckersburg was more than 20 miles away. The single road to town, Decker Street, is comprised of asphalt put down many years before, now broken with the passage of time, compressed dirt and newly placed stones. The road is built down a steep incline and includes sharp turns without barricaded edges. It is a two-way road, but in a number of spots, only one car could safely pass at a time, making the trip into town hazardous in good weather. In bad weather, it became nearly impassable.

Deckersburg

Deckersburg is a micro town, actually incorporated as a village but everyone calls it a town. It's in New York State near the Canadian border; not even on a map. The nearest large town is Vermontville, NY, more than forty miles drive. Deckersburg has just one main street and no traffic lights or stop signs, just a twenty mile an hour speed limit.

Cars traveling through the village have an actual reason to be there as there is no purpose for anyone to come off the thruway to pay a visit. There are no antique stores or special attractions. It's just a faraway place where retired people come to live up at the lake, or working people live in the village itself, serving the community and the surrounding farmers and farmhands. No one makes much money so you will never see fancy items in the few stores or expensive autos.

It's a shirt sleeve and dungaree community, like so many thousands of very small towns and villages across America.

Main Street has six central shops, a number of empty store fronts and a few that have become clubhouses for the local fraternal groups. The centrally occupied shops are a bait shop, barber, rural Post Office, butcher/market, real estate, a bar and a sheriff's office. Across the street are two churches, one Evangelical and the other Lutheran, and a small park/sitting area that is between the two.

A Greek style diner is just to the south, outside of town and is attached to the motel. A small drug store is attached to the diner. The pharmacist's assistant is a nurse practitioner and can handle minor emergencies for the community, provide flu shots, and other lesser medical procedures. All the shops and stores in town are small two-story buildings, unattached but near each other, each separated by an alley. Above the few shops are the living quarters for the owners.

Located behind the shops, separated by a two lane road, Cemetery Road, and with its' own entrance, is the town cemetery. The cemetery is a 70 acre partly wooded area of land with a two-foot wooden picket fence. The fence was white at one time as it's possible to still see a few splashes of white paint embedded in the worn grains of the wood. The fence is in a state of disrepair.

The village owns the rights to the cemetery; making it a village property and it seems no individual really cares about its condition. Old man Joshua, as he is known by everyone, takes care of the area, mows the grass, trims the greenery the best he can and attempts to maintain the fence. In return, the village pays for a small room for him to live in above the bar and gives him just enough money to eat and take care of a few personal needs. Between that and his Social Security, the old man seems to do okay.

The cemetery gate has been missing for a number of years but no one, not even the growing number of teenagers, seems interested in going into the cemetery; and others enter for no other reason than burying someone in a family plot or visiting a deceased relative.

Driving down Cemetery Road from its beginning at the crossroads near the motel and looking to the left, you can see the rear of the town shops and the alleys between. Because each alley is wide enough for a truck to stop and deliver packages and then drive through the other side to either the next stopping point or to go back to the main road, the traffic in town is circular in nature with trucks driving and delivering down Main Street and back around through Cemetery Road to the crossroads for the trip back to Vermontville. The town shopping area is just two streets in length and the cemetery gate, although missing, is located at the center of the two streets.

From the opening where the gate would be, you can see the rear of the Market, the shop owned by Ivan Pochenko.

Ivan owns the butcher shop and market. He calls it Ivan's Market because his name is Ivan and it's his store. He is possessive and proud of his shop. Ivan stocks fresh fruits and vegetables and the small grocery area on the right has enough diversity to satisfy the town's needs. He is also the butcher and has fresh meat delivered weekly. He uses his finely honed skills to cut the meat into superbly proportioned sections. He positions the cuts appropriately in the refrigerated counter glass cases at the left of the shop. This makes it easier for the customers to make selections.

Any meat that does not sell or have the appearance of being fresh, he grinds into hamburger and sells it as pre-made burgers to the diner or Jesse's Tavern. Everybody loves his burgers. Since he does well on the grocery and fresh fruit section, he keeps the meat prices down so his customers can afford a good cut.

He has it firmly in his mind that his customers are also his neighbors and friends even though he has few emotions or feelings about anything.

He also delivers to the general store at Decker Lake and provides groceries and meat selections to Jesse's Tavern.

Ivan is proud of his shop and his status in town.

Ivan is in his mid-sixties, and like many of the people in the area, came from elsewhere. He was born many years before as Karl Romanz in Neag, a small town in the Carpathian mountainous area of Romania.

The Russian army had a small base just north of the town. Periodically, runners would come to the army base to deliver messages by hand. Once they completed their tasks, they would move on to wherever they had come from.

Many years before, when the Russians first came to the town, they questioned many of the residents, a number of which never returned. If any in the town stepped forward to inquire of the missing, they also were gone. Karl's parents and grandmother were taken away when he was just nine years old. He never saw them again and was raised by his grandfather who told him to be quiet and never speak of this again.

He hated the Russians; hated them with a passion so deep that nothing would be beyond him to take revenge. As Karl grew into manhood, his hatred became more intense. He stood at 6'5" and weighed nearly 300 pounds. But he was solid muscle from all the years of hard work in the fields, downing trees and chopping them into firewood, digging trenches and many other menial tasks.

He worked at the Russian army base now and then, lifting broken machine parts and hauling trash to the dump just north of the base. While he worked, he mapped the base in his head and took note of the activity; activity which occurred at regular intervals. He also discovered that the messengers were not Russians, but usually from some other area of the Soviet Union, possibly Kazakhstan or Uzbekistan.

His grandfather, who owned the small butcher shop in town, taught him the trade. By the time Karl was twenty-three he was an adept butcher, was fully grown and had a good knowledge of the Russian base. He also developed a thorough and fully active sociopathic personality and was incapable of remorse or compassion.

He wanted revenge and began to formulate his plan, but he must wait until his grandfather died and the butcher shop was his.

A few short years later, his grandfather passed away and the shop was his. The plan he developed in his mind could now be made into reality.

He built a small storage area about three meters by four meters in size, created an opening in the back wall of the shop and attached the storage area so it became an extension to the existing building. It was made extremely sturdy, with double layers of wood and sheep skin as an insulator between the layers. He then built a new wooden block table for butchering meat and added shelving to stock the items. He needed a place to hang his cleavers, knives and other utensils, so he took a wooden shaft and using metal strapping at each end, nailed it to the ceiling above the cutting table, so that the shaft was just above eye level positioned horizontally.

The internal furnishings being completed and with the double wooden walls and sheepskin as an insulator, the storage area was nearly soundproof and perfect for the next part of his plan.

One day a messenger rode his bicycle through town to the Russian camp and delivered his package to the Commander. The next day, following the usual pattern, the messenger left the base at 6 o'clock in the evening.

Karl laid in wait for the messenger, hiding behind a tree at a particularly deserted stretch of road. As the messenger passed by the tree, Karl slammed him on the forehead with a tree branch larger than a baseball bat. The messenger literally flew from his cycle and landed with a thud on the ground. The impact of the branch cracked his skull, rendering him nearly dead and totally unconscious. Karl finished the task with a quick knife thrust under the chin and into the brain. The slender blade would penetrate and not produce much blood.

Karl then hid the bicycle in the woods for disposal later in the evening. He wrapped the body in an old rug and making certain that no one saw him, carried it to the storage area behind his shop. The grisly task of slaughtering and butchering the body did not bother him as he contemplated the next phase of his plan and the eventual results. But before he began, he needed to dispose of the bicycle. Taking tools with him, he made his way back into the wooded area where he hid the bicycle. He disassembled it and brought it to the old cemetery just west of the town. He had found the perfect place to hide the metal parts, in an old mass grave from World War II. When he completed this task, he looked at the area and was satisfied that it still looked undisturbed. Now he could go back to the shop and work on the Messenger.

Looking down at the body, he made mental notes on the best action to take and how it must be done.

He butchered and trimmed all the usable meat from the messenger, created steaks and cuts that resembled the cows and pigs in the field and ground up the rest into chop meat. The skin, bones, organs and unusable parts were taken later that night to the cemetery and buried into existing graves, carefully covering the fresh dirt with the older dirt so no one would notice any disturbance.

The Russian commander came to the shop every two weeks or so to buy meat for his troops and he was sold what was left of the messenger. The commander praised Karl on his delicious offerings and would not know what he was eating for many years. No one missed the messengers as many of them would periodically just run off and go back to their own lands. The Russians knew that this desertion was a regular occurrence and there were plenty more of them to be had.

And Karl was very good at his task, his plan and the production of meat for the Russians. The Russians paid him well to enjoy their dinners.

As the years went by and Karl neared forty-five, he decided it was time to leave. Everyone was talking about the soon ending Russian domination of his country and he believed it was in his best interest to leave as soon as possible. He applied for a visa to America and organized the journey with the help of the American consulate. He had information from his grandfather that there were relatives in New York City, in a small area called Brooklyn.

"Although they were shady characters," his grandfather said "if he ever made his way to America, he must contact them."

They could do almost anything. He had the money from the Russian Commander, saved for all those years and would use it to change his name to Ivan Pochenko and buy a small butcher shop, in a remote area in America, where no one would come looking for him.

He would also have the satisfaction of knowing that the Russians would eventually come to the knowledge of what they have been eating for so many years. He would see to that.

Karl, now renamed Ivan Pochenko, searched for a remote location where he could open a small shop and live undetected. Many of the Ukrainians and Romanians that fled from Europe and entered the United States with visas changed their identities and moved into the countryside.

His 'friends' in Brooklyn were very helpful, for a price. Using them and others, he was given the name of a small town in New York near the Canadian border called Deckersburg that actually had a market, but did not have a butcher. In fact the nearest butcher was forty miles away. Most of the meat products sold in the market were frozen items, hardly palatable. An older fellow owned the store and was nearly retired. Purchasing this place might not be very difficult.

Karl made his way to Deckersburg and met with the owner who quickly agreed to sell his store to such a 'nice man'. A pile of cash was extremely convincing and caused a quick sale of the property.

Karl, now Ivan, was the proud new owner of the market, which he would turn into a butcher shop and market, 'Ivan's Market'.

"I am free at last," he declared with a wide smile, "I am free at last. Grandpa, you would be proud."

A year after he arrived in America and finished accomplishing his goals, he sent a letter to the commander with the story and the location of the uneaten remains. Although he might never know if his letter reached the monsters that ravaged his town and killed his family, it was satisfaction, nonetheless.

To the right of the butcher shop/market owned by Ivan, is the real estate office. The real estate office is owned and run by Derik Manheim, an attorney who no longer practices law. The word on him is that he was indicted for unethical practices associated with the embezzlement of two non-profit organizations, a volunteer fire department in Vermont and a Veteran's charity in Pennsylvania.

Although indicted, the case did not proceed due to a lack of credible evidence and the disappearance of two witnesses from the fire department. Even so, his license to practice law was suspended for two years. Although he was eventually re-instated, his disreputable behavior followed him from town to town and state to state and he decided that changing his profession was a sound idea. He purchased the real estate office, and his legal knowledge helped him to get customers as well as offer some consultancy to a few businesses outside of town. He made certain that no one overtly knew that he had a license to practice law.

Derik Manheim is a middle aged man, 5'9" tall, heavy set, balding with a fading purple scar that runs from the tip of his left eye above his left ear and ends in a nasty faded greenish knob at the back of his skull. He was borne Derik Aikenhead. As a youngster, he was bullied and laughed at because of his name, which his young friends shortened to 'crap head' which was just one among other more vicious iterations. His parents told him to ignore the insults as their family name originated in Ireland and was considered one of status in the old country. For Derik, it was impossible to ignore.

The continual harassment pushed him to the point of tears. As a result, he became sullen and angry and he became an offensive, self-centered and arrogant child, teenager and young adult. One evening, while drinking in a local bar, he made a comment about someone's girl and received the scar in return. The scar left a mark in his demeanor as well. He was able to masquerade the arrogance and the erratic behavior when in public using laughter as a shield but allowed it to display itself in his shady dealings in college, selling hash, and essays. His persona became as ugly and scarred as his face.

When he came of age, at twenty-one, he legally changed his name to Manheim, the last name of his high school English teacher. He admired this particular teacher for his balanced approach to teaching as well as a no tolerance policy for bullying.

He attended the State University of New York and decided to major in Law. When he received his law degree and eventually passed the Bar, and attempted to try cases, he found that his lack of quick thinking developed into a thought stammer; something that happens when you can't find the words but need to continue speaking. Others typically overcome this problem with practice but not Derik. It just became worse.

The result was an inability to speak effectively in court. He was considered a buffoon by his peers. In fact, he was actually laughed at during a court hearing where he stammered attempting to ask questions of a witness; to the point where the witness leaned away from him to avoid being spit upon.

He began to believe that the whispering in the court was about him, the laughter was about him, and the side glances were about him. He could imagine those around him calling him a 'crap head' or worse. His paranoia being openly evident, he again became sullen and angry, with a penchant for revenge which he managed to keep well in check. Another side effect of his internal anger was the lack of social activity. He could not maintain a relationship, so after a while he just didn't try and if he needed anything special, he just paid for it and went home.

Eventually, he used his non-speaking legal ability to assist the embezzlers in the two non-profits to continue their thieving ways while at the same time covering up his participation in the illegal activity. It's true that being ugly, both inside and out, may have caused him to act inappropriately and he may have been an ineffective courtroom attorney, but no one said he was stupid. Having sociopathic tendencies made you unable to understand the damage to others. Those he assisted weren't sociopaths, just thieves.

As far as the missing witnesses were concerned, never to be found was a good condition.

The sheriff's office is located to the north end of town, set apart from the other stores and two story buildings by 100 yards of empty lots, a few small storefronts, a knitting shop, consignment store, used clothing, and such.

The sheriff position was unfilled for a number of years, but with the growth of the farming community, a nearby high school and other general issues, the Deckersburg town council decided that filling this position was an imperative. They decided to place an ad in the local Newspapers and place another onto the Internet using Linked In as the agent. A number of resumes came in to fill the opening but one stood out from the others.

It was the age and experience of the applicant that led them to respond, interview and then hire Bob Winkler, just a few years before Jesse sold his Tavern.

Bob Winkler came to the town to become the sheriff five years earlier. He had retired from the Philadelphia Police Department at the age of forty-five as the Chief of Detectives. He was well known for his skills and cleared more cases in Philly than any other detective in recent memory. After winning many service awards, he came into political disfavor from the Chief of Police, who believed that Bob was after his position.

Bob suffered with two years of frustration, no pay increases, and detrimental comments in his police record so he decided to pack it in and retire. He never married and had no family to reckon with, so when he read an advertisement for a qualified person to be sheriff of the small town of Deckersburg, he jumped at the chance, applied for and was given the opportunity. It didn't pay nearly as well as the police, but he had a nice monthly pension and along with the sheriff's salary could support himself quite nicely.

He was offered a rental house in Decker Lake but feeling it was too far from the town, and particularly in inclement weather; he rejected the idea and took a small apartment on the second floor of the only motel. He decided not to live above the sheriff's office, even though the space was available. He felt it would be like working full time, twenty four hours each day, if he lived where he worked.

Most of the sheriff's duties were to oversee real estate foreclosures, a few unpaid parking ticket liens or repos, legal notice delivery, and such mundane matters, but he still fancied himself a police officer, a solid detective and could not or would not end his focus on the matters of illegal activity. Should he find something of worthwhile attention, his position dictated that he contact the State Police, not take action himself. He also had a direct link to a number of officials in Vermontville, including the District Attorney.

In the meantime, his gentle smile and pleasant personality appealed to many of the residents and they began to refer to him as Sheriff Bob rather than Officer Winkler or Sheriff Winkler. Bob liked the familiar reference.

He became friendly with a number of townsfolk and up at Decker Lake with Jesse and with George, one of the residents who moved in just about the same time that he took the job.

George was something else, intelligent, honest, moved like a cat. Mary was nice but kept to herself. He knew all the shopkeepers, even though they were but a few and he met the owner of the motel outside of town. It was there that his jurisdiction ended. Everything seemed normal, as normal as any small community could be.

The lake residents came into town periodically where they had their hair cut, shopped at Ivan's, bought some bait. The bar served coffee and sandwiches so they could sit around and talk about whatever inane things the elderly talk about. If you listened in to some of those conversations, you might hear a group at a table talking about five different things at the same time, answering one question with a completely different answer. The strangest part about the conversation was that they all knew what they were talking about and enjoyed the verbal interaction.

What was very noticeable was the general demeanor of the lake people. They were happy, thoughtful and enjoyed each other's company, at least when in the town. The smiles on their faces were real.

And then things began to change. It started about a year after Jesse sold the Tavern to Harvey, the lake people stopped coming to town as often. Bob could understand that they were getting older, but they were always getting older. Homes up there were sold and bought by other elderly people. Overall, nothing should be changing this drastically. Things were becoming different. It was just strange.

Nowadays, it was a rare occasion when someone from the lake came into town on some errand. When they did, they were always accompanied by another, usually a Decker Lake board member, walking close by and somehow preventing any random conversation with local town's people. It wasn't a physical prevention, but in some way a noticeable mental aversion was placed against holding a conversation with someone. All the answers were given by the companion.

The lake resident seemed to want to answer, but either stammered, or stopped in the middle of a word. A palpable, projected fear could be felt as the two walked by, did the errand and went back to the car for the trip back to the lake.

Or maybe Bob just imagined it. It was true that many of the elderly residents of the lake did not drive even though they owned cars and many of those that did drive were afraid to drive down that treacherous Decker Street, so the younger residents, at this time the younger residents were the board members, brought them into town.

It was also true that when someone is doing you a favor, you didn't want to take advantage of the favor by having long conversations with town's people and holding up the person that drove you.

To some of the people in town, in particular Sheriff Bob, the strangeness of the lake community, its people, the isolation and perceived fear on the faces of those that have been seen, demanded some sort of action.

Bob was determined that he must tell someone, but who could he turn to?

"Certainly not the State Police."

What would he say? "Hey, guys, the Decker Lake people look sad. There must be something wrong up there."

No, he would talk to someone who might understand even though he knew it would likely be just a one sided conversation.

As long as he told someone, he would have done his duty and maybe have a clear conscience; maybe but not likely. He decided to make an appointment with the District Attorney in Vermontville. The DA's secretary told him that the DA would be in the office in the morning and had appointments in the afternoon. She scheduled him for 10:00AM and said "please don't be late."

Bob drove to Vermontville the next morning to make the appointment and 'would not be late'.

Bob thought about the DA. "Somehow this overweight, slovenly, loud mouth and generally uneducated fellow, Izzy Duggin, had won the election for DA. It was common knowledge that Duggin was as closed minded and lazy as most of the residents of the area."

"Don't make waves, do as little work as possible, keep your mind narrow" were appropriate slogans for much of the community and this applied to Duggin as well.

"I suppose that's why he won the election," thought Bob, "he reflected the thoughts and habits of the community."

Bob waited outside Duggin's office for what he thought was an eternity. Duggin's secretary told Bob that it would just be a bit more time and the DA would see him. Inside the office, the DA was just finishing reading the latest issue of Mountain Men unleashed. He knew Bob was outside, but would make him wait, make him upset, put him off his game and then when Bob was overtly disturbed, he would let him enter, listen to whatever story he had, tell him "no" and send him on his way. Duggin loved treating the hicks that way, look at the angry faces when he finished with them and knowing they could not say anything. "These people were easy pickin's for a smart guy like me."

When he finally gained entrance to his Excellency's office, and relayed the story about his concerns about Decker Lake, Duggin, with the typical smug politician look on his face and smirk on his lips, narrated a stock answer which included telling Bob it was better minding his own business and other nonsense and he was summarily dismissed. Then he looked directly at Bob's face, waiting for that angry look in return and didn't see any anger, just pity. "Well, that sucked," thought Duggin.

Bob decided to let it go for now, but kept it in his mind for future action. Everyone knew that the DA was an asshole and hopefully someone would replace him; hopefully with someone who cared to do the job rather than sit on his fat ass.

Of course, besides this guy being a jerk, he knew that his story was basically unsound. “The people at Decker Lake are sad. They don’t talk much. They only come to town with a younger person who drives them.”

“How do you relay a feeling, a sense of something wrong, and an emotion, to someone who can never understand? Like this guy Izzy.”

Chapter 2

December 15, Harry and Merle Henderson, retired and nearing 83 and 81 respectively, fell behind on their Dues. Their medical bills were enormous and taking a toll on their finances and savings, so the last bill they thought of paying was maintenance for Decker Lake. Even after receiving a number of arrears notices, and being taken to court, they still could not pay.

Harvey, the Home Owners Association President, was coming after them with the same ferocity that he displayed when the Murphys ran into the same problem. Harry didn't know what to do. He was friendly with George, so one day while both were walking along the lake shore path, he brought up the situation.

"George, what should we do? We can't pay the dues. We are in arrears three years. They won't take a payment plan. They are demanding that we sell the house and move into a facility or anywhere that we can afford. They want their money! Of course, they're recommending the home in Florida, It seems okay but we have a few friends in Utica. I think we'll go there."

"Harry, can you borrow the money from family or some of your past associates? I wish I could help, but we're all in the same situation. I'm also retired and after Mary left, I spent our savings trying to find her, using detective agencies and anyone who might know anything. I wish I could be more helpful."

George kept to his story as part of his and Mary's cover. He liked the old neighbors but wasn't in a position to assist them, even if he could.

"I understand, George. What makes this worse is the look I get from Harvey and the other board members. They can't wait to get my property. I feel like a piece of meat when I talk to them. What kind of people did we let in here? Why did we elect them as board members? They seem to be there for life. We haven't had an election for years and even if we did, I believe everyone would be too fearful of running against them."

"Harry, things will work out. Peg and Joe Murphy have moved down to the Home about two months ago and seem to be happy with the surroundings. Sometimes our own frustrations make things seem worse than they are, make attitudes seem harsh. I'm not saying that you are misinterpreting Harvey's attitude. I don't like him either, but what really matters is your own future, not someone else's mercenary motives. You need to do what you feel is best for you and Merle."

"George, that does make sense. I'll talk to Merle and see where that takes us. If I don't see you, try to perk up. Like you said, things have a way of working out for the best."

Since Jesse sold the tavern and Harvey took over a couple of years ago, a number of residents of the lake had sold and moved to the Sunshine Forever Home. The turnover was large at Decker Lake with so many homes occupied by seniors, so it was not unusual for sales to take place once or twice per month.

Derik was the prime realtor involved and Harvey typically helped the sale along. Housing prices were stagnant and in many cases were sold for less than the original purchase price, but with the seniors' understanding that Medicaid would eventually be paying the cost of their residency in Florida, they were less concerned about the money they received.

The last residents to sell prior to the Henderson's were the Murphys.

Peg and Joe Murphy, both in their late 80's, had a similar problem a few months earlier, but unlike Harry, they called the Sunshine Forever Home and decided to sell their lake house and move to Florida.

Working closely with Derik and Harvey, they managed to recoup what their house cost them and had a little extra to buy a few furnishings when they arrived at the home and their new duplex apartment. With any luck they might outlive their money and get onto Medicaid.

As was usual with the sale, the Sunshine Forever Home organized transportation to take them and some of their personal belongings. Peg and Joe were told it would arrive the next afternoon, right in front of their house.

At 2:00PM the next day, a small moving van, called a Transport, with a 'Sunshine Forever Home' decal on each side, pulled up in front of their house, and packed whatever the Murphys felt they could bring with them to the facility. The rest was moved to the consignment store in town, actually a part of the motel complex.

They stepped into the Sunshine Forever Home Transport, left without even saying good-bye. But that was the way it was in Decker Lake. There were few relationships and even less camaraderie. What really mattered and what mattered to Peg and Joe Murphy was living the best they could into their old age.

Two weeks after they moved to Florida, a postcard arrived at Jesse's Tavern from Peg and Joe, describing how happy they were in their new digs. It was well worth the quick sale to the Board of Directors.

The senior residence was reasonably priced, and eventually they would be on Medicaid and not have to worry about the costs. The card was signed Peg and Joe Murphy and placed onto the bulletin board at the clubhouse for all to see.

Harry and Merle, having read the card, began to feel encouraged by the seemingly good thoughts by Peg and Joe and made a decision. They would contact Harvey and try to get the best price possible for their Decker property, organize their way into the Sunshine Forever Home and reunite with the Murphys.

Everyone knew that it's always better to know someone when moving to a new place. They had no children or family to speak of. They outlived their real friends from the old days. The only people they actually spoke to at Decker Lake were George and Mary and with Mary gone, George had seemingly been depressed and kept to himself.

"It's time to let go and move," said Harry, and Merle quickly agreed.

Just as the Murphys did, Harry and Merle organized the move to the Sunshine Forever Home. Since neither could drive, The Lake Board of Directors organized the Transport to come and take them with their smaller furniture and personal items that would fit, to the Sunshine Forever Home. It would be a two day journey, but in the end, they would be in a better place and with the Murphys.

Time passes quickly in a small community and just as with the Murphys, a post card arrived to Jesse's Tavern from the Henderson's, describing how great it was at the home and how they were enjoying the company of the Murphys, the activities offered and the general sense of well-being. This post card, signed by Harry and Merle, and like the previous one by Peg and Joe, was pinned to the bulletin board in the clubhouse.

A few months after the Hendersons moved to the Sunshine Forever Home, another couple, the Goodmans decided to sell and move and then a Mrs. Magon, Sue Middleton, and Carl Peters, all during a nine month period. Although others living at the lake had also moved, they went elsewhere, either to the nursing home in Utica or to places like Arizona and New Mexico where the weather was more suitable, dry and warm.

George didn't go to Jesse's Tavern very often but as he walked the lake grounds, he did stop in the clubhouse on occasion. Looking at the bulletin board, he noticed that there were many postcards from residents that had sold their properties and moved away, some to the Sunshine Forever Home and some to other places. There was something unusual about the postcards, something he could not put his finger on. He decided to take a picture of the cards and review it in the privacy of his home, not wanting to draw attention to himself.

He was also concerned about the Hendersons. Even though they sent correspondence about their arrival at the Sunshine Forever Home and their surprise to how nice it was, there was no further contact. He went into town to the diner and while there he decided to place a call to the Home from a local pay phone. He was told by the clerk, a woman named Henny, that they were not available at that time. A message would be left for them. Still, there was no response. Strange but not unusual for the elderly to forget about the past and just continue on with the present.

"After all," he thought, "they were not actually friends, just in-passing neighbors who said hello." Yet, he had that nagging thought that Harry was concerned about Harvey, Harvey's venal attitude and even though they made the choice, it would just seem natural that Harry would call him and let him know all was okay.

George returned home and sat on his couch, put on the television and prowled deeply into his own thoughts.

It's not easy retiring from the Agency. Most of his colleagues did not retire. They were killed in the line of duty, or otherwise. The management needed solid convincing that George was a safe bet to retire and not be retired.

This was not the CIA, FBI, NSA or other familiar name that the public was aware of; but a clandestine group acting under a separate authority. It was highly unusual for any agent to survive to the age of retirement. George was the best of them, with firearms, hand to hand combat, edged weapons and makeshift weapons. He had a visual eidetic memory and was able to analyze disparate scenes with clarity that others could not.

Even though he 'retired', he never left the Agency. No one left the Agency. He was contacted a number of times to analyze circumstances, assist with operations, take out an enemy. There are some things that you can't leave behind, things that you immerse yourself in to the point of losing your own identity. The Agency and the work was one such thing.

Mary also worked for the Agency but in a lesser position as a field analyst, not an operational field agent. She provided material support, backup and a back door. She was also trained to finish whatever needed finishing, if that were the circumstance. The fact of her recent disappearance could mean a number of things. Someone from the past found her while she was working an assignment, since she used the 'Mildred' term. The Agency could not provide him information, or would not. In either case, she was gone.

One thing he was certain of that once working for the Agency, even though you were "retired" you were always an Agent. And that included Mary. But he never received the 'found the earrings' message.

He and Mary moved a number of times due to circumstances that might conflict with his 'retirement'. "This lake house," he thought, "might be the last, best place to lose themselves in themselves". He didn't want to think about it, but with Mary gone, he could not put the nagging thoughts about those postcards behind him.

George and Mary took the last name "Flynn" to pose as a married couple wherever they decided to live. They were not married but truly enjoyed each other's company whenever their assignments allowed them to get together.

Many times they were apart for lengthy periods and in a few situations it was years before they saw each other. They agreed, in the beginning, that their work would never allow them to make their arrangement permanent. They also agreed that they could share a life by having a settled location to meet whenever the circumstance allowed.

A number of times, when they were younger, they were forced to leave one location and move to another, for the sake of security; but they always managed to find each other again and share the moment. Now that they were older, they thought they might be able to spend more time together and so they purchased the lake front house at this remote community, Decker Lake.

George went to the bathroom in the hallway between the master bedroom and the office. He looked into the mirror and staring back at him was the face of a 55 year old man, not many wrinkle lines other than a few at the corner of his eyes. His green eyes still had that glaring look and when he stared at a subject, they seemed to feel he was looking into their heads, not at them. He was still square of jaw, a slightly cleft chin, eyes wideset, narrow nose. He could be anyone, but his 6'2" , 215lb well-muscled frame hadn't changed much and he still exercised and practiced each day to keep himself limber.

George unpacked his analysis tools, the large white boards, Agency laptop and satellite transceiver. He began building the visual aid to better understand the nagging reference to the postcards. He had a bedroom set aside for just this type of work;

windows had been blacked out from the inside and looked normal from the outside. Electronic eavesdropping countermeasures were in place. The house was secure and he was armed. It actually felt good to be active and he felt positive for the first time in years. He loved having a 'workroom'.

Chapter 3

George studied the center white board for what seemed like hours. He placed the picture of the postcards on the board and drew a direct arrow drawn to Harvey Paul, who as President of the Association was the organizer and prime individual for moving the residents to the Sunshine Forever Home in Florida.

He drew an arrow from Harvey to Barry, whom he believed had known Harvey for a lot longer than thought. Who else had a hand in the sales of the properties?

There was Derik. That was one remarkable character. Even when speaking softly, he could make your skin crawl. He had the habit of looking right into you. None of the other residents could stand to be around him for too long.

George's first inclination was to look at this entire scheme to be nothing more than a land grab con, but something didn't make sense.

As he continued his gaze at the picture, he began focusing in on the individual postcards themselves. What about them seemed out of place? What?

Suddenly, like the proverbial lightbulb being lit above your head in a comic strip, he saw it. Two years earlier, when someone went to the Sunshine Forever Home, there were a number of postcards, typically spaced from the first two weeks, then a month, then two months, then four months and none came after the first year. All the dates were randomly spaced.

That was characteristic of human behavior. As time passed by, particularly with older people who didn't have much in the way of friendly ties in the first place, contact would start and then taper off until it stopped completely. Those who remained at the lake would begin to forget those that left, particularly since they had little contact with them anyway.

The unusual was what he was looking for and there it was. Just four months ago, beginning with the Murphys, only two postcards were sent from every departing resident. The first one came two weeks after entering the Home and the next and last postcard came two weeks after that. He could understand if this pattern was intermittent or spaced across the entire two years, but the first eighteen months had this random pattern and the last eight months had the same static two postcards spaced at two weeks and two weeks later. That was more than strange and indicated to George that the post cards were either not being sent by the new residents or were being encouraged at those intervals by the staff. Either way, something felt wrong.

In addition, the postcard anomalies began just after Evelyn Jones disappeared. “Coincidence?” he thought, “not likely.” George did not believe in coincidences, particularly when criminal behavior was involved. Somehow, everything had a meaning, a cause and effect, just like the air displaced by the wings of a butterfly.

Motive, opportunity, intent, were all aspects of a crime. But this was perplexing because of the systematic approach that was occurring. He needed to somehow cause a change, or put a break in the sequence.

By adding a placeholder into the sequence, he might be able to determine where or when the criminal event, whatever that might be, took place. He needed to do this quickly, because every now and then, one of the elderly residents would sell their house and move to the Sunshine Forever Home. Whatever was going on, he needed to intervene.

Deep inside the recesses of his analytical mind was the thought that the old people were missing. He noted that one other couple, the Goodmans, three other residents, living alone, two women and one man, had moved to the home and their postcard sequences were also the same.

Edna and Bill Timmins were meeting with Harvey on a regular basis. Harvey had them at the Tavern as guests for dinner and gave them the full sales pitch for the Sunshine Forever Home. Their meetings did not go unnoticed by others and others began talking about Edna and Bill Timmins and how they would be selling and moving soon.

*　　　　*　　　　*　　　　*　　　　*

Harvey sat in the recliner in his living room, in front of the open fire and looking up to his 65" flat panel TV.

He thought back to Jesse and offered him silent congratulations on his furnishings and the entertainment system. As he slowly contemplated everything that brought him to this place, he realized that just four years ago, he was sitting in a Miami apartment, barely large enough to fit this chair, with just enough money to get by day by day.

Now, look at him. He is the owner of a great food establishment, the President of a Home Owners Association and bringing in large sums of money for his future.

It's amazing how far he's come and all it took was a great idea and a little cooperation.

He thought about some of the unfortunate consequences and the collateral damage but set it aside as nothing more than casualties in a war; a war between himself and society.

*　　　　*　　　　*　　　　*　　　　*

It was just a short four years ago that this all began.

Just a short four years ago and as he thought about the circumstances that brought him here, he drifted off to sleep and dreams about how it all began.

Chapter 4
Four Years Earlier

Four years earlier, before he bought Jesse's Tavern, Harvey was just a full time con-man looking for something bigger, better, more lasting. Harvey's parents were both in a minimum security prison for fraud, embezzlement, and a number of other white collar crimes. Neither was a violent felon, but they would not see the light of day until they were way past 80. They taught him the trade, the art of the phony deal, the big con, and he learned quite a bit more. He learned what not to do, how not to get caught, how to ply his trade on unwary subjects.

In between small cons, generally convincing older people to buy siding from non-existent companies, helping them with their banking while helping himself to their funds, he worked in a restaurant as a chef, sometimes as a short order cook in a diner and other times preparing items in a bakery.

His mom taught him how to cook when he was a young boy and he loved making those meals, from breakfast to dinner, from pies to buns. For some strange reason, when he watched people eat his presentations, it made him feel as if he were feeding the next animals to be taken; strange feelings for a young boy and then a young man. Some might call it psychopathic, but in his research, he never found the word for it.

He stood by the window in his small apartment in Miami, Florida and stared into space, attempting to focus on the next strategy to develop the best con ever. He was tired of making small change; he needed something larger or he may as well get a job. Living hand to mouth was not something he strived for.

"I need an unwary subject or a foolproof scheme," thinking and asking himself a question, "Who are these unwary subjects? Who?" and then he answered his own question, "It's always the elderly; it's always the elderly but not just any elderly will do. I need to find a special kind of old bugger. They have to be old without relatives, without friends, without resources. They have to be isolated. They have to have something worthwhile. I'm not looking to sell them magazine subscriptions."

He stared out of that window for some time thinking of every con and grift that he knew and how he might apply it. It always came back to the elderly; the elderly. The problem was to find these perfect subjects and this was the problem that he knew he must solve.

Harvey decided that the only play to make surrounded itself with the isolated elderly, those he could take for everything they had and no one, absolutely no one would be around to help them or to know what was happening. This was the only play to make and he would not perform any lesser cons until he found the way. "Old and alone with assets."

"The problem; most of the old bastards don't have much, just some retirement funds or they're living on Social Security, eating dog food." But then it dawned on him.

"If they get ill and can't support themselves, they get taken to nursing homes, where Medicaid pays the way. Medicaid pays until they die and then it stops. They even get a burial stipend. The nursing homes get it all and if they manage their care, they make a hell of a lot of money."

"Nursing homes, nursing homes," he repeated this to himself over and over like a mantra.

Looking into this scenario more closely, he discovered that the nursing homes usually get the Power of Attorney from the residents until their funds run out. They even get their Social Security money. All of it ends when they die.

He saw the con opening in front of him like a double doorway to heaven. "What if they die but are not dead. Dead and buried could mean 'undead and maybe buried'. There has to be a way to get the money after they're dead. There has to be a way."

Pensacola Florida is located in the western side of the northern panhandle of the Sunshine State. Pensacola itself is a nicely laid out port city and those who might visit there could enjoy some of the amenities offered. The future location of the Sunshine Forever Home, although listing Pensacola as its' primary location, was in reality, just outside the smaller town of Foley, located on a dead end street in a desolate part of that town.

Much of the area in the Florida panhandle shows how the lack of an economy creates a third world country look and the lack of work has depressed the entire area. Nearby is the Alabama city of Mobile.

Cap and Henrietta Folsom are the owners and managers of the 'soon to be' Sunshine Forever Home. With most retirees moving to south Florida, to places like Boca Raton and Ft. Lauderdale, getting business to the place was more than difficult, but manageable.

Cap's real name was Tim but everyone called him Cap since in by-gone days he was the captain of a small container ship. When the shipping line retired him, he had nowhere to go. The salary from the shipping line wasn't great, but it was a middle class existence. Cap managed to supplement his income with a bit of smuggling. If you were real careful and stowed the stuff away properly, the random searches and drug sniffing dogs wouldn't turn up anything.

He deliberately avoided smuggling illegal drugs although the legal kind he didn't shy away from. For the most part he smuggled artifacts, handguns and jewelry. Much of the stuff was stolen and he offered a two way service, smuggle in or smuggle out. A pure cash business, Cap managed to also stow away a large chunk of change in the fifteen years he was the captain of the container ship.

Henny worked as an office manager in a hotel and used some good money management techniques to save or prepare for retirement. She was smart and capable and learned the ways of the business, how to plan room occupancy to get the most revenue and by selling extras or adding extras that unwary guests wouldn't realize were unnecessary.

She managed to maintain the hotel with less staff by organizing the crew in shifts and bringing in just the right number of illegals. She knew that when Cap retired he would be looking for something to do and some way to invest the cash he stowed away all those years. She kept track of real estate in the area and became aware of a property that was up for a tax sale by the bank that held the mortgage; the Pensacola Savings and Loan.

Cap and Henny surveyed the building; Cap mentioned that it looked like an old age home he visited many years before.

"They make a lot of money, taking care of the old bastards. Why can't we do the same?" he asked Henny. Cap believed he could make a go of the senior citizen business, since Florida was pretty lax when it came to rules, inspections and policy and he could take advantage of that. Henny agreed.

The PSL bank branch manager, Mr. Jones, stayed at her hotel each Monday evening with a woman much younger than he and Henny made certain to treat him with the utmost courtesy and respect and gave him the 'Suite' with a second TV for the same price as a king size. She also checked on his actual status, which was married with two teenage children.

When Mr. Jones began the check-in this last Monday, she asked him how his family was, to which he replied, "they're doing just fine, thank you," and he lost a bit of color in his face at the question. She then mentioned casually that she was interested in the property that was on sale for taxes but she knew that it might be more expensive than she could afford.

"Is there any way that I can get a handle on the lowest acceptable bid for this property? A heads up on that would be helpful and I am certain that only good things would come to you and your family (emphasizing family) if you could find your way to help me."

Mr. Jones agreed that it is always best to have local people investing in the local industry and he would do his best to assist her, discretely, of course. He knew exactly what she meant by being good for him and his family. One week later, at the sheriff's auction, the sealed bids were entered and the acceptable bid was just over the minimum value required by the PSL Bank. Coincidently, the acceptable bid was by Cap and Henrietta Folsom.

Two weeks later, the deal was finalized and Cap and Henny stood in front of the entrance to the old Howard Johnson's and smiled at their good fortune.

The history of the condo style building was kind of clouded, but it was believed it was originally designed and built to be a Howard Johnson's and never made the grade. Likely that was for two reasons. The first being its location and the second being its location.

Even though it was in a state of disrepair when they bought the place, it had a nice frontage with a circular drive and parking area. The circular drive led from the road to the front door access to the lobby and continued on to a second parking lot and back to the street. The paving was still in good shape and would only need a partial resurface and sealing. All the concrete edging needed replacement, but this was rather easy work and would not cost much. The parking lots would have the spaces repainted and a few well-placed signs would lead the way to the registration desk.

The double glass front doors opened automatically to let him in and the registration desk was at the left. Still in great shape, it wouldn't take much to make it resemble a 'Senior Citizen Center'. The lobby space was large enough to hold at least six eight foot sofas and a number of tables and chairs, a nice space for the elderly to sit. A few flat screen TVs would accommodate the background entertainment.

Continuing down the hallway, the restaurant and seating area was on the left and to the right were a number of conference rooms and offices. The five elevators were running well, and all were equipped to support the handicapped. An inspection of the more than 500 guest rooms presented the opportunity to reduce the size of many and expand others to provide a single occupancy and multi-room occupancy, depending upon the need.

A nearby hospital could support whatever medical requirements and emergencies that might come. And of course there were a number of funeral homes for quick body removal and a convenient cemetery association.

Doc Fremont was an old time local fixture and was amenable to bend the rules for a little extra cash. He didn't have an actual practice and was mostly retired, for reasons that no one actually knew but he was still accredited and could perform the function.

Cap enlisted him to be the on call physician once the facility was finished and occupied.

Cap and Henny liked the idea of the senior facility, liked the fact that it was theirs to pursue and not some fantasy scheme thought up by others. They knew it would be hard work and take a while to open itself up to better opportunities, but likely worth the wait and it was risk free, from the viewpoint of going to prison.

The Folsom's were old friends of the Paul's, Harvey's parents. Periodically they called the prison, which was a white collar facility, and were able to talk to their old friends. They didn't say much on the telephone, because all the calls were monitored, so most of the conversation was general. This time Cap talked to Gary.

"How's it going? Are you managing to get by?"

"Sure, every week, they let me see Louise," Gary added. "We can meet in the common area and then afterwards, she is taken back to the women's section."

"That sounds sad, but I guess it's better than not."

"Yea, I guess so, but that's our lives from now on. What's happening with you?"

"Henny and I have purchased and are prepping a senior citizen center. It'll take some time, but we feel it's going to be successful. Hopefully, we'll all be around when you get out."

"I have to go now. Try to come by if you can."

"Take care of yourselves. Bye for now."

Of course, Harvey also called periodically, just like a dutiful son. His dad told him about the Folsom's new project and told him to stay in touch and "if you can call more often, try to talk to mom. She's very sad and alone most of the time." His dad added that the Folsom's are really nice people and if they are doing something positive, he should maybe give them a call and see if he can fit in.

"Let me know if it works out."

Harvey began adding up the new scheme in his mind, but he really didn't have a complete handle on it. But here it was, a whole place filled with old people. Old people by the hundreds all gathered in one spot. Easy pickin's ready to be taken. He knew that the Folsom's could help.

"I need to speak to the Folsom's and get a better understanding of the old age home and what it does, how it works, and where do they get the money to pay for the place."

Somehow, deep in the recesses of Harvey's dark mind, he knew that this was an opportunity that he couldn't afford to dismiss.

Calling Cap was the first step.

Then the Folsom's received that call from Harvey. "If it's okay," Harvey said, "I'd like to stop by. We could go for lunch and talk for a while."

Cap thought about that call. It was no coincidence. Harvey was the son of his old friend Gary and had called now and then about some great ideas. He continually expressed a way for all of them to get rich; another great Harvey scheme. Most of Harvey's schemes never came to fruition, particularly after his parents had gone to prison.

Harvey was cold and calculating, had a sharp mind and was likely sociopathic, but he was also pragmatic and Cap knew that he didn't want to join his parents. Whatever scheme he came up with had to be as foolproof and risk free as possible. Cap also knew that Harvey would always have an escape plan and that Harvey's escape plan never included anyone but himself.

You needed to be extra special careful when dealing with Harvey. Cap told Henny about the call and the request. "I'll call him back and tell him its ok. That he should stop by for lunch tomorrow. We'll eat in so we can have some privacy."

On his way to meet the Folsom's, Harvey began thinking about his parents. What a coincidence that he called his dad just a day after his dad received a call from Cap. His parents were old friends of Cap and Henrietta and his dad told him they had just purchased and were in the process of renovating an old Howard Johnson's to make a retirement home. He thought about that phone call with his father and realized that his father never really understood him.

"Maybe they could find you something worthwhile to do?" his dad offered, "something on the straight so you won't wind up in here."

Harvey dismissed that as just commiseration in one's own missteps.

:"Okay, dad, give mom a hug from me. Talk to you soon."

As he was driving to Pensacola, his focus and his thoughts were a rehearsal for what he was planning, to hook them into a scheme.

"I'm pleased that they accepted my invitation for lunch and maybe validate some of my ideas. I know that both Cap and Henny are not averse to making some easy money."

It was only after Harvey's parents were arrested that Cap and Henny became fearful and decided to attempt an honest living. He knew he could easily discuss this with them without worry and they might be able to offer some advice, advice that would include them and their senior citizen center, even if they didn't realize it.

Harvey parked in the closest spot near the entrance to the facility. As he walked to the registration desk, Cap met him and escorted him to a conference room. Henny was sitting at the large table; a pot of coffee and a variety of sandwiches were piled neatly on a large platter. He noticed the napkins, paper plates and plastic forks and knives.

"Harvey, have a seat. Great to see you." They all sat and Henny poured the coffee. "Take a sandwich. We've got roast beef, cheeses ham and turkey. Not much else right now, but we're still in a build mode."

The conversation, of course, began with the typical "how are you?" and "okay." and "where have you been?" and "here and there." but eventually settled into a direct question by Cap.

"Okay Harvey, what's the story? We know that you didn't come here for small talk."

"Listen, Cap," said Harvey who decided that beating around the bush wasn't anyone's style, "Let me give you the particulars of what I'm trying to find and maybe you can help with the finding."

Harvey told him about the real underlying foundation of what he was looking for and that a place that had hundreds of old people might be perfect. It included taking a deep look into the old age home that Cap and Henny were creating. If there was something there, he would find it.

During the conversation, Cap explained how the old age home operated, how it would be funded, who would live in it, the 'finder's fee' deal with the mortuary and the various other medical places in the area. Cap explained how it might be hard work and there would be a large staff, but it would be a good living. He added that if Harvey wanted a real job, he could earn well and have a good life participating in the home. Neither he nor Henny was openly interested in beginning another get rich quick money scheme or running a con.

Harvey, on the other hand, could not even think about honest work, but he did begin thinking about the residents in the home.

"I understand, Cap but let me ask you a question about the people who eventually will be residing in the home. Who exactly are they?" asking and then answering himself, "They're the elderly, but what I'm looking for are those that are old without relatives, without friends, without resources. They have to be isolated. They have to have something worthwhile." And as he spoke, he was tapping his finger on the table to keep their attention focused.

The question was asked by Harvey to Cap, "How would you advertise for those types?" Cap didn't believe you could. "Okay, but where can you find the perfect old person?"

This Cap did know and answered; "The cemetery."

"And you get the money to pay for this place from Medicaid and from the savings accounts of these people?" Harvey asked the question but it sounded more like a statement. "How does that work?" Harvey asked but already knew the answer. He just wanted Cap to give it.

Cap described the financial and Medicaid reimbursements. "After we spend down their funds, we'll get around $4000.00 per month per person from Medicaid and we take all their Social Security, typically averaging about $1300 a month, leaving about

$100.00 a month in a personal spending account. We keep our costs down and earn a good living."

"How about after they're dead?" Harvey asked.

"What you're actually asking", Henny chimed in, "is how can we get the money, the $5300.00 plus without the people?"

Cap looked at Henny, his eyes asking her not to interrupt and continued, "Likely it would take a balance of actual residents and non-existent ones. From past experience we know that everyone who gets caught at this type of scheme makes up phony residents from obituaries. Maybe you get six months to a year at the outside, but then you better run. What you're thinking," Cap added, "is that you think you might have a better way for long term fraud without the liability."

Harvey's mind was racing around that statement and even if he didn't have an idea yet, he will have one. He knew it. And it came to him in a flash, like he had this plan buried deep in the recesses of his mind forever and all it took was little coaxing to let it out. When Cap used the word 'might' it signified his interest begin peaked.

Harvey explained the known details. "The Sunshine Forever Home needs Medicaid accreditation. This means it requires that the facility fulfills all the details listed in the requirements documents, including staff, hospitals nearby and record keeping. These are all easy to put together as it's a standard practice and is available and ready."

"In fact," Harvey added, "you could hire a consultant to do all the work for you and it would be perfect."

"The real problem is how do you get the right prospects and turn away the wrong ones. To make my thoughts work as a viable plan, we need the elderly without relatives, friends, or anything or anyone that might be nosing around. Medicaid is comparatively easy."

Harvey had researched the general methods that Medicaid used and explained to Cap and Henny. "Medicaid requires a signature now and then. We know that each signature, although resembling each other, are never identical, so if a computer comparison is performed, identical copies meant that something was irregular and an investigation might occur."

"How do we get over the top of this? It's simple. All we need to do is have the applicant sign about twenty different forms. Signatures are never required more than two, three times a year, so we have many signatures to use over a period of years. Computer comparisons rarely if ever went back more than three years."

Harvey became animated as he was reviewing all this information, waving his hands and nodding, staring directly into Cap's eyes for effect.

"The real issue is the elderly themselves. We need the sickest, the oldest and the near death ones so we can continue getting the Medicaid payments after they're dead. We have to be careful about the average length of life each of these marks have so we don't surpass it after they're dead. Maybe two years of payments and then we send in the Death Certificates and proper cremation or burial forms. And", he reiterated for effect, "these elderly must be alone, isolated, no relatives, friends or associates."

Harvey was emphasizing certain words so Cap would feel more of his passion and maybe get some of that passion himself.

Cap looked at Henny and both understood that Harvey came by looking for answers but he already had much of it thought out and answered. He came by to run the scheme by them to see if would take.

At first Cap and Henny gently refused to listen about the scheme, waving their arms and hands in a dismissing motion, but then, after a while, it began to make sense. It was fundamentally about committing Medicaid fraud, but in reality it was about how do you commit Medicaid fraud and not get caught? It's true that once a con always a con and the Folsom's had a hard time not listening and considering this plan, particularly since Harvey laid out a really good scheme.

"If we could make a pile of money quickly, we can sell the place and get the hell out; just retire to some nice island somewhere."

"That's exactly right," added Harvey, "and I believe I have quite a bit of the details and just need some filler."

Cap listened intently to Harvey's story and had questions concerning the Death Certificates and financial forms, such as tax returns.

"Okay Harvey, these sounds like a simple plan concocted from a complex topic. In reality it's a very complicated governmental issue to be alive and just as complicated to be dead. We need to have real funerals because even if these people are alone, they have met others and likely made friends in the Home. We can't place the bodies into the caskets. We need to hold those bodies in cold storage for when we actually 'confirm their deaths', bury them and send in the Death Certificates. This way they don't look as if they've died two years ago and were just buried. We can't give banks and others the initial death certificates and of course we have to continue doing their taxes."

Cap continued, "We'll need a doctor to write an original death certificate for a relative who might be in the home but the certificate will not be sent in to the government or registered. In this way, no government agency will know that the person is dead. Since we have Power of Attorney and financial responsibility for many of the residents, we will also be their in-house accountants. We continue filling out the tax returns of any 'joint' survivors."

Henny decided that she needed to add some preconditions. "We won't be involved with any who have relatives elsewhere. We won't be involved with any who are paying their own way. All of those will be legitimate."

Henny continued, "And you know it's hard and nearly impossible to turn people away just because they don't meet the requirements of our scheme. That means that we use their history and track their mail and if they keep touch with anyone, we persuade them to go elsewhere, or we keep them as regular residents, not the ones we plan to store for future use. Once the Home is full, we should get nearly twenty to thirty "undead" per year. That number can double if we can get enough really sick and elderly residents without family."

Harvey added to the conversation, continuing in the same vein of logic, "We also need a place to put the bodies; you know, the ones that aren't actually 'dead' yet. You talked about storage. It may not be easy to find a mortuary or cemetery that has spare space or can and will hide the bodies. And always remember that the more people involved the more likely we are exposed."

Harvey emphasized the following, "Avoiding exposure is the most important issue because anything can go wrong, but nobody can survive a rat. I, for one, do not want to be in the slammer with my parents. The best way to avoid a rat is to pay everyone generously and not bring anyone in who doesn't have the composure for this."

Cap and Henny asked Harvey to relax for a while, maybe go for a ride to the Gulf and look around and come back in about an hour. They needed to talk about this.

Harvey left and said he would be back in about an hour. In the meantime, Cap and Henny discussed Harvey's plan.

Cap began and left it for Henny to put her thoughts first.

"What do you think?"

"I think it's a good plan but I'm always worried about these seemingly innocent and easy fraud schemes. Somehow they always go wrong." Henny raised her eyebrows into a worried look.

"I know and I agree. But what could go really wrong, other than exposure. And we should be able to get away if we plan a time limit on the plan. Say, two years at the outside."

"Two years is a long time. We need to recover our investment up front, so if it totally collapses, we don't walk away with nothing."

"Okay, so we get a mortgage for what we invested after we get the Medicaid accreditation and stash the cash overseas. Crap, if this works and I have made some calculations, you're looking at maybe a quarter million a month. That's big cash and if we do this right, and I mean right, the percentages of success is really high. I think we both agree that working this hard until we die is just pure crap."

Henny thought about this for a short time and agreed that they were both getting older, had no children and no one to leave the home to, so what the hell, the best plan was to make as much as possible in as short a time as possible and get the hell out.

"Okay, Tim, let's go for it. Just remember how twisted Harvey is. We need to keep him in check and not let him plan his own way out at our expense."

"Okay, we agree on all these points, particularly the last one. When Harvey comes back, we'll set up the details. But we'll limit this to a trial run and see how it goes."

Harvey returned to the conference room after driving around for an hour, sitting by the beach, and contemplating his next steps. He knew that Cap and Henny would agree on the plan. He could tell by the look in their eyes.

So they all sat around the conference table and Cap agreed as did Henny and they concluded that the premise was sound. The balance of the details could be worked out and all it needed was a little time and a bit more thought about the structure and a place to store the bodies. They all agreed to a trial run. Tomorrow is a new day and it looked quite bright.

Harvey was proud of himself and knew his parents would also be proud of his play with the Folsom's. His dad always said "the easiest mark to con is one who cons others and lives to make easy money."

Cap also made a great offer to Harvey while the place was being renovated and the plan was in progress. "We're still in construction but part of the place is complete. Why don't we get you a nice duplex room on the fourth floor? The room has all the furnishings you need, good food is served in the area and you can be close to the action. What do you say?"

Harvey was happy to have the invitation. He hardly had any money left and this might have been his last stand.

"Yes ……. and thanks."

Chapter 5

Before the Folsoms could do a trial run or have any valid talks with owners of a mortuary that they might collude with, they needed to complete the renovations of the Sunshine Forever Home and obtain the Medicaid accreditation. It was quite a bit of construction, more than they thought, that had been required to complete the renovations, but most of the lower floors were now complete, elevators were ready for the disabled, the front desk and lounge area looked great, the parking lot was re-edged, newly topped and lined. Within a few months, everything was ready for Medicaid and the State to inspect.

Harvey looked at the mostly finished product, "Cap, this place looks great and looks ready for residents. How soon can you get approved by Medicaid and any other care agencies so we can move the plan forward?"

Cap responded to Harvey's question and wasn't in a real hurry because the details were important and hurried work was bad work.

"We're working on the final details now. One thing is certain. We don't want a rejection."

Harvey continued, "You told me about Phil and May who own the EverRest Funeral Parlor two streets down and have a direct connection to the EverRest Cemetery. You said they appreciated the fact that you would recommend them as the funeral directors of choice and were giving you a fee for referrals. Whatever you call it, the fee is a kickback."

"I suppose you could look at it that way."

"Think they would be willing to make a bit more money storing bodies and urns and preparing obits and funerals later on. They might even have a method of keeping track of everything, like a database. What do you think?"

"Harvey," answered Cap, "Phil and May have been around a long time. I'll ask without being too obvious. They seem to enjoy the good life and if the risk is not too great, I don't see why they wouldn't agree. I'll also keep it simple and just tell them we'd like to store bodies and urns for a time, maybe hold a mock funeral now and then and then do a funeral with obit, nothing about the Medicaid. They're smart enough to know that the less they know the better. Storing bodies and urns is not exactly illegal, mock funerals might be something, but if they know nothing about the reasoning and are getting paid well for the work." He trailed off his words, not needing to say anything else because everyone understood his meaning.

Henny made a call to May and asked if it would be okay if they came over for a chat, maybe a cup of coffee. Of course, May agreed and told her that 1:00Pm would be a good time, if it was good for her.

As Henny and Cap walked to the EverRest, they reviewed how they would broach the subject. Henny asked Cap to do the talking.

Once they arrived, May brought them to the outer office, which was actually a generously appointed lounge with easy chairs, a leather couch and a low table which held beverages and a plate of cookies.

"Pull up a chair," Phil offered to each of them. "Pour yourselves a cup of coffee and I might add that the cookies are delicious."

"Thanks, they look great." And everyone sat down around the table. Cap began the conversation with just a general discussion about the mortuary and some of the needs of the Sunshine Forever Home. "We have a need to store some of the elderly when they pass, prior to them having a funeral."

"Sure, we can do that," responded Phil. "We have plenty of room. At least fifty open shelves."

The number of shelves surprised Cap but Phil added, "This place was at one time the morgue for all the police in this area, so they built it to hold a lot of subjects. Later on, each precinct built its own and put this place up for sale. We picked it up for a great price but we still have the storage".

Cap continued after thinking that this place was perfect, "There may come a time when we would want someone stored and not actually buried. We would need to have a 'mock' funeral. What do you think?"

"Sounds interesting. What's the purpose of this?"

"Let's just say that we would rent the space of these unburied and give you a favored compensation ….. say, three times your normal fees."

May looked directly into Henny's eyes and said, "Why not just tell us what you would like us to do? If we think it's okay, we don't mind bending the rules."

After Cap explained the deal to Phil and May, without going into too much detail, both agreed to the task. They had a large facility, crematorium, refrigerator compartments that would hold sixty.

Typically only four or five were used at any one time, so the others were available. They didn't care to know anything more. They would keep a second database of the storage to keep track of future obits and burials. Both had that inner feeling that there was a lot more here than meets the eye, but so what? Getting paid three times as much for the storage and for long term meant a good revenue stream with almost no risk. Easy to get rid of everything quickly, if need be. A mock funeral would be good practice for the part time gravediggers.

The Foley Funeral Parlor had been in business for quite some time. Phil and May purchased it a number of years ago because it was one of the few funeral parlors and mortuaries in the area and it had a large morgue which served the Police Departments in the local region.

Aside from regular funerals, the large refrigerator section was a significant source of revenue since all the local Police used it for a holding area for their Medical Examiners.

In addition to the funeral parlor, they later purchased the controlling interest in the EverRest cemetery so they could offer a full service package to the bereaved. Phil thought it was a good idea to rename the funeral parlor to 'EverRest' from 'Foley'.

Eventually the Police local precincts built their own morgues and didn't require the use of the EverRest any longer. By that time, the EverRest had established itself and became a prime fixture for mortuary and funeral services in the area.

Both Phil and May loved the game, that they could make big money from other's tragedies. They loved it, regaled in it, wanted more and both believed that they could make millions in this business. Death was wonderful. It may be a tragedy for others but for them it was a joy. It may be inevitable, but at least for now, it would keep them in the lap of luxury, eating in the best places, having the best home in the area, the finest autos and when it came time to retire, it would lead them to the lap of luxury.

Phil and May met in Dallas some twenty years earlier. Phil worked for a funeral parlor and May came in one day to support her family when one of her cousins passed away. Phil, aside from greeting the visitors, also had a hand in dressing the bodies and doing other preparation work. At first he felt it was a grizzly business but after a while he became emotionally immune to the death as well as the crying and suffering of the families.

Objectivity in this business was the word of the day. He noticed May at the back of the room, sitting on a bench and staring into nothingness. She didn't walk up to the casket as others had done, nor did she act as if she had any aversion to it. It was likely that this person was just some distant relative that she hardly knew and that she had just come to pay her respects to the family.

But she was good looking, a striking brunette with a slender figure, well-proportioned in all directions and he had to say something.

Phil approached May and started up a simple conversation with the typical "sorry for your loss" with her response being "thank you, it's appreciated," and then he heard himself saying "how about we go get a cup of coffee" and just as quickly she responded with "sure, it's better than hanging around here."

From that simple meeting, he learned that she was an anatomy major in college and was looking forward to a career in medicine. Once she had found out the cost of that career and having very little resources, she had deferred the 'doctor' part and needed to decide which other occupation in medicine might be more readily available.

Phil explained the requirements for work in the morgue, preparing the bodies and that a degree in anatomy might be sufficient to pursue that opportunity and also that the Police Medical Examiner's office did not require a Doctor to assist with performing autopsies. Both were good paying careers and it would keep her in the business she was pursuing. Maybe with enough time and savings, she could get to medical school.

May loved this conversation, one she had never had with her parents, as they believed she should go get a job at Sears; that her father said she was wasting her time in college; that she should get married and have babies and let her husband worry about the money.

She loved her parents but the one aspect of college life she loved was the open thinking of her generation, not the closed thinking of her parents. No, she would pursue her future without becoming dependent. The conversation with Phil proved that he had the right attitude and, she thought to herself, "He was good to look at also."

From that simple, first conversation, they struck up a relationship and within a year were married. She went to work in the Medical Examiner's office in Richardson, Texas, where she learned the autopsy trade, how to prepare and store bodies for long term. Phil taught her the embalming process and the financial linkage between funeral homes, hospitals and cemeteries. Phil also showed her the enormous profit to be made selling caskets, sympathizing and conning the bereaved to part with as much money as possible.

A year later they had a daughter whom they named Veronica. She was a beautiful baby, born with a full head of hair and eyes that stared right through you. As Veronica grew and reached the age where she should be speaking, at least a few words, May noticed some strange behavior. Veronica would stare at a wall for fifteen minutes to a half hour without moving and then began to play with a toy and then stared at the wall again. She didn't speak but a few words but understood everything.

A decision was made to get her tested. Phil and May waited outside of the doctor's office until the examination was complete The Doctor had them sit in front of his large desk, rubbed his chin in a thoughtful manner and then explained that Veronica had some autism and that most likely it was Asperger's syndrome. He wouldn't know the extent of the condition for some time, but it was good that they caught this early so she could receive some special schooling.

This was devastating news for Phil and May but they accepted the situation with the same objectivity they used in their work and focused on Veronica's schooling.

Years later, Veronica proved to have a mild Asperger's but was fully functional and extremely intelligent, with a savant like quality when it came to assisting her dad in the funeral home. She accepted hugs from her parents, understanding that they needed to do the hugging; she didn't need the hugs. It didn't matter what condition a dead body was in, she could reassemble it so that others could view it without becoming ill. She showed no emotion and no feelings whatsoever. If she had existed in feudal times, she would have been a person 'without a soul' and either ostracized or killed.

Veronica stood at 5'6," slightly taller than her mother, had a slender figure but since she loved to exercise, she was well muscled for a slender girl. Dark hair, raven black as May would refer to it, looked exactly like May's raven hair, but Veronica had deep eyes that looked black in the dim light and dark blue at other times. When she stared at you, it was if she was looking into your soul and sucking life from it. It was fortunate that she typically looked away from most people, but there were a few that she seemed to stare directly into them, not at them.

Most of Phil and May's acquaintances reacted with unease when in Veronica's presence and became less likely to call for a dinner or a get together. Eventually, Phil and May lost these relationships.

Not having any real ties to Dallas, with the exception of the funeral home, they decided to find a place of their own. They looked into funeral parlors for sale and came across the Foley Funeral Parlor near Pensacola and after reviewing the place, made an offer, which was accepted by the realtor.

Moving to Florida was easy compared to raising a child with Asperger's.

Chapter 6

Within a few weeks, the State building inspectors came to the newly renovated and mostly completed Sunshine Forever Home and performed their work. Two weeks after the physical inspection, the facility received a State Certificate of Occupancy for the function requested; A Senior Citizen Center and Nursing Home, functional with support for the fully disabled and inclusive of assisted living residences. Unlike other facilities of its type, this one had a fully functional emergency generator system with automatic transfer switch, should there be a power failure.

The Certificate of Occupancy was then registered with Medicaid and an inspection was requested by the Sunshine Forever Home to review the documents and requirements.

Medicaid agents reviewed the paperwork and came to the building to discuss the practical requirements of the Sunshine Forever Home. Cap and Henny sat with the local Medicaid administrator and reviewed the staffing, on-site nursing, assistants, doctor availability, nearby hospitals, dining requirements, room requirements, and the balance of a full list of reporting documentation, health administration and financial reporting.

The Medicaid administrator thanked the Folsom's for their excellent paperwork, documentation as well as the pristine living facility being readied for the elderly. She indicated that they should hear from Medicaid within two weeks and as a side note, she didn't see any reason why they should not receive accreditation.

That being said, she left and filed the paperwork. As she indicated, the Folsom's received their accreditation eight days later and the Sunshine Forever Home was certified for occupancy.

"It's full speed ahead now," sighed Henny, "Hoping for and very thankful for a quick turnaround." She still had quite a bit of apprehension about this plan of Harvey's but didn't express that to Cap.

Cap agreed and told her that "we need to get the staff ready for the first occupants." Cap was also apprehensive about the whole scheme but decided he wouldn't express his reservations to Henny.

Within the first sixty days, they had twenty-two rooms occupied, ten dual and twelve singles. Three months later, the home had two hundred and fifty occupied rooms, about two-thirds of them single occupancies and the balance dual. A few months later, the first natural death occurred to Helen Fineburg, a woman in her nineties who never received a telephone call, a letter or a visitor. This made her a perfect sample for the trial run

Cap called Phil at the EverRest and organized a 'funeral' since a few other residents on her floor would love to be at a service. Doc was called to write the Death Certificate, leaving it undated. It was to be a closed casket service. Her body was transported to the funeral parlor, where it was promptly placed into storage and the data base updated with the first entry. The Casket with one hundred pounds of filler to simulate the weight of a body was placed into the viewing room where twelve or so of the residents came to listen to Phil give the eulogy and the local rabbi talk about the afterlife.

Of course the casket was closed as per the instructions provided by Mrs. Fineburg prior to her death. After the service was completed, the casket was driven to the EverRest Cemetery for burial. The part time grave diggers, finished opening the grave site, lowered the casket and closed the grave. The rabbi said his piece and all walked away, shaking hands and saying goodbye. The residents were driven back to the Sunshine Forever Home, each with a sad and knowing look that they were likely next.

Helen's unoccupied room was re-occupied by an even older man. The $5000.00 monthly Medicaid and Social Security payments for Helen continued as if she were alive. Cap, Henny, Phil and May all exclaimed how easy that had been, even though

Phil and May did not know the particulars. Harvey had a big smile on his face. They could keep her in storage for fourteen months, according to the actuarial table for age group and gender. That's a cool $70,000.00.

Cap and Henny, later that day, just couldn't believe how easy that had been and expressed were glad they were that they went along with Harvey's scheme. Maybe their worries were for nothing.

As for Phil and May, all they 'knew' was that a body was in storage for which they received a nice monthly stipend and they were paid handsomely for the funeral of the 'filler'.

Within the first fourteen months, there were twenty three full time stored bodies earning Medicaid for the team. That equaled $127,000 each month and now it was time for 'Helen,' their number one, to actually become dead. That evening, Phil and May took the body from storage, went to the Helen's grave site, opened the grave using the trencher and deposited the body into the casket. The grave was then closed and they went back to the EverRest to update the database. Phil dated the Death Certificate and it was sent in to Medicaid and the IRS.

Helen Fineburg was now officially dead.

It was so simple it was frightening. The problem they faced was that the usable deaths, those that had no relatives, phone calls or letters and visitors, were so rare that the total in storage never grew above the twenty three they already had. One died and became the 'undead' and one 'undead' had to be made dead. It was frustrating and limiting.

Harvey had been thinking about the plan and how simple it was to make as much as they had.

"There has to be a way to make use of at least fifty shelves." It wasn't just greed that was doing the thinking; it was the idea of maximizing the profits with the physical structure they had in place.

"It's been more than eighteen months and we haven't been able to grow." Harvey spoke out loud to himself while he paced back and forth in his duplex.

Harvey called Cap to review the plan and to try to figure out a way to maximize the profit or at least break through this twenty-three in storage barrier.

Cap's records show that the Home required two-thirds occupancy to pay for the expenses with a 20% profit and everything above that would be half expenses and half profits. The only real money they were making right now was from the 'undead' in storage. Of course he would like to have the storage number increase and he was trying hard to have the right qualities of particular elderly come to the home, but the ones they really wanted were far and few between. It was also next to impossible to choose the ones you wanted and you were pretty much stuck with the randomness of the arrivals. This random selection resulted in storage of about twenty-three or so, more or less.

Cap and Henny were working hard maintaining the regular facility and the staff which had to be increased to support the growing number of elderly, the taxes, the food, the hospital bills and everything else it took to manage a senior residence.

Cap decided to agree with Harvey and give him the opportunity to find a way to increase the load.

"Harvey's right. We need to find a way to increase the storage number, you know, maximize our money while we can. Everything comes to an end and so will this someday."

"Let's get with Phil and May to discuss the storage aspects, and remember, the storage aspects only, just to make certain they can handle an increase." Harvey tapped the table and spoke assertively to reinforce this aspect of the plan.

Cap called Phil and asked them to stop by and meet them in Conference Room 1 to review the next stages of the plan. Phil and May decided to walk, since it was only two blocks away, and they could enjoy the weather. As they walked up to the renovated entrance, they stopped for a second to take in the changes that Cap and Henny did to the façade. May commented, "They sure did a great job beautifying the place. Don't you think?" Phil just shrugged and grunted something unintelligible as he preferred to stay in the EverRest, not visit an old age home.

Continuing on, they went to Conference Room 1 and saw Cap, Henny and Harvey waiting for them, a tray of sandwiches, soft drinks and coffee on the table. They sat to the left and the others were on the right, Harvey at the head of the table.

Harvey began the conversation with congratulations to them all for a job well done, but now he wanted to expand the plan. He wasn't certain how this would happen but it would be using the same rules as were now in place.

"If it's okay with everyone, I will look for a way to expand the numbers from the twenty to twenty-three we now have to nearer forty to fifty. I will provide more information as it develops or if it develops and I assure you that I agree that no additional risk is acceptable."

Phil and May were generally happy with the revenue they had coming in for storing the undead and keeping the database. They would certainly be happier with more. It was easy work and just took a bit of time to update their dual records. Even though they 'knew' something else was going on, they kept their silence and just went with the flow.

No one asked any questions. It was only a vote of confidence to let Harvey identify opportunities.

Harvey decided to put it to a vote.

"Who agrees that I should make some inquiries as to expanding our opportunity?"

Everyone raised their hand in agreement with the exception of Henny, who tells Cap "the risk is small now, why take a chance?"

Henny pondered the situation and even though she and Cap were working hard, they had enough. She was hesitant but Cap wanted more and he believed that Harvey's scheme, at least until now, was solid.

"Why not try for more? What could it hurt?"

Henny reluctantly agreed, but did not raise her hand.

With the vote four to one abstention, Harvey tells the group that he will begin by calling an old friend, Barry, living up in Pennsylvania; a person that he knows from past experience is very trustworthy and might be able to help.

One thing about his old friend Barry, he was trustworthy, had great contacts and would be an asset to Harvey's scheme. He wouldn't tell them anything more about his friend.

Chapter 7

Harvey met Barry a number of years before in Indiana while he was working an auto sale con on an elderly couple. Harvey had copied a registration for the car and created a Bill of Sale proving he was the owner. Only he knew that the car was stolen.

The couple needed a car and couldn't afford anything new or what they had seen in the used car lot. At the time, Barry was working as a used car salesman and noticed this guy talking to the couple as they left his lot. He was pointing to a car on the street. Being curious, Barry walked nearer to the conversation as the couple was looking at the car and after a short time realized that this fast talking fellow was 'selling' them the car.

Instead of being angry at the situation, he just listened in to the sales pitch; that he had to sell it now and since he saw them in the lot looking at prices, he knew they might be interested. They'd never get a better deal. Barry watched as the old couple agreed they couldn't turn down such a great deal. The fellow said he'd wait until they brought the cash, it was just $800.00. The rest of the conversation was normal. They needed to get the $800.00. The old couple went to a nearby bank and a short fifteen minutes brought the money, were given the title papers, registration and keys in exchange. They looked really happy as they drove away.

Barry walked up in a friendly way and introduced himself and told this fellow that he would make a fine 'used car salesman' if he could sell those two someone else's car.

At first Harvey was intimidated by Barry's size but Barry kept a great smile on his face and invited Harvey back to the sales office. With the cash still in his hand, Harvey agreed and they went into the office and talked about a lot of things; where they came from, their families, and what they had been doing and wanted to do going forward. A few months later, after sharing each other's work efforts, they became more than just passing acquaintances, enjoyed each other's company, discussed how they could combine their efforts to make bigger scores and they quickly became friends.

As is typical of car salesmen, Barry always asked for the names, addresses and contacts of those who were looking. People quickly gave him their Social Security numbers. Whenever he couldn't sell a car, he would aim Harvey at the people who left and Harvey would find a way to close some other deal, at times with some stolen car and phony papers and at other times, with siding schemes or phony insurance policies.

They didn't earn a hell of a lot, but they both loved the game. Eventually they decided to get out. Someone had hired a private investigator to find them and they both knew that the next step was the police. It was goodbye and stay in touch. Harvey went to Florida around the Miami area and Barry wandered north into Pennsylvania. They both changed their cell phones for new ones so that they couldn't be traced and could still be in contact if something came up.

Barry settled into and lived quietly in a community in Pennsylvania, worked in an auto body shop, was paid in cash and brought the least amount of attention to himself as possible. Barry's large muscular frame was very handy at the auto body shop. He could lift and set fenders, hoods, transmissions and other components with ease, saving the shop time and money. Paying Barry cash was an easy consideration for such benefits and no one asked any questions.

Barry had a criminal record which included a number of felonies, fraud, assault and although never convicted of the crime, first degree murder.

The rural community offered Barry the isolation he desired and needed.

The day following the meeting and the agreement that he should attempt to expand their plan, Harvey called his old friend and they decided to meet in Pennsylvania. Barry gave Harvey directions to a small lunch shop on Route 6 near Montrose, on the road to Scranton. Barry and Harvey met at Momma's Bake Shop for a late breakfast.

Sitting across from each other at a small round table, Barry listened carefully as Harvey described the details needed to make this con work. He quickly understood that the Sunshine Forever Home must have people sent to it who are old, alone and ready to die. The question was, "How and where do you get these people?"

Barry told Harvey a short story about an old friend of his, Jesse, who owns a tavern at a place called Decker Lake. They haven't had much contact of recent, but Jesse had talked about the place as being so remote, and so isolated from the nearest town, that no one came through, even accidentally. And not only that, it was considered to be a retirement community.

Jesse said he couldn't recall many visitors and only a few drove even though they had vehicles. In fact, when they needed to go to town, he gave them rides as part of his community service. Generally, the residents kept to themselves, had rare contact to each other and even when they came to his tavern, they typically came alone; nodding to each other as they passed and were seated at separate tables.

As Barry talked about the place, Harvey realized that Barry had not had much contact with this fellow Jesse for a long time, maybe more than a year. This place might be the perfect foil for Harvey's scheme but only if the conditions were the same as Barry described.

Barry was tired of his lonely existence and told Harvey that he would relish the activity. Any help Harvey needed, all he had to do was ask.

"Barry, listen, we need to make a more thorough investigation of this community, just to verify Jesse's conversation. It's best if we send someone other than ourselves, so when and if we move in to take over, we're not recognized by anyone. Since no one actually passes through the place, we could send in someone younger, with 'elderly parents', looking for a retirement community. This way they get taken around, introduced, and get a handle on the place."

Barry leaned forward as to emphasize his words and responded, "I know a smart couple who could go along for a short ride and make inquiries. I'll use a standard, 'I sure could use some help' and I'm sure that they can look around and help for now. It may be worth their while to get a place up there eventually and be part of the front end. What do you think? Ok?"

"Let's give it a try," said Harvey, "This is not a get rich quick scheme, it's for the long run, but I'm anxious to get started. I love the game. But as far as that front end deal, we can cross that bridge later. Let's keep it under wraps."

"Since you know Jesse for a long time, if things seem ok, we're going to want this tavern as a front for our efforts. It could be the perfect place to work from. You know, get the residents on board. What's the prognosis of him selling or do we need to apply pressure? Give him the Godfather treatment. Make him an offer he can't refuse."

"Not a problem," answered Barry, "not a problem at all. Jesse knows me, all too well. If I ask him to sell, and we treat him right, he'll move on. I'll handle it."

It's Saturday afternoon and a nondescript couple in their thirties arrive at Jesse's Tavern. Jesse is behind the bar and makes himself a mental note that these are the first new people he has seen in at least two weeks. The few others that previously came into the tavern, checked out the vacant clubhouse across the way, looked at the inactivity and the lack of any other facilities and left without even saying hello.

That was typical of most visitors. Jesse assumed that most of these general visitors were looking for a lake community for themselves or a retirement community for their parents and the plain vanilla Decker Lake was not for them. First glances said it all.

"Not for me."

He really didn't care since the lack of a lot of people suited him just fine. He had enough of controversy, pressure, lies, arguing, choosing sides and just wanted the peace and quiet of this place, Decker Lake, a place where nothing ever happened and it suited him just fine.

Unlike all the previous, typical visitors, these two came into the tavern, walked up to the bar and greeted Jesse with a warm "Hello, how about a couple of beers?"

They actually wanted to have a conversation and asked Jesse whether he was knowledgeable about the place. They had called the Board of Directors main line and the answering machine responded with a typical message that 'no one was in and they should leave a message at the tone'. No one ever called back.

Jesse indicated that he could tell them what they needed to know in a general way, that the Board was mostly disbanded with the exception of one fellow who got the snow plowing organized.

"So, tell us about this community. Our parents are getting up in years and are looking for a quiet place where they can enjoy the sounds of birds, animals and listen to the flowers grow. In fact, they really don't care about organized activities, horns, sirens or a lot of partying. Dad fishes and I hope the lake is stocked. Mom knits and crochets and loves to sit on the porch in the fresh air."

"We see that this not a gated community. Does this mean that there are only a few visitors? Or no need for notification? If there are gatherings in the clubhouse, are most of the resident's elderly? Do visitors bring their young children around to make a lot of noise? Are there a lot of cars coming and going?"

The two rattled off a lot of questions as if they had practice asking them. And maybe they did, with other home developments in the area.

Jesse asked them if they'd like to go for a ride and just look at the overall community and he could answer most of their questions along the way.

Of course they agreed

He then gave them the ten cent tour which included driving them up and down the main roads, pointing at a few of the older homes and then some of the latest Decker Lake versions. He let them know that "Derik, the realtor in town, told me last week that lake front wasn't available at this time. But maybe Derik could give them more detailed information, if they were interested."

They walked a bit at the lake shore and then he drove them back to the tavern for a short and friendly talk. He explained that in all the years he had been at Decker Lake, there were few visitors as most of the people who owned the homes were older and had few relatives. In fact, the remote location of this community actually attracted the loner type of person since it was secluded and tended to limit visitors; unwanted visitors.

Jesse spoke about the community and described the homes, as being set far apart and separated by thick woods. Even though there were better than 600 homes and properties, most were taken and you would hardly know the place had so many residents due to the rarity of seeing anyone.

He told them that his tavern was the prime meeting place for those who wanted some company. Every now and then, someone wanted to go into town and called him for a ride. He would ask them to meet him at the tavern or pick them up at their home and drive them to Deckersburg. Many did not drive even though they owned a car.

This fellow in town, Derik, the realtor, acted as the dues collector, stocked the lake and took care of the few physical aspects that the lake community required. For that effort, he received a monthly stipend.

Jesse also added that should a few homes be for sale, as he mentioned earlier, the transactions were handled mostly by Derik. If they wished, he could show them the properties. He even had keys so they could look around and get a feel for each one.

The couple thanked him for his time and said it would be better if his parents could see the place rather than waste time seeing places that might be fine for them, but not fine for his parents. They were really interested in the community and would be returning soon.

As they left, Jesse made a mental note that they seemed friendly, but a little contrived. Some of the questions were pointed at the remoteness, not the security and comfort that most would be looking for in a senior community. They didn't ask about hospitals or medical support or how long it would take to get a 911 ambulance from the nearest hospital. Vermontville, NY is the closest town with real medical services and more than forty miles away. Older people with health issues were always concerned about security and healthcare access. Most importantly, they did not introduce themselves. He felt remiss in not taking down their license number.

George and Mary came into the tavern for dinner. Jesse always enjoyed their company, as they were not typical of the older people in the community. In fact, even though they were 'senior citizens', they had a vibrancy that belied their ages. Both ordered the same, a Cobb Salad, a Pinot wine and coffee. They didn't mind Jesse sitting with them as the conversation was always gentle yet stimulating. Jesse told them about the couple coming in to look around, the questions asked and the questions not asked.

George felt that although it might seem slightly off, it might just be an oversight. When they returned with their parents, the parents might ask those missing questions that the children didn't. If they didn't return, as was the case with most, it really doesn't matter.

Of course, they might be casing the place for a robbery. They all laughed at that, since everybody was armed with shotguns, rifles and other lethal weapons.

"Jesse, thanks for the salad, See you soon."

"Enjoy the rest of the evening," replied Jesse.

George and Mary took a leisurely stroll back to their home without giving the scenario another thought. George, however, always kept everything in some section of his mind, to be opened at a later date.

Later on that afternoon, the young couple stopped in Deckersburg and located the Postmaster, who at that time was in his bait shop.

Charlie Gross owns the bait shop and barber shop which is actually a single building divided into two stores. He fancies himself as a barber, told everyone he went to a barber school and has one of those turning barber poles in front. He also doubles as the Post Master. The Post Office is only opened from 9:00AM to 12:00noon, so Charlie runs back and forth if someone needs stamps or bait. Since the bait shop is only opened in the summer, he can stay in the Post Office during open hours for the balance of the year.

Charlie supplemented his income by doing some snow plowing in the winter. He's a lifer, meaning that his parents lived in the town, his grandparents lived in the town and even the first residents of the area were distant relations. He never married and has no intentions to do so, nor would any of the eligible women in town even consider Charlie an available catch. Catch being the operational word, as Charlie always had this smell of bait about him. Even the letters he placed into the Post Office Boxes for the residents smelled of fish.

He believes he is a barber, but the aroma of fish permeated the shop and only a few daring men would venture to have Charlie give them a haircut. The fish smell would just not wash out.

Charlie offered a haircut to the young man, explained that he was the town barber and everyone came to him for haircuts, the women also. He would be pleased to take care of their parents. Charlie also talked about the mail.

"No, not much came from or went to Decker Lake. Most of the mail was advertisements for wheelchairs, long term insurance, mortuaries, and such items. There was little to no personal mail."

He knew all the residents by name, but saw very little of them since there were hardly any need for them to come into town.

"Everything they needed was delivered to the 'General Store' at the lake."

They looked at each other after meeting with Charlie and were amazed that this place was seemingly made for Barry. They had no idea that beneath Barry's request for information was a deeper and darker scheme. They just followed instructions and were happy for the payday. One thing for certain, Charlie smelled like fish. No way would they ever let him touch their hair.

Next on the schedule was the real estate guy, Derik. Barry said he was also a lawyer, disbarred for a time, reinstated, but was definitely a shady character. Since he was responsible for real estate sales at the lake and managed their dues collections, he would be an important asset. Getting a line on his operation was an imperative.

The couple walked into Derik's Realty and were greeted by Derik.

"Have a seat," said Derik, "what can I do for you?"

They described the general situation with the parents wishing to buy some Decker Lake property. Derik described the process and added that he might be able to get a non-lakefront home rather quickly. It was a nice one, nearby Jesse's Tavern and the clubhouse and was currently owned by an elderly couple in their 80's, the Mallorys. Typically he received a 6% commission from the sellers on the resales (percentage allowed by the Real Estate Board), but if he could move the property more quickly, would they be willing to pay an additional commission outside the normal contract? He could probably get the Mallorys to sell the house for less and it would more than equal the 'extra commission.'

One thing that Derik did not lack was nerve. Even if these two were plants, nothing he said was illegal, albeit a tiny bit unethical. Evaluating character was part of Derik's delusion. He thought he could. If it were so, he would have recognized a questioning con when he was part of it.

Unlike Derik, the couple understood Derik immediately. Here was an unscrupulous character that would do anything for money and probably anything for just the hell of it. Could be useful information for Barry and he might make it worth their while with a bonus.

Derik, unlike Jesse, was very detailed. He also noted that they didn't introduce themselves and as they left, he gazed outside and took their license plate number, filed it for a later date. He knew that it always paid to have as much information as possible.

On the way out of Derik's Realty, an olive skinned dark haired fellow introduced himself.

"How ya doing? I'm Sal, the town barber. I saw you talking to Charlie, who owns the barber shop, but he's not really a barber, just would like to be. He's always saying how many haircuts he gives to men and women alike, but actually he probably doesn't do any; you know, the fish smell. Word gets around quick around here. I have a small salon behind the bar you passed just as you came into town. If you ever need anything or a haircut, just call for Sal."

Sal is the part time actual Barber and does a good business using the area behind the bar as a salon. Sal offered Charlie an opportunity to sell the barber shop, since Charlie didn't have any clientele, but was refused. Charlie fancied himself a barber and even without patrons, the shop would remain Charlie's; so Sal did all the haircutting elsewhere as he is the only real barber within twenty miles.

Sal also tends bar four nights a week, not because he needs the money, but because it allows him to have a good social life. Aside from the regulars that come into the bar almost every evening, a few of the housewives tend to drift in and say hello. He can afford to buy them a beer or martini and since he has that Italian flare, as he likes to call it, sometimes he manages to do a bit more. Tending bar has some advantages.

The conversation with Sal was short, as he didn't have anything to add to the detail they had already collected. He was just a typical small town guy with nothing to do and enjoyed running around greeting anyone he didn't recognize.

Chapter 8

The information gathered by the couple was delivered back to Barry and eventually to Harvey and the rest of the team. Decker Lake seemed like the ideal community, isolated, many older couples, hardly any visitors, which meant not much family. The proof of the isolation was in the Post Office service. Almost nothing came and went to or from Decker Lake.

Harvey, Barry and the Folsom's agreed that Decker Lake was the target. The next question and integral part of the plan was how to get the old buggers to the Sunshine Forever Home. They already knew how to 'keep them alive' after they're dead, for at least twelve to twenty four months.

"Why store them," asked Cap, "why not just cremate and dispose?"

Harvey responded, "Listen, the details are everything. Just in case someone comes by, asks a question, looks at an obituary, checks the urns or wants to the see the body. Everything is accounted for. We can always say they just died and show the body. A Medicaid investigator looking at the files, sees the timelines, reads an obit, decides to come to a funeral, dig up a body some years later, they see one and we keep them fresh using embalming techniques at the EverRest. Remember, all we want is one maybe two years of money and then we move on to the next one. Greed is bad, consistency is good."

"Okay," Harvey continued, "The next step is to get the tavern. From there we can help form the direction the old couples take, keep track of the community in general, maybe even track who can and cannot buy into the place. Jesse said that there's no real Board of Directors. We can take it over, run the place completely."

"Most of these home owners groups are autonomous. No outside agencies look into them and very few are run by management companies. I know people who have bought homes in them just to run for HOA office. They win and embezzle what they can. It's typically easy pickings. It's our task to make sure that we run this place on the up and up, so if anyone does look, they see a competently run place."

"The residents leave us alone as long as the roads are in good shape, the lake is stocked and they don't have to be involved. We avoid controversy and focus on the task at hand; getting those old bastards to the Sunshine Forever Home."

Harvey, Barry, Phil and May meet at the Sunshine Forever Home with Cap and Henny a few weeks later to finalize their plans. Harvey did most of the talking as the idea was his and the others filled in what was necessary. Everything was moving into its' rightful place.

Barry will take a trip to Jesse's Tavern and procure the tavern for Harvey. Barry was certain that Jesse would take the offer.

"It was one that Jesse would not and could not refuse."

Once that was settled, Harvey would head north, take possession and begin the takeover of the Board of Directors. According to the Decker Lake By-Laws, an election was overdue, so Harvey would contact Derik, who was generally in charge of lake money issues and have him send out a notice. He would nominate himself and since he would be the only one running, his election was assured.

In the meantime, the Sunshine Forever Home was ready for more residents and the EverRest was ready for more storage.

Chapter 9

Jesse is standing behind the bar at his tavern, leaning on the bar with his elbows, gazing up at the 60" flat screen TV which is positioned strategically so the patrons that want to watch must sit at the bar. He knows that when they sit at the bar they tend to order drinks and drinking was the staple of the tavern. He offers a selection of standard pub food, the usual hamburgers, chili, chunks of mystery meats with spaghetti, sliced meat, egg salad and tuna salad sandwiches and prepackaged pot pies, chicken strips and basic house salads.

Nothing real fancy was the order of the day. What Jesse sold could be easily frozen and stored for a long time. Not many people came to the tavern from the outside; only those who might be looking for a retirement community; so he prepared meals that he knew the residents enjoyed.

The older men loved pub food and the older women loved salads.

He was thinking about all the long days and nights working in factories, aboard merchant ships, the tour in Viet Nam and the jobs he didn't want to do but had to for survival. Somehow he managed to save just enough to finally buy a place of his own. He considered it a lot of wasted years that you could never get back. He had regrets and plenty of them but knew that having regrets didn't do you any good.

There was Ruth, whom he didn't marry even though he loved her, but couldn't provide for her. Even though she implored him to stay, his ego was at stake and he left her standing at the door of their small apartment in Scranton. He told her he was going to find work that a man could be proud of, that he could offer to his woman something of value, not a broken down husk of a person who earned minimum wage, needed the VA to overcome PSTD and therapy to avoid alcohol.

He thought he was doing the right thing, but in the end, it was not. Maybe if he was there, she would still be alive, not suffering with the cancer that eventually killed her. It was hard to endure all the recriminations, guilt and regret and even harder to avoid drinking again. He thought he had no children of his own but years later Ruth called him from her deathbed and told him that he had a son, Billy, and begged him to make sure that Billy was okay. He cried for nearly two days after Ruth died, but kept his word.

He contacted Billy, stayed with him until he grew up and he used his meager savings to put him through college. Billy graduated, took a job in the financial section in Scranton and became self-sufficient. Eventually, Billy found a better place to live and a better job in California and relocated. Jesse decided to move on his own again and travelled into New York where he found Decker Lake and the tavern, at that time a run-down establishment. Jesse did most of the work himself and the current look of the tavern, Jesse's Tavern, took shape. He decided to avoid any questions about his history and just tell everyone in Decker Lake that he was a retired fireman.

Billy and he continued to have a relationship, even if it was remote and not often. Someday Jesse would sell the tavern, move closer to Billy and enjoy a complete retirement. He promised himself this a number of times.

Jesse didn't realize how soon that day would be.

Barry walked into the tavern and directly over to Jesse, standing behind the bar, watching TV. Barry glanced up at the set, saw that Jesse was preoccupied with a football game in progress and made a decision to start this conversation off very slowly.

"Jesse, how about a beer, and you can make me a roast beef on rye."

Jesse was startled by the voice as he was daydreaming about his life and lost in thought. When the fog lifted, he was again startled when he saw Barry standing there. A cold shiver ran up and down his spine. He knew Barry as a young kid from Scranton; a sullen, nasty and belligerent oaf, starting fights, molesting women to start fights, pushing his way to start fights.

When Jesse was 35, Barry was just a teenager. He was arrested a number of times but never served long sentences as most would not testify against him. For some strange reason, Barry thought that he was his friend and he would never tell him otherwise. Barry always had ulterior motives and seeing him standing there put him on notice that Barry wanted something and he would have to give it.

"Okay," responded Jesse, walking to the right where the refrigerator stood, prepared the sandwich and on his way back to Barry, pulled a beer from the nearest tap. He also pulled one for himself, which he didn't drink.

Barry saw that Jesse was startled, at first by the sound and then by his presence.

Jesse began the conversation. "What's up? Haven't heard from you for more than a year, no phone calls and then here you are. Been seeing a lot lately, maybe a couple of people you've sent by; got something on your mind?"

Barry, having just taken a bite from his sandwich, hesitated before answering and wasn't going to respond to the obvious statement that Jesse knew the other couple might have been sent in to case the place.

He then responded, "Jesse, listen, you've got a nice place here and I'm sure it's a lot of work. I know that as you get older, it doesn't get easier. So I've decided to make you an offer, one that I know is so good that you just won't be able to refuse. This place and this tavern are perfect for me and my friend; so no reason to beat around the bush. Here's my offer."

And it was right to the point, no frills, no fluff, just Barry hovering over the bar with those big arms resting on the mahogany and the gray eyes staring at Jesse.

Barry pushes a slip of paper to Jesse. Jesse looks at the number and understands exactly what Barry is saying, without him saying it. Barry wants the tavern, likely not for himself, but for another. Thinking about the past week and who came looking, he now understands that it was for some guy he never met. The young couple came in shortly before Barry showed up, casing the place, asking questions. He learned that they went into town to see Derik, spoke to Charlie and asked more questions. None of the questions involved the typical ones asked when looking for a place for the elderly.

Jesse decided he wouldn't say anything to Barry about what he felt he knew. It was healthier to keep much unsaid.

"Barry," give me a couple of days to think it over."

Jesse knew that he must act without Barry suspecting that he was uncomfortable and that he might go to the police with his suspicions. Actually, Jesse wouldn't have, he just wanted time to organize his affairs and get ready to leave. He's got enough money to start over, if he wished. He could visit with his son. Maybe he'd just go to Hawaii and hang out on the beach. Barry told him he'd be back on Wednesday, in the morning and if Jesse accepted the offer, they could go into town and see this real estate guy, Derik.

Barry finished his sandwich and after praising Jesse on the great roast beef, they shook hands. "See you Wednesday" called Barry, as he left the tavern, got into his car and drove to Deckersburg. He called Harvey and told him that the phase 1 of the plan was okay. He knew that Jesse would sell, because he made a solid offer. He and Jesse planned to visit Derik on Wednesday and Harvey would soon have title to the tavern.

Harvey acknowledged the call and responded with just an "okay, talk to you later."

Barry had his general plans previously prepared. First he would say 'hello' to Jesse and then he would meet this realtor, Derik, in Deckersburg. He had his friend Mickey do a 'look up' of Derik and found that Derik had a history, one not actually hidden from anyone who chose to find it. Derik was involved with embezzlement and other unfounded, unproven charges and chose 'not' to practice law in New York, but do the realtor job instead. His suspension from the Bar had been lifted.

Strange that he would choose to become the realtor in this small tucked away place. But there were many people who chose to hide away and live quietly rather than to come out and confront.

"Crap," Barry thought, "I did that myself hiding away in PA."

Barry walked into Derik's office and introduced himself. Then, after all the introductions and platitudes were completed, and they were both seated at Derik's desk, he continued.

"Derik," my plan is to purchase the tavern from Jesse. Naturally, this is confidential and until the contract is signed, no one can be the wiser. Understand?"

"Of course," Derik responded, seated with his hands folded, fingers interlocked and demonstrating trust. "All business of this kind is held in strict confidence. When will this be taking place?"

"Jesse and I will be here on Wednesday morning." Barry was certain that Jesse would sell the tavern. "He can't know that we are having this conversation, nor can he know some of the details."

Derik replies quickly. "Understood, but what are the details?"

"Even though I'm making this deal with Jesse, the tavern will be placed in the name of Harvey Paul. I'll give you his information now so we don't have to do this later. I'll give you a cashier's check for the total amount and pay you an 'extra' commission for being so accommodating later on. Is it necessary for Jesse to know the name of the actual purchaser?"

"No, it's not required and since you want this confidential, I will not ask you the question you are obviously waiting for me to ask, which is" Derik hesitated just slightly with the next word, "why?"

Barry didn't answer the obvious unasked question and said instead, "That's good, so I'll see you on Wednesday and I hope we can enjoy a very long relationship working together." Barry stands up, they shake hands and Barry quickly turns and walks out of Derik's shop without looking back.

Derik just stands there looking out the door and rubs his scar in a way that others would rub their chin, when thinking about what just occurred.

But right now, what Derik is thinking about, is the money he will earn from this sale.

Derik thought it unusual that Jesse, who loved working in his tavern, would sell it to a relative stranger. Maybe Barry wasn't a stranger?

"It's none of my business," he thought, "as long as I can make a few bucks."

Two days later, it's Wednesday and Barry arrives at the tavern in the morning as promised.

Barry offered to drive Jesse to Derik's and back but Jesse explained that he would rather take his own car, and that he might take a ride to Vermontville to pick up some supplies.

Jesse was not getting into Barry's car. Although he didn't know what was going on and didn't want to know, he knew Barry well enough to take his own ride. It was ironic that Barry also knew why Jesse wouldn't get into his car. No matter, Barry knew that Jesse would sell, leave and never contact anyone in Decker Lake again.

What Barry didn't know was that Jesse had a son and that Jesse's mindset about the community gave him feelings of loyalty to the residents. Somehow, he would get a message about his suspicions to George and Mary, who seemed to be the most capable and worldly residents. He enjoyed their conversations and also didn't want bad things to happen to the community.

The meeting at Derik's was uneventful. Neither Derik nor Barry acknowledged each other as having met before. They went into the small conference room just in the rear of the store. The conference room was sparsely furnished with a centrally placed oak table, four rich leather chairs and one bookcase. Derik sat with his back to the rear wall, with Jesse on his left and Barry on his right. Derik filled out the basic title transfer papers. All the finances were in order. Jesse signed as the seller, Barry signed as the buyer. Derik acted as the attorney and witness. Derik would take the paperwork to Vermontville for filing and once the filing was accepted and money transferred, the sale was complete. He would notify both sides of the completion. In the meantime, Jesse could begin preparing to move his belongings.

The transaction being completed, they all stood and walked to the front room where Jesse shook Derik's and Barry's hands and then left the store, got into his car and drove off in the direction of Vermontville. Barry thanked Derik for the quick transaction and his confidence and assured him that it would not be forgotten.

Barry called Harvey soon after the paperwork was signed. "Everything's a go. Paperwork should be sealed and Title transferred in a couple of days. Let's get ready for Phase 2."

Just as predicted, the paperwork is certified, sealed and money delivered. Jesse transferred the money to a private account. Two days later, Jesse loaded his car with his essentials. That evening he left without a goodbye to anyone. He headed west to see his son. From there who knows? One thing is certain; he will contact George to let him know who Barry really is, what he is and who his associates might be. It's the least he can do. Another thing for certain is that no one will know where he is or where he's going. It's time to forget and to be forgotten,

Just after Jesse left, Barry drove to the tavern and entered into the next stage of his life, maybe the final con, but it's gon'na be a good one. He smiled a large toothy smile and wrapped his big arms around himself like a hug. He had prepared a sign for the front door so all will know that the tavern has changed hands. It's a simple and direct statement.

"The Tavern will soon reopen under new management but the name of the place will stay the same. Please, everyone come by for the 'Grand Reopening of Jesse's Tavern on Sunday at 4:00PM' when all drinks will be on the 'House' and dinner will be served."

Chapter 10

What a beautiful Sunday afternoon it was. Harvey could not have picked a better day. It was cool, but not cold. The invitations were sent to all the residents and one was posted in the clubhouse just in case someone stopped in. He even went into Deckersburg to post the invitation at the realtor, the bar and the sheriff's office He prepared all the food, most of which was pre-made and had it shipped in from Vermontville.

He made certain that there was plenty of beer on tap, bottled choices for those that enjoyed store brands and a variety of liquor expressly selected to delight the palate of the senior citizen. This he did by himself, not wanting his 'helper' to be in sight until later on in the plan.

As the residents wandered in, he led them to the bar, to tables, offered them beers on the house, cordials for the ladies, and brought out the menus. He added a second TV so those seated at tables could also watch. The TVs were all on the same channel, tennis matches, which seemed okay for both the women and men. There was just enough action and sound to keep the tavern friendly but not anything that might distract them from the friendly conversations taking place.

In fact, the residents hadn't gotten together like this for years and would not do so again, at least not with his help. His plan was twofold. First, he wanted to meet them all in a friendly setting so when he offered to become the President of the Association, they would jump at the opportunity to have a young and generous person like Harvey as their 'leader'. Secondly, he would then be able to execute the Phase 3 of this plan, bringing in Barry as his helper and then waiting for the first resale, when he could have Phil and May Gruenweld move in.

By that time, he would be able to appoint Phil and May to the Board of Directors and totally control the community. Of course, either Phil or May would have to remain in Florida to run the mortuary and help with the death certificates as the residents of the Sunshine Forever Home died. It made him smile to think about those that would actually die and have funerals; while others would die, but not really be dead and be stored for a period of time; like popsicles or, he almost laughed, momsicles.

He thought to himself, “this was actually fun”. And he had this warm and comfortable feeling inside.

“I bet mom and dad would be proud of me.”

George and Mary were seated at a corner table overlooking the road and watched as the residents came and left, shaking hands with Harvey, the new owner, thanking him for his hospitality and assuring him that they would be happy to enjoy his company in the future.

A few had asked what happened to Jesse, to which Harvey responded with, “I guess he just decided it was time to retire. I was in the market for a place like this, to run a small tavern in a quiet community and it coincidentally came along just at the right time. Sometimes you can’t believe your good fortune.”

George looked at all the comings and goings and knew that this was a onetime event. Everything would be back to normal by the next day. Somehow, as he was listening to Harvey’s words, he came to the opinion that the words were practiced, had little emotion or speech patterns showing any empathy for those good feelings. Strange it might be, but George acknowledged to himself that it might just be the studied expressions of a person who owned a business before and needed to make a good impression, visually and verbally.

The food was good, a better quality than Jesse offered. No one knew that it was prepared professionally elsewhere and delivered. But everyone ate and expressed their opinions that Harvey would be a good proprietor of the tavern. He also told them that he was keeping the name ‘Jesse’s Tavern’ as it was recognized in town and elsewhere and he didn’t want to lose the name recognition.

Everything went as well as Harvey had planned; plenty of shaking hands, camaraderie, smiles and free drinks for all. By

10:00 PM the evening ended and the last resident said good night and left.

Harvey thought to himself, as he finished a half-eaten roast beef sandwich and downed the balance of a beer.

"The next few days will be busy, taking care of the bar, the food and organizing the first sale of property."

I'll need some help with this place, so Barry coming by tomorrow and me hiring him won't be a surprise to anyone. If anyone asks, I'll just tell them that I knew Barry as a passing acquaintance whom I met years ago in a tavern in Pennsylvania. Most of the men know that when sitting at a bar having lunch, you make some small talk with the bartender, who just happened to be Barry. He told me then that he was looking to move on to a place that might not be as busy and where he could also add some cooking to the days' work. He enjoyed cooking and preparing food and talking to patrons. Barry could add the name of the town as Harvey didn't need to know it as he was just passing through. It's an easy story to remember and would satisfy anyone making conversation.

Harvey called Barry and told him to come by the next day and relayed his thoughts about how they met. This all sounded plausible to Barry who knew that keeping it simple was the best practice.

The next two months were uneventful at the lake. Harvey continued to establish himself in the tavern. Barry became the face of the tavern, behind the bar and the server of the meals. Every evening he managed to go for a walk and was not seen or heard of until the next day when the tavern opened.

The Sunshine Forever Home renovation continued and it was able to serve local Florida residents. More than half of the 500+ rooms were filled with locals and referrals from the area. Medicaid, Social Security and long term nursing care insurance were more than adequate to pay all the bills, to hire more staff as well as provide a substantial payday to Cap and Henrietta.

The collaboration with Phil and May at the mortuary and the details for storage, cremation and burial were working well. Phil could demonstrate the dual database methods for maintaining the 'dead' as actually alive and the 'dead' when they were finally pronounced dead for the records.

It was interesting that when a spouse died, the remaining spouse, if capable, would attend the funeral, be driven back to the home and was easily convinced to move to a single rather than a double room without argument or struggle. The death of the spouse typically took all the fight out of the husband or wife.

An insurance database even had an actuarial table of how long a surviving spouse would live after the death of a partner. Phil actually laughed out loud as he thought, "the insurance companies, Medicaid and banking methodologies are actually doing most of the work for us. No wonder there's so much fraud. Medicaid, Medicaid, thank you for all your good works."

All aspects of the con and embezzlement were firmly in place for two years and ready for the first "mark" from Decker Lake.

Phil called Harvey and expressed his delight with the whole operation at his end. All that remained was adding Harvey's new slice of the apple pie.

Chapter 11

A few months later, Harvey had completed the next step in his plan, which was to become the President of the Decker Lake Home Owners Association. He had Derik, who was the temporary trustee of the HOA, send out a notice for elections and as he had predicted, he was the only resident willing to run for the position. He was certified as the President a week later and asked Derik to stay on as the trustee sending out the dues and whatever else he did during the interim. Derik, of course, agreed.

Now it was just a waiting game until the first resident decided to move. In the meantime he reviewed the deeds of the homes already owned by the Decker Lake community. None of them could have been used to support Phil and May as most were too distant from the tavern.

Harvey and the Gruenwelds agreed that they should try to find a place closer to the entrance. Either Phil or May needed to be in the mortuary and it was rare that both could be at Decker Lake. Coming and going would be less obvious if they could just drive out without others seeing all the travel.

Fate has a way of stepping in and introducing an opportunity. The Mallorys had made a decision to sell their lake home and move to a more suitable senior community. Harvey had posted on the clubhouse bulletin board a number of scenic photos and services at the Sunshine Forever Home as well as the telephone number of the registration desk.

The home also provided a bus-like vehicle as a transportation service, referred to as a Transport, with one stop along the way. Not as fast or convenient as flying, but the Transport also took luggage, personal items, some small furniture and other necessities which would make the place more comfortable for elderly people moving in.

It was almost too good to be true, but there it was in black and white in the brochure. The Mallorys, an elderly couple in their late eighties, were tired of the cold weather and made a conscious plan to move to a warmer climate; Florida being the choice for many senior citizens. They had no children or relatives. No one came to visit them. They did not make many friends at the lake and the lake did not have any social events or planned trips or anything that they might want to do. Most people at the lake were those who wanted to grow old and watch the grass grow and the lake ripple and do the same thing every day. They had felt the same way, but with the passage of time, they realized that a little excitement or variation in a daily life might awaken their younger spirits, so Florida and a real senior facility might be the answer.

Since they had some savings, Medicaid wouldn't kick in right away, but they could afford one of the duplex apartments in the assisted living section. All their meals would be prepared. There was a medical facility nearby, not forty miles away like here at the lake. Social events were planned, even day trips. Their money would last about a year and they'd both be nearing ninety.

This was not the time to plan ahead or be presumptuous that they had that long.

"Yes, they would sell and move".

The first call they made was to Derik Manheim., the realtor. Everyone at Decker Lake knew Derik, rumored to be an attorney and the only realtor in town. Since all the commission percentages were the same for all real estate sales, they weren't concerned that they would be paying more for local help than getting someone from Vermontville.

They also had strong ties to the local community and keeping the money and business within it would help everyone. They told Derik of their plans to move to this Sunshine Forever Home in Florida, which had been posted at the clubhouse.

"No, we did not contact Harvey, the President of the Decker Lake Community. We didn't think it was necessary".

Derik told them that one of the conditions of the HOA Title was to bring the lake community in, particularly now that they had an elected president. Oftentimes, a sale could be faster if the HOA was involved as not many outside of here were looking at this time. They may not get the best deal, but it would be quick.

The Mallorys, thinking about the actual time it would take to sell their place, agreed with Derik and asked them to call Harvey and organize a meeting at Derik's office.

Derik placed a call to Harvey and told him of the impending sale. They wanted to haggle a bit, but he was certain that he could bring in the property for ten to fifteen thousand less than book because the Mallorys want a quick sale. This would be only the first, the first of what they hoped were many sales of this kind. Derik was unaware of anything but the kickback scheme to get the properties cheap, and he would reap another couple of points on the sale.

Marty Mallory called Harvey at the tavern. He thought to himself how easy this was to get the quick sale and was happy about the discussion he had with Derik. Harvey answered the telephone call which he knew was coming. All was planned and ready.

"Marty, what can I do for you?"

Marty explained the situation just as he had told Derik. Harvey offered to drive him and his wife into town for the meeting. If it worked out well, they could all go back to the tavern for a nice lunch and celebrate the new chapter in their lives. Harvey would call Derik and set a date and time, preferably in the morning when everyone was fresh and there would be plenty of time for that lunch.

Harvey called Derik immediately after hanging up with Marty to set the date and time and each congratulated the other for this great deal. Both would profit from a simple transaction.

The deal went smoothly at Derik's office. Just as Derik indicated to Harvey, they sold the house for thirteen thousand dollars less than market, so Derik made a cool extra $1300.00.

Derik had a number of papers for the Mallorys to sign and they didn't notice that two were identical, one selling the house to the

Decker Lake community and the other selling the house to the Gruenwelds, the owners of the Florida mortuary.

Derik sent the Gruenweld Bill of Sale to the State for affirmation and the Title was sent in and registered to the Gruenwelds.

Later on that day, Harvey and the Mallorys enjoy the celebratory lunch. Afterwards, Marty called the Sunshine Forever Home and confirmed the entry and prices, etc. They wanted a duplex for two and would pay direct for now, not with Medicaid.

"No, they would not sign over their financial rights at this time or give power of attorney to the home. This might come at a later date, but for now, they could afford the costs."

The home sent some legal paperwork to the Mallorys, which they signed and returned, after Derik looked it over. The home, having received all the necessary paperwork and a two month deposit, expressed their thanks and told them that they will send the Transport at the Mallorys convenience.

The Mallorys packed, had a yard sale for their furnishings and waited for the Transport. Anything unsold would be picked up by the consignment shop. After the Transport arrived, their personal belongings were neatly placed into the lower compartment; they were given seats, which reclined for comfort.

They said their goodbyes to Harvey, thanked him for his service and stepped into the Transport to Florida. The Mallorys arrived at the home the next day, registered and were shown their nicely furnished duplex room. About two weeks later, they sent a nice postcard to Decker Lake expressing how wonderful it was at the Sunshine Forever Home, particularly with the rooms, the events and so on.

Meanwhile, the first resident of the Sunshine Forever Home after the Mallorys arrival had passed away after a short illness. Eugene was 76, single, had no family, no visitors and was generally a loner and on Medicaid. The EverRest mortuary came and collected the body and put it into storage. They had the typical sham funeral with the casket closed and a hundred pounds of material inside so the gravediggers wouldn't notice it empty when they lowered it into the new grave.

According to the actuarial table, this guy should have lived at least three years with the general conditions he had. Phil decides that giving him 24 months would be adequate. He placed a funeral on the calendar set for two years and closed the freezer drawer. He notified Cap who sets aside 16 signatures for use with any form requests that might come in. If Cap determined that there were any additional inquiries, he would speed up the 'funeral' and back off the payments to avoid exposure. This was just another of many residents who were already in cold storage; and a second benefit of this was they could re-rent the room to another – like double billing a client for services.

When he expressed this sentiment to Harvey, May and the others, they all got a good laugh. "A toast to Harvey for this great idea and to Eugene, whom we hope will be comfortable in our cold storage unit." They all raised a glass, those in Florida, and those in New York, celebrating the next phase of their enterprise.

Chapter 12

The Sunshine Forever Home was flourishing with almost all of its rooms occupied. Periodically, a resident died, was 'buried' and otherwise stored at the funeral home. In fact, more than forty shelves were occupied and it was becoming just a bit more difficult to manage all the 'death certificates' for Medicaid, the relocation of the bodies into their coffins that were buried two years earlier, tracking newcomers and attempting to funnel the sickest elderly possible to the home to maximize the profit.

Decker Lake supplied a nice quantity of product subsequent to the Mallorys being the first residents to enjoy the home. Since it was possible for Harvey to market the resale of the lake homes to the oldest people he could find, he would conveniently forget to contact any younger applicants who had interest in the lake. All of this required coordination with the Gruenwelds to ensure that they did not overload the storage system. The shelves weren't capable of supporting two corpses. Periodically, Medicaid sent forms for signature as well as other typical requests for information.

Henny expertly lifted other signatures from the many originals that the incoming residents signed and 'signed' the forms, filled out what was required and sent back the information to Medicaid.

Acknowledgements were received from Medicaid and payments were automatically deposited into resident accounts. As of right now, that was a cool $200,000 each month from the residents of the shelves.

Prior to the Decker Lake project, they had been limited to about twenty-three bodies in storage and now they were up to about forty. The number seemed to be stable and they needed to increase it to take advantage of the fifty to fifty-five shelves available.

Harvey, Barry and Phil decided to have a quick meeting to review what they were doing and how they might increase the 'product', as they liked to refer to the bodies in storage.

The issue was how to create an atmosphere at the lake which would cause some of the oldest homeowners to become more open to the idea of moving to a senior facility. No one had any ideas on that subject and any open malicious intent against anyone, no matter how secretive, might lead to a police investigation. They all agreed to table the subject until someone could come up with something solid, something that might work. In the meanwhile, natural attrition would suffice and maybe some encouragement from Harvey as he met with the residents at Jesse's.

A few days later, Barry came up with an idea.

Barry fancied himself an expert in certain types of psychological pressure. He was a very large man, well-muscled and many of his acquaintances would refer to him as a 'tank'. Even though he could tower above most people and could present his body language in a threatening manner, he learned to use a tone of voice and facial expressions to impose his will upon what he called his 'prey'.

Barry was as smart as he was large and had no issues with using both attributes to gain the advantage. He also believed that technology was the future of any endeavor and he read extensively on subjects that might give him an additional advantage.

Even when he was hiding away in Pennsylvania, tending bar, he maintained his edge by studying police reports, judicial reviews of fraud cases and technical manuals having to do with psychological warfare and advanced interrogation techniques.

He told Harvey about a military study he read that low frequency sound waves, at the right amplitude and intensity, transmitted from a white noise activator and presented continuously, became a silent auditory assault. It created an emotional uneasiness in subjects which allowed interrogators to gain influence. The low frequency sound waves interfered with sleep just enough that those who were under its influence experienced long term, sleep deprivation effects.

When those who had depression experienced this, they became more depressed and had heightened feelings of anxiety. The elderly were particularly sensitive to this as most had underlying depressions about death and illness, even if they were feeling healthy at any particular moment.

Barry explained that even the younger residents would begin to have feelings of paranoia and unease and although the sounds were beneath the audible range, they would be 'heard' in the mind as whispers, as a creepy feeling. Many would experience the feelings that they were inside a horror movie waiting for a monster to jump at them from behind a tree.

As Barry explained all the details to Harvey, his mouth formed a wide grin and his eyes figuratively began to shine with joy. In fact, Harvey had never seen Barry so happy. Talking about torture and mental manipulation actually made Barry happy and joyful.

Harvey thought about his own preoccupation with doing the con, the 'project' as he like to call it. It made him happy but only on an objective level. He didn't become emotionally charged by the 'project'. But Barry, he actually got off on this.

Although he made certain that his facial expressions were controlled, he was slightly disturbed by Barry's pathological behavior.

He just didn't recognize his own.

"That's the best way to express the results of the exercise," Barry exclaimed as Harvey listened intently to the description of this mental form of torture.

Harvey liked it. He wanted to do it. Even if it didn't work, it might be fun to watch the residents creep and crawl around.

He didn't mean that it would be the same kind of fun that Barry enjoyed, just more objective, not sociopathic.

Harvey added only a few words to the conversation. "How do we get started with this? It sounds like it might work and if it doesn't, we haven't lost anything."

Barry begins to describe the plan. "The north end of the lake is nothing but thick woods, no trails with the exception of a few paths for quads. The Pine trees are massively tall and surrounded by Oaks. Between the shrubbery, scrub oaks, Sycamore, Sassafras and Willows, hanging Pine branches and tree fall, no one actively or purposely decides to go hiking in that morass of vegetation.

We'll use the height of the trees to plant the white noise activators, and I know there are some natural caves to hide the low frequency generator. It'll take some time to find the right locations, to provide coverage to most of the community, but the height will give us an advantage. The intensity can be measured to ensure that we cover the housing areas but not reach as far as the entry roads.

We don't want this crap impacting us as well, and it will if we subject ourselves to it. Phil and I will get some camouflage suits and wear Indian moccasins to keep a soft footprint. We'll map out where we want the units during the day and use night vision goggles at night to install the equipment.

I can't add more than that for now, but it's important that we are not (emphasizing 'not') seen doing this work so as we move forward, our plan is safe."

Barry studied the maps of the area and compared them with his previous evening hikes into the woods. He used the maps to verify the positions. He found some of the highest Pine trees, in the thickest brush and noted them on the plan. He also found one cave like structure that was well hidden beneath the roots of a monstrous Oak tree.

He didn't see any signs that an animal was currently occupying the cave, so he noted it for the location of the generator. Once he determined the number and types of devices he needed for this operation, he called one of his 'suppliers' in Pennsylvania to order the components. Some of it is military grade and is not accessible to the general public.

A beneficial characteristic of the generator is it's a battery powered unit that provides a massive inaudible output. The battery could last for up to a month, depending upon the hours of usage. Barry decided that using it from dusk to dawn was best as it would interfere with the sleep periods, as well as evenings, when the dark, animal noises, fog and general appearance of the lake might add to the loneliness and depression of its' residents.

It has no moving parts and offers no audible sounds during its operation. Either he or Phil could go out in the evening to change the battery when necessary. A wireless IP access to its internal operation would allow them to make changes in its characteristics as well as monitor the output.

Unfortunately, the white noise activators, a speaker in general terms, needed to be wired directly to the output. Wireless speakers would not provide the functionally he needed. His installation plan included the thickest tree sections, where branches of one tree merged with branches of the next, almost like a canopy described in African jungles. This canopy would be the hiding place for the wiring between the speakers and the generator.

Many of the speakers would be wired in series. No more than three parallel circuits will be needed to push the non-auditory noise out to the community.

Camouflaging the speakers would be simple as they'll be placed high, were not very large and will be shrouded in the trees as well as have camouflaged coverings. Unless someone was particularly looking for these devices, they couldn't be seen.

"Okay," Harvey added, with some incredulity written on his face. Barry was more detailed than he realized and seemed ready to apply this to the lake community. It sounded like a great idea and if it worked, it could speed up the profits.

"Go for it."

Chapter 13

Barry received a call on his cell phone from his friend in Pennsylvania. Everything was ready for delivery. All Barry needed to do was to tell him where and when. Barry thought carefully about the location of the drop and decided it was best to meet his friend's van on the outskirts of Deckersburg, maybe at the cemetery.

Barry returned the call, "Meet me at the Deckersburg cemetery at 9:00 pm, right near the missing gate. We'll transfer the stuff to my car. There's a good spot just behind the back of Ivan's Market. The location is dark and isolated. We won't be seen or raise suspicion."

Later that evening a dark Chevy van pulled up to the gate entrance to the cemetery and a lone figure emerged from the driver's side. A second person stayed in the van. Noticeably, when the van door opened, the light didn't come on in the passenger compartment so the person in the passenger seat was not illuminated.

A second vehicle pulled up alongside the van. Barry opened the door Also, noticeable was that the light inside Barry's car did not go on. Barry and the other person walked to the rear of the van; opened the back doors and began to take boxes from the van and place them into Barry's vehicle. Once the van is emptied and Barry's car is loaded, Barry and he shook hands, an envelope with the payment is placed into the other's hand and the man entered his van and drives off, leaving Barry to move on as well.

Ivan heard noises behind his shop. He was in his apartment upstairs with the lights off just sitting in the dark and contemplating his life. He could never stop the dreams of his times in Romania and the vicious Russians who killed his family.

He could recall the feelings he had when he was killing and slicing up the messengers for meals for the Russians. For anyone else, these would have been nightmares, reasons to commit suicide, but for Ivan, they were just memories, which came in the form of waking dreams, which he sometimes relished and at other times, just dismissed.

He sat in the dark every night, never watching television or reading a book or holding a conversation or needing any company. In all aspects of his life he was a solitary person and hardly a human being at all.

He peered out from his rear window, keeping himself in the shadow of his curtains so he wouldn't be seen and looked toward the location of the sound. He didn't hear the van pull up, but did hear the sound of the second vehicle. Getting out of the car was Barry. Barry and this other fellow met at the rear of the van and moved a bunch of boxes and stuff from the van to Barry's car.

He thought to himself, "This is a very strange occurrence, to have this meeting in the dark. In front of the cemetery is an interesting location."

Ivan believed in portents, things he learned from his upbringing in Romania and this portent, a transfer of unknown things in the dark in front of a cemetery was an omen of evil. Ivan didn't care about evil; it was just a notation in his mind. He would be thinking about this and would need to make a decision whether to let Barry know that he has witnessed this event.

"By the next time Barry comes to the market to buy supplies for the tavern, I will have made this decision." Ivan considers the timing but does not actually understand why he would be making any consideration at all. But he will wait. He remembers the patience he had in Romania to take vengeance on the Russians. It was years forming his plan and finally getting revenge. Yes, he will wait until he feels it is an opportune time to ask Barry. This is not it.

It was best to leave things alone rather than get involved. There were many times that Ivan forgot that he was in America illegally and actually did not "exist" except in the minds of the people in Deckersburg and his vendors.

His venders he always paid cash and he took credit cards through a thing called PayPal, an internet banking and money handling place. He didn't understand very much about the workings of PayPal but he heard that if you kept the total income in there under a certain amount, they did not notify anyone of the transactions. He managed to have a few PayPal accounts under different email names and the whole thing worked well.

His pseudo identity that he purchased was perfect for a minimum wage; easy 1040 tax form, without too many complications and no one gave him a second glance.

Barry sat back into his car without noticing that he was watched from the upstairs apartment of Ivan's Market. He drove back to the small parking area behind the tavern, took all the boxes and equipment from his car and put them into the tavern's storage shed. In the morning he will inventory everything to make sure all the components are there, not because he thinks that his friend would leave anything out, just that it was a complicated setup and something might be inadvertently missing.

Once he began the installation process, he didn't want to stop because of a missing piece.

The next morning, at first light, he walked to the shed and met Harvey. Barry showed Harvey the equipment and completed the inventory. He assembled the generator and performed a quick power test. Barry noted that the power test was nominal and he reassures Harvey that everything is ready and working. He will begin the installation after dark.

Barry and Phil both knew that no one goes into the woods at the north side of the lake in the evening so they wait until 10:00PM grab the generator components and batteries, load them into his car and include a small rubber wheeled cart. When they get to the parking area just outside the north woods, they unload the cart and then the components. With some difficulty, due to the heavy underbrush, they manage to push and pull the loaded cart to the location near the giant Oak tree. Barry begins the initial install of the generator.

It’s not easy work and walking and working in the camouflage suits and moccasins, although necessary, makes it more difficult. By the end of the first evening they have completed the install of the generator and some quick self-testing proves the generator is working within nominal limits.

They perform a quick IP test of the generator’s remote access and modify the settings. All is working as planned. The next part is more difficult; installing the wiring and the speakers high up into the wooded canopy.

For more than five days, Barry and Phil work through the night, with Barry climbing the trees and pulling the cabling, installing the white noise activators and with Phil feeding the cable, hiding it into the niches of the Oak trees, covering it with soil and leaves using Elmer’s clear glue as a paste.

The wiring being placed from the cave opening under the tree roots and vertically into the Oak tree niches is hidden so completely that no one would ever know that the wiring was there. Once in the canopy, the wiring is spread horizontally among the branches and from tree to tree and begins to resemble moss covered vines. As the project is completed and the speakers are placed, both Barry and Phil look at their handiwork and actually take pride in its’ invisible characteristics.

Phil is pointing at one spot in the high branches that might be exposing a speaker, but Barry doesn’t see anything. They agree that coming back in the daytime would be a good idea. Maybe ask Harvey to take a look, just to be certain that the setup is truly invisible.

The next morning, Barry met with Harvey at the tavern. “Harvey, the equipment is totally installed, tested and ready to go. I’m hungry, how about putting up a couple of burgers?”

Harvey agreed with the burgers and as they grill, waits for more information from Barry. “Okay, we’re going to take a walk today, you and I, just down the path and into the north woods. You know that this stuff is there. Look around and try to spot anything, wires and speakers, whatever. If you can’t see this stuff, neither will anyone else.”

Harvey agreed and after they finish eating, they take a nice leisurely walk down Decker Path into the north woods area.

"I don't see a thing. Where is this stuff?" exclaims Harvey, who is very surprised that his sharp eyes can't spot the equipment even though he knows it's up there somewhere.

Barry, of course, is happy with his efforts and tells Harvey "Good, if you can't see it, neither will anyone else. Let's just keep this between Phil and myself for now. If you want to see the generator cave, I can take you there at night, but not now."

Harvey, of course, agrees with this assessment and adds, "Let's turn it on tonight and watch the game begin."

Chapter 14

New York State near the Canadian border cools rather quickly by the early fall season as Canadian north winds and weather begin to take over the too short but prolific summer season. Decker Lake has the same short summer season as most lake and vacation communities in the region. Vacationers and summer residents come to enjoy the facilities after Memorial Day and tend to leave just after Labor Day, so the season runs from May through the beginning of September.

Tourism also ends as there are no winter sports, snowboarding or skiing in the area. As the weather changes to shorter days and cooler nights, those who are not full time residents leave for warmer climates. Those who are living permanently at Decker Lake, which are mostly the senior community, stay and enjoy the lazy days and evenings in front of their fireplaces, drinking hot tea and contemplating the portion of their lives that are just memories.

The latest technologies allow older people to make video calls to see their children and grandchildren, should they have any, without leaving the comfort of their homes, but Decker Lake doesn't have these services. Each house may or may not have its own antennae Dish for television and the community is wired for land lines for telephone service. Cell service is sporadic in this area and if you have one or two bars on a cell phone, you have the top level of power. Most of the residents at Decker Lake have few relations or friends, which is why they had no issue with selecting such a remote location and don't really care about the latest technology.

The residents, generally, have not come to the conclusion that warmer climates might be more suitable. Only a few of the very old, those who are past 80, are making decisions that might lead them to move on.

But recently, many have been experiencing an anxiety that they have not had before. Those few that meet at the tavern have talked about nightmares, loss of sleep even though they seem to be sleeping just as many hours. They wake up tired and anxious. Some are depressed even though they haven't felt that way until this particular fall.

In the early evening, just before dark, the cool evening air touches the slightly warmer lake water causing a cold fog to form on the lake. The fog spreads outward into the community and anyone who is subject to its touch feels that chill in the bone and shivers in the spine. Now the fog is causing fear among those that it touches.

Some of the residents who see the evening fog rolling slowly in their direction attempt to describe the anxiety but find it difficult to express themselves. No one can put a name to it or fully explain the feeling, but it's like an itch in the mind that can't be scratched; nagging….. and….. maddening.

Harvey, tending bar and delivering sandwiches and other items to the patrons overhears the discussions and now completely understands that the constant barrage of the low frequency white noise is having an effect on the most elderly among the residents.

Of course he relays this information to Barry, who has been outside raking leaves, clearing the area around the tavern of brush and other debris. Barry smiles and suggests that the evening barrage is working. He doesn't mention to Harvey that this woman, Mary, has been taking early evening strolls to the north end and sitting by the lake shore. Barry doesn't believe that he and Phil were seen, but they needed to change the batteries at the generator and believed it would be a good time to go. It's much easier to work without the night vision goggles.

"Mary," he noted to himself, "looked around and even walked to the spot where she might have seen them walking. It wasn't near the generator but even so, seeing them in their camouflage outfits would have been damaging. He saw her looking at the spot where they had been, but he knew the Indian moccasins hardly left a trace of their presence on the forest floor."

One fall evening, Mary was sitting by the lake shore near the north end. This was a regular habit she had for a few months, contemplating her and George's 'retirement' from the Agency and missing the action, but not missing the action, both feelings happened simultaneously, and it was difficult to actually understand how both conditions could happen at the same time.

Mary turned her head quickly. She thought she heard noises in the woods behind her. Looking closely through the thick underbrush and tree fall, she believed she saw something stalking through the woods. Feeling more apprehensive than normal for her, she slowly stood up and walked to the area that she believed was where she saw something and found no signs; no footprints, no broken twigs, nothing. The only thing she was certain of was the silence that had been invoked by the presence and the return of the forest noises upon the departure. This and the whispering in her ear when she sat by the lake shore, demanding that she leave or suffer the consequences.

When she turned her head to see who was speaking, there was no one there, but the whispering returned when she faced the lake. It was all too eerie. She wrapped her arms around herself in a protective manner and shivered internally. She wanted to scream "stop it, stop it already". It was like being inside of a horror movie, waiting for the creature to leap out and grab her with its razor sharp teeth, or a ghoul feasting on her flesh.

She thought about her feelings and wondered if George was experiencing the same. During the evening, when they both were in bed, she would waken suddenly from whatever nightmares she was having, looked over at George and saw the motions of his mouth, like silent screams, the agitation on his face and knew that he was also having nightmares.

Mary was deep in thought, "I don't know what the hell is going on, but I don't want to take this crap anymore. I'll tell George it's time to leave. I love the bastard and I know he'll agree. Anyway, it might be just a coincidence but the Agency contacted me for an assignment, something I can't tell George directly but I can tell him the code word ‘Mildred’, so he’ll know I’m leaving again. But no matter the assignment or not, moving on is the right thing.”

The next evening, George and Mary were sitting on the couch in front of the fire and watching television. He wasn’t actually watching the TV but was staring into the fire and at the flames moving from left to right and dancing on the logs. She loved doing that as well and when they sat together on the couch, huddled under the blanket, they both watched the dancing flames and hardly watched whatever was on the TV. It was just white noise keeping them company.

She told him, “George, we should leave this place. It’s changed since Harvey bought the tavern. I just feel something is very wrong here and we shouldn’t stay much longer. You know I must go to Mildred’s. In the meantime you can find another place for us. We don’t need to tell anyone why or where we are going. Let’s just leave. Forget about the house. We can sell it while it’s empty.”

George didn’t want to tell Mary that he was experiencing anxiety and felt like he had sleep deprivation, had this continuous creepy feeling, like microscopic bugs were crawling on his skin and just under his skin, so that no amount of scratching could stop the itch. He thought it was only him, and now Mary was feeling the same way.

Neither had any contact with the tavern and didn’t know that the residents, particularly the older ones, were experiencing more severe forms of anxiety and depression. Listening to Mary’s concerns and to his own anxieties, he agreed that they would sell and leave. He didn’t understand the immediateness of her demand to move and even when she told him that she was leaving for Mildred’s and she wanted him to leave as well, he couldn’t bring himself to just walk away from everything that they earned with so much difficulty and tragedy for so many years.

The Agency was a great employer but impersonal. There were no heroes, no massive relocation payments and no special treatment. You earned a salary and your greatest benefit was the knowledge that you were supporting the freedoms that everyone enjoyed and took heart in that. But in all other things, you were just a middle class earner, that's it in a nutshell. It was a career based upon service for the sake of service.

"Yes, he would leave," he uttered beneath his breath, "but in due time and after we sell this place."

Mary left two days later and repeated that she was going to Mildred's. He knew that she was going on an assignment and they used that word just in case someone was listening. But they also understood that when they arrived at the 'assignment location' they would somehow send the second code words 'I found the earrings' and that didn't happen. George decided that he would call a friend to try to find her, just in case the unforeseen occurred. That was unsuccessful as well, so he just had to wait.

George went to the next Board of Directors meeting and let Harvey know that he was looking to sell the place, but Harvey offered less than the place was worth. Coincidently, when George went to town to see Derik, the realtor, he was told the typical asking price was very similar to what Harvey offered and included a commission for the realtor. George went on line to attempt to sell through multiple listing services, but no one ever responded.

After a short time, Harvey approached George and again offered the low ball price. When George declined, Harvey, although attempting to control his body language became internally agitated. George could easily see the tenseness in his demeanor.

"George, you will never get a better offer! Prices are not going up, rather they are declining! You don't want to be alone until the place sells, do you? Have you seen or heard from Mary?"

That last question irritated George to his core, but he maintained his cool outward appearance and just told Harvey in a very calm and clear voice, "Harvey, I'm not selling until I can at least get back the money I invested. That's the end of the story. Okay?"

George saw that Harvey was extremely nervous due to George's calm exterior and light smile. George showed no emotional response to Harvey's deliberate question about Mary. But Harvey knew that he should stop and move on. He will get George's property. It was just a matter of when.

Harvey also decided that George didn't know that he had spoken to Mary about buying their house and advising them to move to the home in Florida. He used every tactic he could on her and even gave her some of the threatening tight lips and smirk smiles that he developed during some of the small con days, but it didn't faze her, at least outwardly.

"Interesting, though," he thought to himself, placing a forefinger against his lips, "was that she kept that discussion from George."

"Okay," Harvey responded to George. "See you soon. Why don't you stop down at the tavern for lunch sometime?" George didn't answer and Harvey turned, waved his hand in a dismissive manner and walked away.

Chapter 15

Periodically, the residents wanted to go into Deckersburg, maybe for a haircut, stop in at the diner, or just to walk around in different surroundings. Many of them who owned cars no longer felt they were capable of driving so Harvey offered a transportation service to those who wanted to go to town. It was just Barry giving them a ride. Less often, a few residents met at the tavern and drove to the town together. A number of them just felt that getting away from the lake for a day might ease some of the anxiety and depression that was so pervasive.

They tended to walk with their heads bowed, a frown on their faces and appeared to shuffle their feet as they walked.

Another side effect of the 'low frequency white noise' was the suggestibility of those who were more susceptible. It wasn't a hypnotic affect, yet it had a similar result.

The older residents, who had more illnesses and frailties and might have been considering moving on, were easily motivated by a range of small talk which included, "how nice the atmosphere was at the Sunshine Forever Home" and "Those that moved recently have written how great they felt and how fortunate they were in their new community."

It helped to add some self-deprecating statements to the conversation, "I sure have been feeling anxious and nervous these past months. Maybe it's time to move to a sunnier climate."

"How have you been feeling?" That usually led to a great discussion about illnesses, the cold, the anxiety, the creeping feeling.

Every conversation ended with declarations by Harvey, "If I had my way and I was your age, I'd want to be in a place where the warmth and comradery overcame any anxieties and illnesses. What does it hurt to look into it? Why stick with something just because you've been doing it a long time? Many of us have bought these houses when they really were inexpensive. Pretty certain you can get back what you paid and probably a bit more. Anyway, Medicaid pays for your living expenses at the home after your own funds are drawn down."

Convincing the older residents, who were under constant assault by the low frequency noise, became easier and easier and one by one they approached either Harvey or Derik to sell their place and ask about the Sunshine Forever Home.

During the next year, nearly forty residents sold and moved to the Sunshine Forever Home, giving Harvey a profit on the resale of their houses to other elderly couples or singles who wanted to live in a lake community for a time.

Derik also profited from the turnover at Decker Lake as he received additional 'finder's fees' from Harvey and always had a number of papers for the sellers to sign, including the duplicate copies of to whom they were actually selling the house.

From time to time Barry would turn off the generator giving everyone a break from the constant unseen and unheard torture. This was done for a number of reasons, one of which was to give the new residents time to acclimate themselves to the lake community and to give the others a rest from the constant emotional assault.

Harvey, Barry and Phil met regularly in the evening to discuss the progress of their Medicaid fraud scheme, and what they needed to do going forward. The Sunshine Forever Home was at capacity rental and the EverRest Funeral Home had nearly fifty of its trays filled. Cap, Henny and May told them to take it easy on the pressure. They had regular customers to serve and needed a number of the shelves for those that came in requesting actual burial services.

They needed some more deaths at the home to open some rooms and the usable morgue trays were nearly full. Cap was taking inventory of the product to see if any were late in their 'demise' for Medicaid to end payments. It would take a short while; in the meantime, they were taking in nearly $250,000 a month from Medicaid and Social Security on the 'undead'. Not bad for a few years of effort.

Barry, on the other hand, was content with his share of the 'earnings' but he wasn't just in it for the money. He loved the game. He wanted more, money and game.

If Barry could have felt the vibrations of another's thoughts, he would have felt Ivan again thinking about the clandestine meeting outside of the cemetery because it was just then that Ivan decided that he would talk to Barry about the nighttime visit behind his shop and the secret exchange. When it first occurred, he thought he would confront Barry the next time he came in for supplies but decided it was not in his best interests. He waited for more than a year when the thought rose to the surface of his mind.

Just as he decided previously, it would be when Barry came into his market to buy supplies.

Chapter 16

Barry took the tavern's small van into town to pick up the regular order from Ivan's Market. Besides all the various cuts of beef and hamburger, people enjoyed pork chops, chicken and venison. Funny how these people liked venison when in so many of the restaurants he had worked in never served it.

Everyone claimed it was too gamey, like badly cooked lamb chops. Barry thought about his childhood. He grew up on badly cooked lamb chops. His mother's cooking, never tasted like anything he would want but never made him sick either. His father worked in the mines all his life and it was a short one. His mother died soon after, leaving him on his own. They didn't have much, growing up in near poverty, but what he did have was some sound advice from his father; a remembrance that he carried with him.

His father told him from his death bed, "Barry, you can work like a dog, be honest and live like a dog, or you can go out and get what you can to live like a person. You're only twenty and you've got a full life ahead of you. Don't waste it in the mines. Help your mom when you can, but never sell yourself short. Check your emotions at the door when you need something. Live well, live smart. Listen and learn and then act."

As Barry entered the market, he saw Ivan off to his right, not behind the counter where Ivan usually stood. Ivan had seen Barry pull up with the van and decided it was time to confront him with the knowledge that he had seen the clandestine meeting outside of the cemetery. It was more than a year and Barry would not be as tense as he might if he was confronted just after the meeting.

Barry gave Ivan a quick nod with his head and moved into the market to gather up the items needed for the tavern. Ivan slowly walked over to Barry as to not raise any suspicion and decided to make it quick and direct. "Barry, I've been meaning to ask you about this and even though it's been a long time, it's been on my mind. I saw you and this other fellow outside the cemetery a while back. You were exchanging an envelope for a bunch of boxes and packages. It was late and dark and afterwards, the other fellow drove off and then you left. Do you remember?"

Barry, always holding his emotions in check, even though the quick and succinct sentence from Ivan could have thrown him off his game, thought quickly about his answer. It had to be direct and sound truthful, but not with any sarcasm that would make Ivan more suspicious. "Hey, Ivan, that was a long time ago. Always looking for something for less, so a fellow I knew had a few things that 'fell off a truck' and I asked him to bring it my way. He doesn't like to deliver in the light and would rather be as unseen as possible when making deliveries, so we decided to meet at the cemetery rather than at the lake. It just helps me make a few extra dollars."

Ivan listened intently to Barry's words, not believing much of it and decided not to press the issue. After all, what did it matter to him anyway, as long as it didn't involve him?

"I hope it works out well for you. If you give me the carving section of the list, I'll get it ready for you while you get the balance of the groceries and I'll help you load the van."

Barry only came in twice a month for goods for the tavern and was a major contributor to Ivan's monthly earnings. In fact, without the tavern and the Decker Lake general store, Ivan would likely go out of business, so Ivan decided quickly not to continue this conversation.

Barry looked at Ivan after Ivan responded and somehow knew that Ivan wasn't satisfied with his answer, and the fact that Ivan didn't press him for more, convinced him of that. Anyone else would have made at least one follow-up question. Barry also didn't add anything to that particular conversation and thanked Ivan for the help, gave him the list of carved items and continued shopping.

Once Barry was finished, he walked to the carved meat section, where Ivan was busy cutting up a large piece of top round into steaks. Just behind Ivan on the upper shelf was a display of very expensive imported Balsamic vinegar and a specialty Calavrio imported olive oil that Ivan displayed but never sold. Ivan understood that all smaller markets, such as his own, had a display of something special, that customers would look at but be unable to afford. He didn't understand why, but evidently it was a marketing tool to entice business.

Barry, his mind not wandering as he shopped, but lingering on Ivan's question, decided that he would take it a step further.

"Ivan," Barry pointed at the bottles on the shelf, "how much for the Balsamic vinegar on the shelf back there? Is it thick like a glaze or thin like some of the balsamic products you have on your regular shelf?"

Replying while he was still carving, Ivan didn't think about the question, but just answered, "It's semi-thick like a glaze and if you like balsamic, it's the best."

"How about giving me one bottle of the Balsamic and one of the olive oil?" Please put them in their own bag as these are for me, not the tavern. I'll pay separately.

Ivan reached up and grabbed one of each, bagged and produced a register receipt for Barry. Barry reached into his left front pants pocket, took out a well-worn wallet and paid cash. Ivan thanked Barry for the sale and in his mind; he was thanking Barry for the cash.

After Ivan finished putting together the meat portion of the order, he tallied up the total, which Barry paid with the tavern debit card. As promised, Ivan helped Barry with the packages and loaded up the van. While Ivan was helping, Barry took the small bag holding the balsamic and olive oil and put it on the front seat. Having finished the loading, Barry said his farewells to Ivan, and drove away.

Once out of site, he opened up the small bag and looked at the two bottles inside. Ivan's fingerprints would be on these bottles. His Pennsylvania pal could get a quick fingerprint check on Ivan and see if he had any old issues that he wouldn't want disclosed. Barry thought carefully about this and he still had the nagging thought that Ivan did not ask any follow-up questions about the cemetery meeting.

"Well, always better safe than sorry."

Barry contacted his friend Mickey and agreed to meet him at the Roscoe diner, outside of Roscoe New York rather than at the Deckersburg cemetery. It's an out of the way spot that would guarantee that no one from Decker Lake would by circumstance or coincidence, view the meeting.

Mickey was probably in his late fifties, an army veteran, fought in Iraq and elsewhere. He reminded Barry of a turkey, the way he walked, looked like he was stalking a chicken, his neck moving and bobbing in a strange way. Mickey might seem strange to those who didn't know him, but he had contacts in military circles and could get just about anything, for a price. He also knew people in law enforcement who would be able to do a complete fingerprint search on the two bottles that Barry brought.

They both ordered a couple of special Roscoe Diner burgers, and before the meals arrived, Barry and Mickey both leaned in to each other to get a little bit more privacy.

Speaking in a low voice, Mickey asked Barry a simple question. "Before I get the scoop on this guy Ivan, what do you want with the information? If he's dirty, do you want him exposed, or should I just have my contact delete the search?"

"Just delete it," Barry answered in an equally low voice, "if it's worthwhile, I'll use it to my advantage and I'd rather that your friends didn't pursue it unless they have to. How soon can you have the answers?"

"Let me think a minute. Okay," responded Mickey, with his typical shrug and bob of his neck. "It'll take two days and we'll be searching through police, military, Homeland and Interpol."

"Good enough," replies Barry, "We'll talk in a couple of days, after you get the results."

After finishing the burgers, they went their separate ways; Mickey off to his lair to order the fingerprint results and Barry driving back to Decker Lake. He had decided not to tell Harvey about this unless it brings results that are useful to the team, or, as Barry thinks about it, “Useful for me at some future time.”

Meanwhile, Ivan began to close his shop for the day, prepared an evening meal and went upstairs to his apartment. As is his typical preparation for the evening, he did not turn on any lights and sat in his chair near the window; that same window that he looked out from when he spotted Barry and the other person exchanging boxes for an envelope.

His first thoughts, as always, dwelled upon his days in Romania, the death and destruction of his family and village, the death of the messengers and the look likely on the Russian commander’s face when he learned that he had been eating a special meal each night.

Ivan relished in the thought that he provided a lifetime of horror and memories that would never be erased for those evil monsters from Russia.

He felt a chill running down his spine, as if someone was stepping on his future grave; a chill that happened just about the same time that Mickey lifted the fingerprints from the two bottles and asked his contacts to begin the fingerprint search. Ivan didn’t know that within just a few days, his life would be changing again.

And Barry didn’t know what effect that would have upon the team.

Chapter 17

Evelyn Jones enjoyed walking on the dirt path which ran east, south and west of the lake. Her place was almost to the north end of the eastern occupied section. She didn't live at the lake front, but two paths to the east of Bleeker Road, where many smaller lake homes were built to be summer homes, not for year round occupancy. Her small cabin had been converted for year round a few years earlier and she loved her new life.

Even though she didn't have a lake front she had a lake view. There were rights of way paths that ran between some of the lake front properties, allowing the other residents to gain access to the water and one of these was directly down the road from her house. Some of the rights of way ended in a small beach with a boat launch for canoes, row boats and other non-powered vessels, but not this one, it was just a beach.

Living alone had its' advantages. She didn't have to worry about taking care of some ridiculous man, who couldn't even wash his own clothes and wanted to be mothered. She had her fill of that and made a conscious decision to avoid any future entanglements; particularly since her divorce from that cheating bastard in Pensacola. Once her children were out, so was she. If she needed anything of that nature, she could go to the bar in town where Sal worked now and then. He filled the bill and she also enjoyed the freedom of no entanglements.

Fifty-five wasn't a bad age if you kept yourself in good shape. Standing at 5'4," still weighing only 120lbs, and lightly muscled, kept her looking fit and desirable. She kept out of the sun to avoid wrinkling and dry skin. She ate well, took her vitamins, visited her doctor regularly and was in great shape. She wore appropriate clothing, but kept her blouses just a bit transparent and her skirts slightly short and flowing. She enjoyed being looked at and she could feel the older fellows looking at her as she walked away.

The walk each way on the dirt path was great exercise and she did that every day. But this day, she left her home for the walk just a bit later than usual and as it became dusk, with the sunlight becoming dim as it worked its way through the dense forest, she decided that she might take a short cut home by hiking through the woods at the north end.

Recently, the dusky part of the day made her feel uneasy, as if something was watching her from the tree line. She could feel the eyes upon her, and even thought she heard whispering, but when she turned quickly, no one was there. She was more tired than usual and believed she wasn't sleeping well.

"I will definitely tell the doctor about this when I see him next week."

She didn't feel it was an urgent matter, a little tiredness and some anxiety. It probably had more to do with aging than anything else.

She moved slowly and deliberately into the thick woods, climbing over the massive tree fall and growing underbrush, hoping to find some sort of trail around the north woods and back to her house in from the eastern shore. As she wandered a bit deeper into the woods, she kept solidly in her mind that she must not lose sight of the lake shore; then she heard a sound, a rustling that reminded her of clothing rubbing together as when someone is walking. Looking toward the sound, she believed that she saw a shadow moving just about a hundred feet ahead and to the left, deeper into the forest.

Ignoring her cautious nature and her determined decision not to lose sight of the lake shore, she followed the rustling deeper into the forest. She moved to the left around massive Pine trees and to the right around twisted Oaks and Sassafras. It was becoming increasingly dim as the sun went down and the forest quickly became more impassable. The underbrush was entangling her feet and legs as she walked but she continued to follow the sound.

At the same time she felt the anxiety return, hearing the whispers in her mind and an inner voice telling her to run, get away as quickly as possible. She felt the turmoil rise within her and knew she could not continue. She must turn back. She will turn back. And as she made that decision, the anxiety eased just a bit.

Just then, without a warning, a large figure jumped from the woods behind her, grabbed her by the upper torso with one arm and the other around her head and with a single twist of those massive arms, snapped her neck and threw her to the forest floor.

As she felt her neck snap and the life draining quickly from her body, she thought about the hopes she had for her future, how she missed her children, how well she was doing and then everything went black and she was gone.

"Phil! Phil! Get over here!"

As Phil walked quickly through the woods to the sound of Barry's voice, he saw the woman on the ground.

"What the hell?" Phil exclaims with surprise, "What the hell?"

Barry tells Phil that he saw this woman walking through the woods and she must have seen him because she was on his trail. He had no choice. It was either that or let them be discovered. She was that close to the generator.

Phil's in shock, not because of the dead woman, which he has seen plenty of in his business, but now this simple fraud scheme has become murder.

"Shit! What the hell do we do now?"

"Well, first we tell Harvey and then figure a way to get rid of the body. We can't leave it in the open for the animals to eat, so we'll put it in my camouflage suit and stuff it in the generator cave until we can sort this out. Who is she?"

Looking through her clothes, they find the small carry bag that Evelyn had strapped around her waist but inside her clothing.

"Her name is Evelyn Jones and she lives on the eastern shore, at 105 Camille Drive. What the hell is she doing walking around the woods? What the hell?"

Having completed wrapping Evelyn into the suit and stuffing her in the cave, they trek back to the tavern where they tell Harvey what happened.

"Harvey, we had no choice but to dispose of this woman, Evelyn Jones, who was that close," Barry holds his hands two feet apart, "to seeing Phil at the generator."

"She lives on the eastern shore, at 105 Camille Drive. Right now, we have her hidden in the generator cave. We need to go to her place and gather up her personal belongings, to make it seem that she left of her own accord. Phil agrees that we can call his daughter Veronica to get up here ASAP, put the body in the Transport and bring it to the EverRest morgue for storage before we cremate her and eliminate the ashes."

Harvey is visibly upset as he also realized that the simple Medicaid fraud has now become murder, but if they get rid of the body, no one can put the murder on them and if there is no body, there is no murder. "Okay, okay! Let's get this done and not waste time."

"Phil, call Veronica. Have her get up here pronto. Tell her to go to the dirt road just north of the lake woods. Send her this map of the area. We'll meet her there and put the body in the Transport. Barry, get over to her place. Make sure you wear gloves. Get her clothes, jewelry and her personal items and bring them to the cave for now. It will take Veronica at least one full day, maybe two to get up here."

Harvey calls Cap at the Sunshine Forever Home and tells him to get the Transport ready for Veronica to head up north. He can't say why on the phone, just that it's urgent. Cap agrees and readies the Transport.

Phil calls Veronica, who immediately, with robot like precision, walked to the Sunshine Forever Home, spoke to no one, climbed into the Transport and began the long drive to Decker Lake. She has seen the map and has memorized the location. She has a mobile phone to make the last contact.

Chapter 18

Barry waited until midnight to take the long walk to the Jones' house. Everyone is sleeping and only a few night lights are on in some of the homes. It's a totally clear evening and if you gazed upwards you could see a sky filled with stars. He thought to himself, "This is what people in the city miss, the sky filled with stars. All they ever see are the few bright ones, the lights of the city obscuring the volume of stars viable here in the woods."

The half-moon provided just enough light for him to walk along the path but not enough light to cast a shadow. His dark clothes provided him with moving cover should anyone happen to glance out a window. All they might see is a dark figure walking and with the deer, bears and other animals occasionally seen in the area, they likely wouldn't give him a second thought. Everyone knew that no one walked around at night.

As Barry neared the Jones' house, he began to move more deliberately and slowly, looking around just to be certain no one was watching. His night vision goggles, although providing a visible spectrum, made everything into an eerie green, reminding him of a few horror movies he had seen where the monsters always looked green and everything they saw was either green or edged in haloes.

He had the key from Jones' carry bag, opened the door and looked slowly from left to right to make sure he wouldn't fall over anything. The field of view of the night vision goggles was limited to the direction of the field of vision. Even though he was familiar with their use, he still had to walk carefully.

First stop is the bedroom, where he gathered up her clothes from the closet and her single dresser. He remarked to himself that she didn't have much in the way of selection but in a good way, it made the job of carrying this stuff out much easier. He found a large suitcase and stuffed all the clothing inside it. He then found a small jewelry box and emptied it into the suitcase. His last stop was the bathroom, where he gathered up all of the toiletries, medicines and other personal stuff and put all of that into the suitcase as well.

He looked slowly around the small cabin just to make sure he took everything of personal value, any personal pictures, notes, address books, papers, mail and such and after he had everything in the suitcase, walked slowly to the door, took a last look and left, making sure he locked the door behind him.

Barry was satisfied that with Jones gone and all of the personal belongings gone as well, there might be some concern but she will have disappeared and without a trace. When Veronica arrived with the Transport, they'll pack Jones into the luggage carrier with this suitcase and have her transported to EverRest where May will cremate the whole mess and drop the ashes into the nearest river or better yet, the Gulf.

As Barry walked back to the generator cave with the suitcase, he thought about Jones, not that he had any remorse, but just about the complication it presented.

Having completed his task, he met Harvey at the tavern and they reviewed the next steps. Veronica had called and said she would be up near the lake by 7:00PM the next day. They talked for a while about Veronica. She was the perfect assistant, unemotional, responsive and reliable. It seemed fitting that Phil and May ran a mortuary and funeral home and had a daughter who had no feelings, emotions or caring about anything. She just followed directions of those she believed had the authority to give them.

Barry still didn't mention the inquiry he had made about Ivan as they were only suspicions. In fact, by the next day, he should have the results of the fingerprints.

Barry and Harvey parted for the evening. The next day, Harvey opened the tavern as usual, Barry was behind the bar and serving lunches and Decker Lake life went on without the knowledge that there was at least one less resident.

Later on that evening, but before he was scheduled to meet with Veronica, Barry received a telephone call from his Pennsylvania friend, Mickey, who gave him the complete scoop on Ivan. Mickey referred to Ivan as Ivan, The Terrible, since he knew exactly what the Russians reported to Interpol.

Mickey discovered that Ivan was actually this guy named Karl Romanz from Romania and that he entered with a visa some ten years earlier. Homeland had no information as to his returning to Romania and had no current location or address.

This was not an unfamiliar story as many who came on visas somehow managed to overstay and it seemed no one cared. The inquiry did not raise any eyebrows at Homeland since it was fulfilled as a clandestine action, not an official one. Homeland also did not have any history on this Karl as the connection to Interpol was incomplete on this character.

The inquiry through the police records found nothing on Ivan, just that nothing existed about Ivan prior to ten years. Without any current information or criminal activity from Ivan, the Police and other military records would not have flagged this person that everyone at the lake and in Deckersburg knew as Ivan.

Interpol, on the other hand, had a Russian warrant for Karl Romanz, wanted for multiple murders of Russian citizens in the town of Neag, Romania.

The detail provided by Interpol included a portion of a message sent by this person Karl to the Russians, admitting to the murders and to where they could find the bodies.

Interpol was very interested in the apprehension of Karl Romanz but did not pursue the case as it had implications and involvement with the ending of the U.S.S.R. and the freedom of Romania from Russian interference in 1989.

The politics involved might color the actual circumstance surrounding the warrant and Interpol had more nefarious characters with which to be concerned.

Mickey did not know, nor did his source truly understand that an inquiry, no matter how clandestine, would leave a slight trace on the Interpol servers. Of course, this unknown information could not be relayed to Barry. Of course, the missing facts from Karl's note to the Russian commander concerning the meals could not be included as no one knew except for Karl and the Russian commander and possibly a few others that the commander might have told.

Barry thought as he reviewed what Mickey had told him, "Ivan is someone else and is wanted for multiple murders in Romania. In fact, he's not even Ivan, but Karl. This has got to be useful; a serial killer living and working in front of a cemetery in Deckersburg; a man sitting in the dark looking out of his window; I had better be careful."

In the meantime, Barry had much more to do to complete the task of eliminating the Jones body and her personal effects. He called Veronica to confirm the time of arrival at the dirt road at the north end of the forest. Once confirmed, he called Phil to have him meet at the generator at 6:30PM and to bring a body bag. For some reason known only to Phil, he always had at least two body bags with him at all times, likely due to his past and training in the mortuary, "always be prepared".

Phil and Barry walked along the hidden invisible trail that led to the generator and the Jones body. Once there, Phil removed the body, still inside the camouflage suit and replaced the suit with the body bag. Barry reclaimed the large camouflage suit, as it didn't have any damage associated with hiding the Jones body and he still needed it for those times when he or Phil had to maintain the generator, or replace the batteries.

Veronica was on time to the minute, which was her nature. She arrived just as Barry and Phil carried the body bag with Jones and her personal items to the dirt road north of the woods.

Veronica said nothing, not even a "hello" or "can I help you" or "see you sometime". She just nodded her head after the body bag was stuffed into the luggage carrier at the lower level of the Transport and drove down the road to get back to the New York State Thruway for that long 24 hour trip back to Florida. Of course, she called her mother and gave her the approximate arrival time.

Her mother, May, was ready to receive the body and items and was just waiting for her daughter to return. She knew that Veronica would not stop in any hotels along the way, likely just pull off the road in some secluded area to take a nap and then be back on the road.

She had an uncanny ability to stay awake and concentrate until her assigned task was done. True to her nature, she could only handle one task at a time, but it was always handled with precision.

Veronica arrived at the EverRest the next day and pulled into the receiving area at the rear. The receiving area was an internal garage space so it was an easy matter to remove the body bag, with a little help from her mother, carry it to the crematorium, place the bag containing the Jones woman with her personal effects on the motorized slab and let the furnace do its job.

Once the ashes were collected, May drove to the Gulf and poured them into the calm waters. Evelyn jones had effectively disappeared and left no trace.

May thought to herself, as she drove leisurely back from the Gulf, "how easy it had been for the murder and elimination of a possible witness, how easy it had been to dispose of the body and how she should be worried about herself and Phil, should Barry believe they were a threat."

She continued her thoughts as she turned into the funeral home, "This was supposed to be nothing more than storing bodies for their future burial, now it was murder and my daughter is an accomplice."

She shivered even though it was very warm for a fall day, as if someone was walking on her grave.

Barry telephoned his friend Mickey to arrange disposal of the Jones' car. This was the last piece of traceable property.

"Mickey, how soon can you make a cube of scrap?"

Mickey replied using the same code wording to avoid incrimination. "Just bring your scrap over, you know where, and we'll take care of it."

One thing was certain about Mickey. He did not fool around when it came to product, like sell it as a stolen car rather than make a scrap cube. Mickey was trustworthy for a low level criminal.

The evening after Veronica left with her 'package', Barry delivered the car to Mickey and within the hour, it was nothing more than an unreadable metal cube, sitting in a pile of other metal cubes, waiting to be melted and formed into a new product.

Chapter 19

Barry and Phil separated as they reach the crossroads. Phil went home and Barry walked slowly to the tavern to update Harvey on the success of eliminating the Jones woman. He understands that he must measure his words carefully. He has to make a decision whether to let Harvey know about Ivan, that he's not Ivan but Karl from Romania, a wanted murderer. Although it is a difficult decision to make, he believes that telling Harvey about this is the wise thing to do.

Harvey is in charge of the scheme, not he or anyone else on the team.

Together they can come to a conclusion of how to best use Ivan should the need arise. At this time, with Jones' body in route to cremation, they have nothing to worry about. Knowing about Ivan could be beneficial, if the need arises.

Barry and Harvey sat at one of the tables near the door of the tavern. Its past the dinner hour, all the residents have gone home, no one is at the bar and the tavern is totally empty and quiet. They have the place to themselves and can speak openly.

Barry relates the story of how he obtained Ivan's fingerprints and sent them to a friend in Pennsylvania. The only useful information that came back was from Interpol, not from any American agency. Actually, the Police, Homeland and other U.S. agencies only displayed an old data card with Karl Romanz' name on it for a short term visa. There was no information of this person Karl returning to Romania. In 1988 -1989, computer systems were limited and they didn't always track the comings and goings of visitors. Most went home but many stayed. This Karl was one of the stayers.

Somehow the fingerprints on the American systems were replaced and Ivan's didn't raise any alarms. This meant that Ivan had help.

It was the Interpol system that raised the alarm about the fingerprints. It was an alarm only due to the fact that the prints match the Russian government warrant for the arrest of Karl Romanz for murder, not an Ivan. Interpol was not aware of an Ivan, just Karl.

Whatever assistance Ivan or Karl had obtained when entering the country could not help him with Interpol, or possibly the Interpol warrant came after Karl was already in America? Barry didn't think it mattered either way. What did matter was the fact that Ivan might be useful in the future.

Harvey agreed with Barry's assessment and as Barry was leaving for the evening, Harvey figured he would have a last word. "Barry, let's keep this completely to ourselves, not tell Phil or anyone else. Okay?"

Barry responded quickly and he pointed his right thumb upwards, "Okay."

One week after her disposal, Jones had missed her scheduled doctor's appointment. The doctor's office had called a number of times, but there was no answer and no response to the messages left on her answering machine. The doctor feared that she might have taken ill and living alone, she might be unable to respond.

The State Police were contacted by her doctor since she missed an appointment and had never missed one before. The State Police, decided to contact the Deckersburg sheriff rather than travel up there for no particular reason other than a missed doctor's appointment.

"Hey, Bob, do you think you can get up to the Jones' house at 105 Camille Drive and see what's what with this Jones woman? Her doctor said she missed an appointment."

"Of course," Bob agreed as anything outside of his normal boring duties was an exciting adventure. When he arrived at her address, he found the place locked and dark.

"If anyone asks why I broke in to the house, it was because I heard something suspicious, like a moaning sound." He announced out loud to himself.

He forced open the front door entered and looked around. He discovered that her clothing, her personal effects and other toiletries were gone, as well as pictures and other personal things. He didn't see a car out front, in the garage or in the driveway.

He called the State Police to notify them that the house looked as if she had moved; no clothing, personal items, or car. He let them know that he was going to knock on a few of the neighbor's doors to see if they knew anything, but he believed that the State Police should open an official investigation.

He then canvassed the immediate community to determine if anyone had seen or spoken to her and all had answered with the same shrug of their shoulders

"Sorry, but we haven't seen her for many months. She kept to herself and I believe she went into town to the bar periodically."

That's about all anyone knew. He inquired at the tavern and Harvey remarked that Ms. Jones rarely came in to the tavern. She had been known to go to the bar in town. Another of the residents mentioned that he had seen her weeks ago walking from her home to the lake path.

The sheriff, with help from the State Police, organized a search team to go into the woods on the north side just in case she decided to take a hike and became injured. Searching wasn't easy due to the tree fall, the thickness of the underbrush, the lack of trails and just the general condition of the woods that made it unsuitable for hiking.

Bob wasn't surprised when George volunteered to be on the team and worked tirelessly during the search period and afterwards. After all, a few months earlier, his wife had disappeared. The search team never came across the well camouflaged cave under the giant Oak.

It wasn't long before the sheriff decided to call off the search. Neither he nor the State Police decided to dredge the lake as it was one of the deepest lakes in the State and would rarely give up its secrets. The State Police filed a missing person's report, which was issued to all federal, state and local authorities. After three weeks, nothing was found, said or returned. Evelyn Jones became an OMP, Official Missing Person.

Evelyn Jones was missing without a trace, despite the authorities best intentions to find her. Inquiries at the bar led nowhere. All the residents and anyone knew was that she was missing. That and the evening low frequency generator and white noise activators disturbing their sleep patterns made them more edgy than ever.

Harvey told Barry to adjust the output because he didn’t want any suicides and he wanted to be able to sell the properties, didn’t want the place to get a reputation of being malevolent.

Chapter 20

For the next few months, Barry shopped at Ivan's and Ivan prepared the twice monthly shipments of meat and other products for the Tavern. Ivan never mentioned the meeting at night by the cemetery again and Barry did not mention that he knew who Ivan actually was; a wanted murderer by Interpol and an illegal alien disguised as a butcher. Barry anticipated the time when he would confront Ivan about his past, but that time had not yet occurred.

Harvey, on the other hand, worked closely with Cap and Henny filling slots at the Sunshine Forever Home, banked their Medicaid payments and attempted to expand their business. Phil and May were busy storing and burying and reburying the bodies of the dead.

Harvey, Phil and Barry decided to have a meeting to decide what to do next. It's been two months since they disposed of Jones.

Harvey made breakfast at the tavern; scrambled eggs, bacon and sausage, toast, jelly and butter. Harvey knew that talking business over a great meal made for better conversation. The meeting was short and hardly lasted beyond finishing the first cup of coffee.

Even though things were going well with the overall product, they were again stuck at about forty to forty five units occupied. Even with the generator, they couldn't seem to advance and stay beyond this number. May was becoming quite accomplished at maneuvering the stored product in and out for burial and Henny was extremely efficient contacting Medicaid with the updated death certificates.

Being extremely detailed about relatives and visitors, they avoided any questions concerning the 'undead'. For more than three years, their scheme was actually successful and with the exception of the Jones girl, there had been no further complications.

Phil and Barry both congratulated Harvey on a great con, and Harvey and Phil congratulated Barry on his technological prowess with the generator.

And then along came Peg and Joe Murphy.

Peg and Joe Murphy, living on just their Social Security, were barely able to afford the mortgage and Decker Lake Association fees and eat at the same time. Joe didn't earn much during his working life and Peg cared for their one child, who passed away from leukemia at the young age of thirty six.

They weren't able to afford decent medical coverage, so they went into massive debt, mortgaged their small home and borrowed from relatives and friends until they had nothing more to give. Their daughter died anyway, not having been cared for by the best doctors, not having been able to get the best treatment and no one really cared.

Their lives being crushed by the loss, both worked hard to save just enough to get this small retirement home at Decker Lake and now in their old, old age, medical bills were again crushing them, they had nothing to fall back on and they outlived their friends and relatives.

Looking at each other with the saddened eyes of many years of burdensome memories, they agreed that selling to the board and moving to Florida was the best course of action for what few years they had left. Joe continually reminded her with a simple statement.

"Why am I still alive, without my little Dorothy?" and he cried until he had no more tears to shed. His bent shoulders heaving slightly with each sob. Then in a few minutes he became composed, and with a smile on his face told Peg how much he loved her and they could be happy anywhere, and maybe happier in a warm place, in a nice place, in Florida.

Peg, Joe and Harvey met with Derik to organize the sale of their home to Decker Lake through the Decker Lake Board of

Directors. Derik had them sign about twenty different sets of papers, which had massive fine print, but one page was written to clarify all the others.

That page gave the Sunshine Forever Home Power of Attorney over their funds and their Social Security at the time that their savings would run out. It also provided them with minimum funds each month to purchase personal items, about $100.00 each. Their duplex room, meals and basic toiletries were provided by the home. They were able to buy a certain amount of essential furnishings, such as a new television, a couple of very comfortable easy chairs and had some of their own furnishing that would fit in the duplex, delivered to the home.

All the details being settled, the Sunshine Forever Home was notified and Harvey told the Murphys that the Transport was on its way. Two days from now, Peg and Joe would be traveling in style to their Florida destination. Cap and Henny were notified by Harvey of the impending new tenants and he asked them to call May and have Veronica drive north, meet the Murphys at the clubhouse and drive them to the home.

Just like clockwork, Veronica pulled up to the clubhouse and saw Harvey standing in front of the tavern with the Murphys and their two large suitcases on the left curb. She parked the Transport, walked to the tavern just in front of the group and introduced herself.

"My name is Veronica. I am here to transport you to the Sunshine Forever Home. We will have one stop along the way which is about halfway to our destination. We will sleep over until the next day when we will travel directly to the home. The Transport has refreshments on board, in a small refrigerator but there is no bathroom. Should the need arise, you will notify me and I will make the next possible stop."

As Veronica was placing the luggage in the bottom of the Transport, Harvey explained that Veronica had a mild case of Asperger's and they should not worry about her speech patterns. This was normal in such situations and he exaggeratedly expressed to them that Veronica was extremely intelligent, despite the outward atypical behavior.

"Don't worry," he told them with a large smile on his face, "she has transported many of the residents to the home and is completely capable of getting you there on time and in comfort."

Veronica knew that it would be getting dark about 4:30PM this time of year. She urged the Murphys to board so they can get on their way. Peg and Joe say goodbye to Harvey, board the Transport and found that the interior seats are semi-reclining and very comfortable. They also noticed the small refrigerator and when Joe looked inside, he saw the typical airline size liquor bottles, and two single serving size glass flasks with a pinot wine.

Snacks and finger size cheese and meat sandwiches were also stocked in a small cabinet just above the refrigerator. He believed that this would be a nice trip for both he and Peg, probably the last one they'll ever make.

Veronica pulled away from the clubhouse with her passengers and luggage neatly tucked away and began the long trip back to Florida. By 5PM as it was getting dark, Peg asked to stop again for a bathroom break. Joe complained about the pain in his hips. Peg began complaining about her leg. Both complained continuously and then they started arguing about their dead daughter, whether they could have done more. Then the crying and consolation began. The noise was deafening and disturbing. She had to do something as it was intolerable to be in the presence of such a disruption.

Veronica had watched as her mother prepared a valium cocktail for some of the bereaved in the EverRest Funeral Parlor. She crushed up the valium and mixed them into a sugar bowl. Then she offered the truly upset mourners a cup of tea, to which she added two teaspoons of the mixture. They didn't know that they were being mildly sedated and no one ever knew what her mother had done.

Mom told her that many funeral homes use this procedure to keep the crowd calm and avoid some of the older mourners throwing themselves into the coffins.

She decided to make up a valium mixture at the next rest stop and offer cups of tea to the Murphy's. The Transport had a coffee/tea maker which made tea and coffee by the cup. Whichever they wanted, she would add the mixture.

Her plan came together at the next rest stop. Both Peg and Joe went into the bathroom facilities and Veronica crushed the valium into a sugar bowl. When they came back to the Transport, she offered them each a cup of tea, to which both accepted. Having heated the water and making the tea, she placed three teaspoons of the mixture into each cup.

"Here you go," Veronica said with a forced smile on her face. It was 7:00PM, dark and getting colder. She hoped the rest of the trip would be smoother. Shortly after drinking the tea, both Peg and Joe fell into a deep sleep. The mixture was just supposed to make them calm, not put them to sleep. What Veronica didn't know was the extent of their other medications, their toleration to sedatives and the interaction to the other drugs they were taking.

Even though she was, to some extent, smarter than others her age, she was inexperienced and didn't have the inquisitive qualities which might have made her think about complications. All she thought about was the quiet and what her mother made for her more excited clients. She might have seen her mother make the mixture but was unaware that the total valium per teaspoon in her mother's mixture was no more than a half part to one and what she had made was closer to four parts to one.

It was less than a half hour from the rest stop when she pulled to the side of the road and checked on Joe. He was dead and Peg's breathing was shallow.

It didn't personally matter to her that Joe was dead, just mattered as an objective exercise that this person Joe could not be taken to the Sunshine Forever Home in this condition. She also could not bring Peg to the home with her husband dead. Objectively, unemotionally and without any malice, she covered Peg's mouth with a thick towel and held it there until Peg stopped breathing. Peg's body convulsed instinctively as it fought for life, but the sleeping older lady didn't have a chance against the strong youthful woman covering her mouth and nose. It didn't take long for Peg to join her husband.

Now, both were dead and it would be just another task to determine what to do next.

The choices were twofold, call Harvey or call mom. She decided to call mom for instructions. In the meantime, she would prop them up so they looked comfortable to anyone passing by or noticing people in the Transport.

"Mom," Veronica said using her normal conversational tone, "Peg and Joe Murphy are dead. I made them tea with a valium powder to calm them down. A half hour later, Joe was dead. I decided to kill Peg as having one alive would be very complicated. So both are dead and I have them in their seats, propped up and looking comfortable. What should I do?"

May was taken aback by this turn of events. She never thought that Veronica could be deadly in so matter of fact sort of way, but it made sense. She didn't see people as living beings but as objects, easily replaceable or to throw away when broken.

"You stay there and I'll get right back to you." May called Harvey and explained the circumstances with complete objectivity, very similar to how Veronica explained it to her.

Harvey was visibly shaken by this, having two more dead people to handle, but he didn't do the killing. And yet, he couldn't have the deaths exposed or the entire scheme would be blown.

He thought quickly, "We don't want to send the two bodies to Florida for cremation and dispersion. It's too long a trip and it poses too much of a risk. We need to keep the bodies local and dispose of them here."

Suddenly it dawned on him, "Ivan, Ivan the butcher, a runaway murderer from Romania."

"May, hang in there. I'll get right back to you. Call Veronica and tell her to stay where she is for now."

Harvey was anxious with the timeliness of this and realized that he needs Barry to contact Ivan and coerce him to participate in getting rid of the bodies.

"Harvey calls Barry immediately and tells him what happened with Veronica and the Murphys.

"Shit," Barry exclaims, "what's next?" his question alluded to the necessary murder of Jones and now the murder of this old couple.

"Okay, I'll go over to Ivan's right now. He's not closed yet. I'll let him know that I know about the murders in Romania and who he is. Just know that if I don't come back, it was Ivan who did me in."

Barry drove quickly to town and parked in front of the market. He saw through the large window that Ivan is closing up and putting the meat into the freezer, other items that might spoil into the refrigerator and generally cleaning up the market. He's carrying an old style broom, whisking the dust to the rear of the shop. Likely he will whisk the dust out the back door when he is done.

Barry walked into the market, watched as Ivan neared the refrigerator door and casually walked up to him, stopping about six feet away. Before Ivan can say anything, he looked directly into Ivan's eyes and said as strongly as he could,

"Ivan, I know that your real name is Karl Romanz. You come from Romania and you are wanted by the Russians for murder."

Barry handed Ivan the copy of the partial note to the Russian commander that Ivan had sent him after leaving Romania. Then Barry stepped a foot back to be certain he is out of the big man's reach.

Ivan looked at the note and noticed that the part about the butchered bodies and meat was missing from the note and only the part about the murders was there. He looked up at Barry with his eyes glaring and his jaw clenching, as if to stop himself from tearing this person apart.

Then Ivan spoke in a voice just a bit louder than speaking normally, "So what do you want? You are going to turn me in?"

Ivan has his voice raised just enough to invoke a shock into the person he is talking to and leaned into Barry as he is speaking. Barry moved back another foot, shakes his head from side to side and says "No!" as emphatically as possible.

"We need you to do something for us. You'll be paid well."

"Spit it out. What can I do that will prevent you from turning me in?" and this was said with a veiled threat that if it did not meet with his approval, he would do what was necessary to prevent being exposed.

"Listen, you live in front of a cemetery, mostly dark and rarely used. We need you to bury two bodies and make sure that they can't be found. Just like you did in Romania. That's it. But we need it done this evening. Will you do it?"

Ivan thought for a few seconds and understood that this is not a question but a directive. He's not being asked to kill anyone, just to bury them. If he says no, it will go badly and he'll have to run again, but quickly. If he says yes, then he can stall the fact that he must run again and make a better plan. He knew that he would not allow anyone to blackmail him to perform this nasty work. Not for long, anyway.

In fact, he suddenly had this feeling of exacting revenge against Barry and the other guy, probably Harvey, for exposing him when he had such a good thing going.

"You said 'we', who's the other? I will not work for an unknown."

Barry confirmed Ivan's initial thoughts, "It's Harvey. Will you do it?"

Barry decided to expose Harvey's name so he wouldn't be the only one with skin in this game.

"Yes," answered Ivan, glad that Barry confirmed Harvey as a conspirator, "Bring the bodies around the back to my shed. I'll take care of the disposal into the cemetery. You will bring me $10,000 tomorrow."

Barry agreed and called Harvey to tell him the news. Harvey immediately called May and relays the information to tell Veronica to drive the Transport to the rear of Ivan's Market in Deckersburg. "Ask her to estimate the arrival time so they can tell Ivan when she will be expected."

Veronica, sat in the driver's seat of the transport, just staring into the windshield and likely not thinking much about anything, was just waiting for the call from her mom.

May, having received the call from Harvey, called Phil and told him the story, as best as she knew it.

"Veronica has accidentally killed both Joe and Peg Murphy."

"It doesn't matter how right now. I'll tell you later. Some guy named Ivan, who owns the market in Deckersburg, has agreed to dispose of the bodies. I'll contact Veronica to give her the information so she can get back to Deckersburg while it's still dark. After I call her, I'll call you back and we can talk about this. I just want to let you know the story."

"Don't call anyone right now, because if they haven't called you yet, they didn't want you to know about something. If they call you before I call back, make believe its news to you."

May said goodbye, called Veronica and gave her detailed instructions. Veronica agreed, just as May knew she would, and began the long drive back to Deckersburg. According to her time sense, she should arrive there at 2:00AM and would notify Harvey of the arrival time once she is closer. She knew that when she arrived at the rear of this market, a fellow named Ivan would be there to remove the bodies from the Transport. She would then begin the trip directly back to Florida and return the Transport to the Sunshine Forever Home.

Chapter 21

Ivan is sitting upstairs in his room looking out the rear window at the cemetery.

"It's been so long a time that I have forgotten how it feels to deal with the dead. This woman Veronica will be here in a few hours and I am expected to remove two bodies and dispose of them in the cemetery. It doesn't surprise me that Barry trusts me with this task as he believes he has me locked in to his every wish. Yes, I will bury them in an existing grave so no one will ever find them. I will put them into coffins with the others, cover the dirt with leaves and brush so they will disappear from the earth, just like those messengers so long ago."

"And I will take souvenirs for future use."

Ivan began rapping his fist on the arm of the chair in a drumming motion and with a frown on his face, his eyes pressed into a stare, speaking aloud to reinforce his thoughts.

"I will not disturb these old people any more than I have to. They are just victims of crime, not criminals, not even unwilling conspirators like the messengers. But I must make plans to leave. The $10,000 will be a good start to prepare a payday for my friends in Brighton Beach to make me a new identity otherwise I will be subject to the whims of these criminals."

It's ironic that Ivan (Karl) did not think of himself as a criminal since he was only taking revenge on the Russians and their assistants, the messengers, as they murdered his family, so long ago.

He always believed that in a society where there were no rules but dictates from tyrants, revenge was not a crime but a justice. The same could be said of America, in their old west, in the struggle for work and pay from the rich and powerful, in the lack of justice for the poor.

"We are all the same," he thought, and then he spoke out loud. "We are all the same. Revenge is more than a human motive." And then he spoke even louder, "It is justice where there is none. I hope I have the opportunity to exact vengeance upon Harvey and Barry."

Time passes quickly for Ivan and he saw the Transport pull up, at 2:00AM just as Barry told him it would. He picked up two heavy-duty extra-large, black plastic bags, that some of the larger meat products come packaged in and met Veronica at the back door. She tells him that she has placed the bodies in the baggage area for easier delivery and speaks so unemotionally that Ivan begins to wonder about her.

Putting the wonder aside, Ivan unloaded them from the Transport and brought them into his shed. He tells Veronica to leave. She immediately returned into the Transport and followed her mom's instructions to get back on the road to Florida. Ivan looked a little bewildered as the Transport pulled away, without even a "goodbye" or "what will you do" or anything.

She delivered and turned and left just like a robot. He remembered seeing a movie, Stepford Wives or Westworld or something with people created like robots, called androids. Setting aside these useless thoughts, he knows he has a lot of work to do this evening.

He placed both bodies into the plastic bags in his shed. Before he brought them into the cemetery, he must locate an appropriate space.

When he first came into Deckersburg and purchased the market, he spent the first evening staring into the cemetery. He didn't know it at the time that someday he might need the information, but cemeteries always held a fascination for him. Maybe it was all that blood and gore from the old country, his parents, grandparents, villages, being murdered by the Russians and his revenge, murdering and butchering the messengers.

His second evening in the town he decided to take a walk through the cemetery where he found the new section, walked by the old section and then into the wooded area at the rear. He discoverd a number of graves in the wooded area likely belonging to those who could not afford a plot or those who just made a decision to bury their own and not tell anyone.

It was in this area that he made the plan to bring these two. He took a shovel and an old carved wooden walking stick with him and walked into the cemetery, in the total darkness, feeling his way along on the old path until the beginning of the wooded area.

It was there that he turned on a very small flashlight, just to light the way beyond and into the underbrush. He pushed onward into the underbrush and to the location where he remembered he saw the old graves. He was just about fifty yards into the wooded area when he saw the twin plot, likely dug in the 1700's since a few nearby headstones still had a readable date. He spent at least an hour digging and found two old wooden coffins, with the lids still intact. Lifting each lid, he found that the bodies inside were mostly decayed and gone and the interior had enough room to place the two plastic bags.

He walked quickly back to his shed, got the wheel barrow, loaded up the two bagged bodies and returned to the cemetery and the newly opened graves. After dumping the bodies into their coffins, he closed the lids, repacked the dirt and recovered the graves with the underbrush.

Only if someone were directly looking into this spot would anyone notice the reopened graves.

Ivan returned to his shed and put the wheel barrow in its place, the shovel back on the hook and the walking stick into the corner.

The evening's work was hard and even with someone who was in as good shape as Ivan, all that digging, re-digging, lifting and hauling took its toll. He was tired, more tired than he'd been in a long time. He climbed the stairs to his apartment and sat down in his chair, again looking out the window. This time he looked far into the cemetery, in his mind to the spot where he buried those two innocent victims and it reminded him of all the victims in Neag, victims of the Russian oppression and he was angry, angrier than he had been for many years.

He called Barry and told him that all was taken care of and then hung up before Barry had a chance to answer.

Chapter 22

Harvey awakened the next day after a fitful sleep filled with nightmarish images of the dead, the dying and piles of money. He rarely remembered his dreams but this one was vivid in his mind. Even though the dream would have been a nightmare for someone else, for him it was just an active dream and was not an emotional issue. What he remembered most about the dream was the pile of money.

He never thought of himself as a sociopath, but he didn't kill the Murphys, Veronica did. All he did was hide the bodies. In fact, he didn't hide the bodies, it was Barry and Ivan. They were the real sociopaths. Ivan was a wanted murderer, a sociopathic killer. Barry had not thought anything about this at all.

"No," Harvey thought, "I'm not a sociopath, just a guy who likes to make money the easy way." Another thought enters his head.

"I had better call Cap and Phil to make sure they're still on board."

Phil is still at the lake, so Harvey called him to come over to his living area at the rear of the tavern. Once Phil arrived, Harvey called Cap and the three of them review the situation and how to address the future.

Cap is really upset. "What the hell do we do? This couple is dead and gone and their room is unoccupied. Medicaid was notified of their arrival, the doc is ready for the initial visit. Banks were given Power of Attorney forms. Man, this is a freakin' mess.," Cap's voice was getting louder as he spoke and Harvey could tell he was getting himself out of control.

"Getting wacked out is not accomplishing anything. We need to get over the top of this and quickly," answers Harvey. Phil is eerily quiet and says nothing.

"Over the top?" Cap responds loudly and sharply, "Over the top? Veronica killed two old people. This is out of control."

"Listen to me, Cap, What's done is done and we can't change what happened. We can only try to resolve it and move on. So you've got a choice. Pack up and run or let's put a plan together to absorb this and move on as if nothing happened."

Cap is beside himself with worry as he doesn't want to be implicated in a murder, but decides to listen. Phil still hasn't said anything.

"Ok, we all agree that this sucks, but we need to get this in control. First, the bodies are buried and gone and no one knows where they are. Second, they're supposed to be in a room at the home and they're not. So we have to put them there even if they don't exist. Otherwise they're going to be missed, by someone or something.

We already have the Power of Attorney for their bank accounts and their Social Security money is direct deposited into the home account in their name. Once their regular finances run out, Medicaid will kick in.

We need doc to fill out the medical exam forms as if he did them. He's done this before with some of the older patients, so it shouldn't be a problem. Think of it this way. They're not dead. They're living at the home. We'll treat them as if they are living residents. But no one living or working at the home will know who is supposed to be in the empty room.

Two weeks from now, Cap sends a postcard to Decker Lake so I can post it on the bulletin board in the clubhouse like the others. A couple of weeks later he sends another so that everyone at the lake knows how much they enjoy their stay at the home. The only thing that's changed is that they are invisible and we don't have to store the bodies.

May will add them into the actuarial table so at some time in the future we can officially kill one of them, have doc sign the death certificate, send it in, cancel the Social Security, and all the other things we do when we 'let one be actually deceased'.

In the all in all, this seems like a disaster to our scheme but it may actually be an enhancement."

When Harvey finishes, Cap begins to think about the whole thing and agrees with Harvey's assessment. "Ok, we can make this work. But we didn't sign up for murder or to be accessories to murder. This is bad. I'll talk to Henny and we'll begin the cover up process. Doc is good and really doesn't care what he signs. We'll do the financials, continue with tax returns, and stay with the plan."

Phil is quiet during this whole conversation, just taking it in. His daughter committed the murders and May knows about it. They have no choice but to go along with the scheme, so there is nothing to say. When Harvey asks him his thoughts on the subject, all Phil says is, "sounds like a plan."

When he gets back to Florida, he intends to have a long talk with May and begin to organize the escape plan. They can't tell Veronica because she has no capacity to understand what intended secrecy is. Although she will never tell anyone about the two she killed, she might talk about the escape plan.

Deep in the recesses of his mind, he knew that eventually the whole plan would unravel and this may be only the beginning. If he knew Harvey and he did, Harvey would be thinking about the next sale and the next residents coming from the lake. How could he let them go to Florida and not see the previous couple who presumably live there?

"Not alive and not dead," he thought, "and likely only the beginning, especially if this works out."

Chapter 23

Two months after Peg and Joe move to the home, Harry and Merle Henderson decide to do the same. They saw the postcards on the clubhouse bulletin board stating how happy and good it was to make the move to Florida. It's a much better place to be than spending the cold winters here at Decker Lake.

"Wish you were here." This convinced the Hendersons that a move was inevitable so why not make it while they could still enjoy the weather and maybe the company of some friends. They also agreed that it was getting more difficult every day to take care of the small cabin and the land. Enough was enough.

Harry called Harvey and told him that "maybe the lake board could assist with the sale of his cabin and help organize a move to the Sunshine Forever Home."

Harvey, never being one to hesitate, quickly agreed and told Harry that he would call the home to find out when a duplex room could become available and that Derik would be in contact very soon about the sale of their property. Harvey realized that this was the first request since the disposal of Peg and Joe Murphy. The Hendersons knew the Murphys so even though they wanted to go to the home, certainly one of the reasons was to be with the Murphys.

Harvey's first inclination was to a comedic thought, "The Hendersons want to be with the Murphys. Yes they can and they will. There is no other way."

But maybe he should fold up the plan here at Decker Lake, not let anyone else move to the home and just get the hell out. Harvey wished he could talk to his parents about this, but he knew he could not. He also knew that his parents never hurt anyone physically, nor were they accomplices to anyone being hurt. It was just about money. When he thought more deeply about his parent's motives, it wasn't just about money, it was about the con.

Why was he so conflicted about this? If it wasn't about the murders, then it was just his thoughts about his parent's judgement upon him. He knew what they would say. "Stop now and close it up. You didn't do it the first time and you weren't responsible the second time. Don't have anyone else do it again, because if you do, it will be on your head."

Harvey thought carefully upon this and decided that he could keep it going for a short time. He wanted the money, and the money and the scheme meant more to him than another couple of old buggers who already outlived their usefulness.

It was just then, that Harvey finally realized; he couldn't give a crap about anybody as long as he enriched himself. Not his parents, not Barry, not Phil and May or Cap and Henny.

He would know when to get out; when and how to organize the escape plan; and it would be for him, not the others.

Harvey called May and explained that they had a great opportunity to add to the coffers. The Hendersons were in their mid-eighties and wanted to be with the Murphys in the home. Naturally, they can't go there but why shouldn't we avail ourselves of another invisible couple. We have nothing more to lose and if we don't, they might become curious as to the Murphys disposition and make some unwanted inquiries.

Harvey didn't actually believe that, but he wanted May to agree and the best way was to press May into believing they really had no choice.

"We need Veronica to do what she seems to do best. Put people to sleep, permanently."

With nothing happening since the disposal of the Murphys, Phil had gone back to Florida to be with May and talk about their next steps. They agreed that they couldn't tell when this entire scheme would come crashing down. It was getting too complicated and nasty.

Harvey was right in one respect. They couldn't refuse the Hendersons without good reason and no matter what they were told; they might try to contact the Murphys.

No one who worked in the home even knew about the Murphys, only that there was one empty duplex on the third floor.

Unfortunately for the Hendersons, space would be made for them as well.

In the meantime, however, they needed to cooperate with Harvey until they could extricate themselves from this mess and disappear.

Veronica could not be in more trouble than she was already in, so they agreed. The cover up must continue at all costs until they could finalize the plan to get out. But the plan would be for them not anyone else

May agreed and told Harvey that all she needed was a couple of days' notice and she would send Veronica to pick up and take care of the Hendersons.

Barry contacted Ivan and explained to him that he must be ready for another two bodies for disposal. Of course, he will give Ivan another $10,000 for the effort. Ivan agreed without voicing his reluctance and if Barry could have seen Ivan's face, the curve of his lips and the narrowness of his eyes, he might have thought twice, but he did not.

Ivan just calmly agreed and told Barry to give him a heads up on the time of arrival. Ivan knew that protesting or attempting to convince Barry to leave him alone would not work. Ivan also knew that the threats about turning him in were idle ones. If they did and he was caught, they would all become exposed.

In fact, even if not caught, they would be exposed. In reality, they needed him to proceed with their schemes.

"Yes, it was better to collude with them until he had enough to get away."

Chapter 24

Derik contacted the Hendersons and asked them to come to his office for a review of the sale. Harry and Merle enlisted George's help to get to town and to please stay while they were inside the real estate office. They would need a ride back afterwards. Of course, George agreed and after bringing them to Derik's Realty, George parked his car and walked down to the sheriff's office to say hello to Bob.

Harry and Merle entered the office and Derik stood from behind his desk to meet them at the door. "Let's go into the conference room where we can review what you're planning to do."

Derik explained to Harry that the comparative selling prices for lake cabins has remained fairly static for a number of years and that there were presently no prospects to buy the property. He also let them know that in the past, the Decker Lake Board of Directors purchased the properties at a small discount until a buyer could be found.

If they were interested in this, just let him know and he will contact Harvey, the President of the Lake Association, to make an offer. They both agreed with this option since they were looking forward to moving to the home and seeing the Murphys. It would be nice to have some acquaintances in their new place.

George and Bob were having a general discussion about life and sadness. Bob explained how difficult it was to move from a big town police force to a small town sheriff's position. It took a while to get used to it. He had met a number of nice ladies in the area but none presented a long term commitment.

George, always expecting to live by his cover story, explained how much he missed Mary and how he would never stop looking for her. He also mentioned how sad it was up at the lake, the difficulty sleeping, nightmares, and just plain depression. It seemed everybody felt the same way.

Bob explained what he thought to George. "It might just be the facts surrounding a community of senior citizens; A part of the aging process." Bob didn't really think this but he felt it would be better for George if he told him this.

George didn't agree with this assessment and he said "the whole place changed shortly after Harvey bought the tavern." George didn't add anything else to the statement, just waited for Bob to have it sink in. Bob just rubbed the area above his upper lip as he thought about what George had said.

George looked out the window and saw that the meeting with Derik was over and Harry and Merle were outside looking around. George said his goodbyes to Bob, left the office and walked back to where the Henderson's were standing.

"Everything go okay?" asked George, with a smile on his face, "How'd Derik treat you? Okay?"

"Thanks for asking" replied Harry, "Everything is good. We didn't get as much as we thought we would, but so what? We'll be on Medicaid in about a year. Sure had to sign a lot of papers, though, more than I thought. Derik said that it is typical that we need to sign a Power of Attorney when going into a senior citizen home, so that our finances are then under control of Medicaid. You know, we pay down our own money until it's gone and then Social Security and Medicaid pay our way until the end. What a deal?"

"Sounds about right. How long did they say this would take?" asked George, but George made it sound more like a statement. George contemplated to himself. "All this uneasiness at the lake is causing the older folks to move away so quickly. Homes are selling for big discounts to the lake association. Some things just didn't add up" and now it was making the hackles on his neck stand up, and he felt a shiver in his spine.

"Not long," replied Harry. "Everything should be ready to go in about a week."

"They said they needed the time to organize a duplex room and the Transport to take us down. Other than that, it's all ready and we're ready to go. As of right now, George, it doesn't seem as bad I thought it would be. Just a sign of aging, that's all. It's not fun but it's the way it is."

George nodded his head in understanding. He has seen many a retired person go along this way. It's sad because as you get older you realized you're next. He wished he had Mary by his side; Made him even sadder with the thought, yet he still felt slightly off as his trained mind began considering the timing, his inner feelings about Harvey and, of course, Mary.

The drive back to the lake was uneventful and very quiet. No one made any conversation because everyone felt saddened by the next phase of life for Harry and Merle and the future phase of life for George.

"Life sucks and then you die," thought George, but with that thought he made a decision to live to the fullest. He wasn't going down without a fight.

"Harry," asked George, his hand on his chin in a contemplative manner. "How about coming to my place before you leave, You, Merle and I can share a few beers, have a light bite and talk about the future. It's a lot better than going to the tavern and standing with Harvey waiting for a bus. Don't you think?"

"Sounds okay to me and I don't think Merle would mind either. It's better to be with people you know rather than those you don't when making a long trip. Probably never see you again, unless you decide to do the same and we're still alive. Do you think you can help us bring our luggage over to your place, while we wait for the bus?"

"Absolutely," replies George, "Be happy to help and I would like the company."

This being arranged, Harry calls Harvey and tells him of the change in plans. Harvey has a few concerns about the change as he doesn't want anyone else involved with the Hendersons' travel plans. His face shows the unease but his voice is calm as he says, "Sounds like a plan. When the Transport gets here, I'll give the driver directions to George's."

Harvey decides that he needs to pass this new information to May who would pass it on to Veronica. Veronica was too strange and Harvey didn't know how any change in a plan would affect her. Better to leave it to her mother to tell her and avoid any last minute issues.

Chapter 25

Veronica was already on the New York State Thruway, nearing the exit for Deckersburg and then onto Decker Lake. Her task was to pick up the Henderson couple, load their luggage and personal belongings, make them comfortable in the reclining seats of the Transport and begin the drive back to Florida.

She had already formulated the plan in her mind, including how she would make them relax and then drug and dispose of them.

Her mom explained that no other people could come to the home from Decker Lake but they still wanted to come, so she must provide them with the sedatives and the suffocation that she accidentally did to the Murphy couple.

Mom said this so objectively that Veronica felt it was her duty to perform this service. Veronica had no emotional feelings or thoughts about the killing of these people, any more than she had any thoughts about the deaths of people in floods, fires or acts of terror.

"Everybody dies," she thought, "it's just a matter of when. It's important for the Hendersons that they do not go to the home and better for them to be with the Murphys."

Veronica decided that she would stop at the same rest stop as she did previously and offer them tea or coffee. She would make certain that they had enough sedative to kill them both, but if for some reason they did not die, she would suffocate them with the heavy towel.

Once the task was completed, she would call her mom who would make the arrangements for her to meet the man by the cemetery and he would take it from there. As before, she would not say anything, just get back into the Transport and drive back to Florida.

She made the call to her mom, who told her that she would be meeting the Henderson couple at this fellow George's home, not at the tavern. It's just a pick up location change and does not alter any plans.

If she stops at the tavern, Harvey will give her the address and she should proceed as if nothing has changed. Veronica understands and acknowledges the change in plans with her usual precision-like thought process.

"Yes, I will stop at the tavern where Harvey will give me the address. I will drive to the address and pick up the Hendersons. All things remain the same from there."

Veronica arrived at the tavern at 4:00PM. Harvey has been looking out the window of the tavern waiting for the Transport to arrive. May called and gave him the approximate time of arrival and knew that barring unforeseen circumstances, Veronica's assessment would be extremely precise.

Harvey walked out of the tavern and to the driver's side window where he gives Veronica a slip of paper with George's address and the Henderson's first names, so she could greet them with a more personal tone.

Veronica says nothing, looks at the paper and returns it, then drives onto Decker Lane, where she will turn left on Bleeker and to George's house. Harry and Merle should be waiting for her to arrive and will be ready to leave right after saying goodbye to George.

Just as she anticipated when she pulled into George's driveway, Harry, Merle and George were on the front porch with the luggage. She exited the driver's seat, walked up to the three and greeted them with the practiced "Good evening. My name is Veronica. I will be your driver. Please let me take your luggage. I will place it into the storage area below."

George studies Veronica's eyes and speech and realized that she has Asperger's, but it is mild and she is fully functional. He said goodbye to Harry and gave Merle a hug and helped them into the Transport, where Veronica showed them to two comfortable reclining seats.

"Please sit and make yourselves comfortable," Veronica continues with her prepared statements, "We will be making one overnight stop on the way to the Sunshine Forever Home. As there are no toilet facilities on the Transport, if you need to stop, just let me know. Beverages and light snacks are available."

As the Transport pulled away, George waved goodbye, even though neither see him waving as they are preoccupied with the comfort of the recliners. He knew that he will never see them again because as with all the older residents, once they're gone, they're gone. It just seemed sad that this was the future for them all.

"Crap," he thinks, "this place is getting to me. I can't get any sleep. I can't stop thinking about Mary. I'm getting old. This sucks."

Veronica is on the road driving within the speed limit as she always did. She held no conversation with the couple sitting there and unless they addressed her directly, she wouldn't.

A few hours later, they asked to stop for a bathroom break and when the two left for the Rest Area, she prepared the tea and coffee with the sedatives already included. Upon their return she offered them a light snack of tea sandwiches and either coffee or tea.

Both accepted with smiles and thanked her and shortly after drinking the beverages, they fell into deep trance like slumbers. Neither seemed likely to die anytime soon, so Veronica, understanding that she must be at the cemetery by 2:00AM to meet the big man, suffocated each of them.

Once she confirmed that they are dead and comfortable in their recliners, she called her mom and gave her the arrival time. May promptly called Harvey. Harvey hasn't had any contact with Ivan, nor does he want any. Barry is the front man for this task and was waiting for the call. Once the call is received and relayed to Barry, Barry called Ivan to let him know that the Transport will pull up behind the market at 2:00AM. Ivan grunted in agreement and advised Barry not to forget about the $10,000 and began the preparations for the arrival of two more innocents.

It's 2:00AM and Ivan was waiting inside the rear door to his market. He had prepared the shed as well as the location in the cemetery for the two bodies. When the Transport arrived, Veronica exited and assisted Ivan with the removal of the two bodies. Ivan brought them to the shed and told Veronica to leave.

Veronica, without turning around, walked to the driver's side of the Transport, opened the door, sat in the driver's seat, turned on the engine and drove away. All this is done in a robot-like precision manner, without any words or human like actions.

Ivan watched her as she left and still wondered about this young woman. "What must her parents be like to have such a daughter as this? She drives away with the living and drives back with them dead. She has no thoughts about what she is doing."

"Very strange" he mutters under his breath, "but I have seen worse and in fact I have done worse. I am not one to judge."

Chapter 26

Ivan has both bodies in the shed and decides that the time is coming when he will be finished serving Barry and Harvey's needs to dispose of their murdering of these innocents.

As he contemplates the end of this savagery he is leaning against a wall, pounding the side of his large fist repeatedly into the wall, making a soft wooden drumming sound. Someone outside of his market would think he was playing a Native American percussion album but no one was outside at this late hour. He stopped his frustrated pounding because he knew he must complete this task and get on with it.

He decides that it would be much easier to place the bodies into smaller plastic bags, partially unassembled, so he sections them and puts the parts into separate and smaller bags for burial. The smaller bags are easier to carry and manipulate into the existing coffins in the old section.

Just as before, he takes his wheel barrow, shovel and walking stick and walks deep into the cemetery to where the others are buried. As before, he opens an existing old grave, lifts the old wooden lid and places the bags into it, leaving an equal number of bags for the next coffin. He replaces the covers, shovels the dirt back into the grave, places old leaves and brush over the grave site so it seems undisturbed, says a few words as he once heard a priest say, and smiles.

He recalls that as he was sectioning, he was just absentmindedly stuffing parts into bags and likely mixed and matched parts of each. What a joke it will be someday, if anyone digs up these people and finds them intermingled for eternity or tries to put one together without the other.

He remembers to take his souvenirs.

On the way back, he smiles. He knows that he can and will take some measure of revenge upon Barry and Harvey, not just for discovering who he was, but as justice for the innocent people they are killing.

It seems like old times and he knows that before he can, he needs to accumulate enough money to move on. "Soon," he thinks to himself, pondering what may be next. "Soon," he says in a whisper to himself so he can hear the word. He knows that these won't be the last. He just needs to know when it is time to disappear and "the time is coming, it is coming soon."

Upon his return to his apartment, he calls Barry and tells him that all is complete. Barry thanks him and wishes him a goodnight, with a sarcastic tone that once again justifies what Ivan has been thinking about taking revenge.

Ivan sits into his chair that overlooks the window and the cemetery. He leans forward as he stares into the night and wonders why fate has brought him to this state. He believed he could escape his past and it has caught up to him. These evil men, they are no better than the Russians but worse in so many ways. Murdering old people reminded him of the murdering of his grandparents and so many others.

It's always the old, the weak, the poor. "Well, this time they are dealing with the wrong man."

And he thought about the messengers. "Yes, the messengers. They were so many, but the thirty seventh one, he was the one who almost escaped. He had a motorized bicycle and rode low and I missed him with the first swing. It is fortunate that I set up the fallen tree in the road so he fell from his bike and did not escape. They were so many that I lost count but whether it is one or a hundred, it is all the same. Fate brought me to this place and involved me with this and fate will take me away. It was meant to be."

Barry came for the package of meat for the tavern the second Wednesday and at the end of each month. Ivan always had it prepared and ready for him for pick up. This time Barry will bring him another $10,000 as payment and Ivan will give him the large package of boneless lamb chops, hamburger and other meat products. Tomorrow is pick-up day. It is rare that Barry calls and asks for a delivery and with the payment due, he is certain that Barry will come in person.

Just as Ivan predicted, Barry came in early on the Wednesday, handed Ivan an envelope and picked up the large package of meat and other items. Ivan mumbled something to him which Barry would take as a 'thanks', turned and retreated back behind the meat counter. Barry left the market, walked down to the Post Office to inquire if there was any mail, just like all the other residents do when in town. He waved at a few of the townspeople, smiled and then walked back to his car and returned to the tavern.

Once back in the tavern, Barry unwrapped the package and placed most of the meat into the freezer leaving about a quarter of the package for the refrigerator to feed the lunch crowd.

During the next two months, Ivan has been the recipient of one more elderly couple, whom he decided he would just bury intact as he was too busy to be bothered.

Then during the next few months, Veronica brought three more elderly residents, two ladies and one gentleman. Since they were transported by Veronica individually, he surmised that they likely were single people living up at Decker Lake.

He never met any of them. As was typical for Veronica, she came and left each time without saying a word, not offering to help, not saying goodbye or "see you next week." Ivan decided that, in each case, the elderly women and the old gentleman were small and light enough to place each into their own large plastic bag and buried intact.

He never forgot to take his souvenirs.

For each, he received $5,000.00 for a single and $10,000 for a couple. Barry was very prompt with the payment as if he believed that the payment would be enough for Ivan to keep up the good work.

Ivan had more than he needed to make contact with the 'friends' in Brighton Beach and to begin his new life. He decided that it would not be long before he must leave. When he did, he would leave the shop intact and somehow get a message to the authorities.

Meanwhile, George was working on his whiteboard, moving the pieces around to understand what was going on at the lake. He understands that the Timmins' couple was contemplating moving to the Sunshine Forever Home and he decided to formulate a plan with Bill Timmins, if Bill agrees, to verify their arrival.

Chapter 27
NOW

Harvey had dozed in his easy chair in front of his fireplace and had dreamt about the circumstances that led to this remote place. He awakened with a start as if something had gone wrong but he doesn't know what it is.

"Nah, it's just my nerves getting to me. The dead bodies are beginning to pile up."

George heard about the meetings that the Timmins' were having with Harvey about selling their house and moving to the Sunshine Forever Home. He decided to call Bill and ask him to meet for a cup of coffee in town, maybe at the diner.

The next day, just as George had asked, they met at the diner. George attempted to dissuade him from selling his home to Harvey and then moving to Florida.

"Bill," exclaimed George, "stay in the area where at least some people know you. After all, Edna is not as well as she might be. Just because it gets cold here in the winter is not a reason to move. You can always just bundle up and relax in front of a good fire. It's damn hot in Pensacola and even hotter than that when the wind blows from inland."

George tried to discourage Bill with as many objections as possible, with the lack of four seasons, the general third world scenario of Pensacola, maybe the lack of decent medical facilities, but in the end he failed.

He just had this dark feeling that neither Bill nor Edna would be seen again. He couldn't say that to Bill. It would be an insane assertion without any foundation and utterly ludicrous and it might also be relayed to Harvey. Instead, he asked Bill to do one thing for him and not mention it to anyone.

From all the postcards that came from the home and were posted in the clubhouse, it was evident that everyone who moved there sent back a card about the home, how nice it was and how they should have moved earlier. He gave Bill a slip of paper. Drawn on it was a small diagram of a Masonic symbol, easy for Bill to copy. He asked Bill to copy the symbol on the lower left corner of the first postcard and mail it when he found the time after moving to the home.

"Above all, please don't show it to anyone". If Bill decided to mail a second postcard, he could do the same.

Bill thought it was kind of a strange request, but he knew George for a while and he seemed to be of good character and a 'straight shooter'.

Bill agreed and also agreed not to tell anyone and he thought to himself, "I won't be telling Edna either."

He thanked George for his concern and went back home to get ready to move.

Edna and Bill Timmins have made the decision to move to the Sunshine Forever Home. Bill didn't understand George's concerns and felt it was just his way of trying to maintain friendships, now that he's alone, with his wife gone. He understands George's loneliness but his and Edna's own needs must be put first and living more comfortably into their later years sounds like the best plan.

George gave Bill the sketch to put onto the first card he will send. He puts the sketch into his wallet and promises himself that he will do this for George. Everyone at the lake feels a heavy anxiety and it's likely that this is a sign of the anxiety representing itself in George.

As with the previous residents who were relocating, Bill and Edna met with Derik to discuss the sale of their property. They signed the typical paperwork, many copies of it and Derik organized the date when they would be picked up by the Sunshine Forever Home Transport.

They asked why they couldn't just fly down and be picked up at the airport. Derik didn't have the answer to that question, even though he was acting as an agent for the home but would make an inquiry and get back to them.

Prior to the Murphys, some of the residents would ask to fly down and others would ask for the Transport as either they didn't fly or didn't have the money. All of those that asked to fly after Veronica's unfortunate murder of the Murphys, were persuaded not to and all had agreed to take the Transport.

Persuasion was generally easy, since the nearest airport was two hours away and had no direct flights, so the trip by air took more than eight hours, with the driving, the waiting and the flying time. Harvey and the team decided that offering an option was not a choice for a number of reasons, particularly since they needed to control the where and when of the 'sedation and disposal' of those who were moving.

It would be the Transport. The Timmins were not offered a choice; they were given the Transport as the option.

But Bill Timmins said "No, thanks. We decided to take our personal belongings on the plane and buy all new when we get there. Anything else, we'll ship."

"Well," he thought, "it doesn't matter to me. I'm getting a good commission on selling these homes to the lake association, which is actually Harvey."

Derik wasn't aware of the problem associated with the couple flying into Pensacola and had no knowledge of the murders or the Medicaid fraud. As far as Derik was concerned, it shouldn't make any difference. But to Harvey and the team, it added a complexity for which they weren't ready.

Derik called Cap at the Sunshine Forever Home and explained that the next couple are looking into flying down rather than taking the Transport. All they need is to be picked up at the airport and brought to the Home. Their personal items will be shipped separately.

Cap isn't happy with this revelation as he knew that no other living people can come to the home from Decker Lake. Derik doesn't know about any of this so his question must be answered correctly.

"Derik, I'll get back to you with any arrangements they would like to make. Talk to you later."

Cap called May at the Funeral Parlor and they discuss what the next couple wants to do. "How we gon'na handle this can of worms?"

May responded, trying not to let her concern be a 'tell' in her voice, "Cap. Hang in there, we'll handle it."

Phil has remained in Florida for the time being as everything seemed to be running smoothly up north and he wanted to organize their escape plan.

But May cannot control herself, her voice becoming louder and more urgent.

"Phil," she uses a flat and directive voice, "Phil, get over here. The whole thing is coming down. This next couple wants to fly down and be picked up at the airport. How're we going to handle this twist?"

Phil, rubbing his hand on his chin and squinting as if the sun is shining brightly in his eyes, answers as best he can.

"Listen, we pick them up at the airport. We can't say no. When they arrive, we tell them their apartment isn't ready and we need to put them up in a motel for the evening. There are a couple of motels on the road from the airport that are really isolated. We bring in some dinner to the motel room and eat with them making sure that their drinks are drugged."

"Once they're asleep, we get Veronica to finish them off. We wrap-em-up, get them in the Transport, bring them to the crematorium and proceed as before. When their stuff arrives, we sign for it and bring it to the crematorium for disposal."

"I don't like the idea of all the loose ends," replied May, "This is bad. Airline flights leave traces of where people went. Shipping companies leave traces of stuff being sent. You tell me Phil, you tell me. This is really bad news. It's over, or am I wrong?" and she had a tone of finality in her voice.

"No, you're not wrong. Let's make ready to get out. I think we need to leave the country, maybe Costa Rica." He continued with a list of other places and problems, "Too many dead bodies that aren't supposed to be dead; too many loose ends, too many loose lips."

"No, you're not wrong." Phil adds, "I'm going back to the lake right after we get rid of these two. Veronica will drive the Transport to the EverRest crematorium and I'll get up to the house as if nothing is wrong. In the meantime, start making preparations to get out. I believe we have maybe four to six weeks." and Phil adds, "Don't say anything to Cap or Henny; and don't tell Veronica anything yet. And above all, say nothing to Harvey or Barry."

Derik called Bill Timmins and told him that he and Edna can fly to the Pensacola airport where the Transport will meet them and bring them to the home. Since their larger personal belongings are being shipped separately, they can sign for them when the shipment arrives.

He told Bill that as part of the Sunshine Forever Home service, they will fly them first class and send the tickets. Of course, Bill agrees.

When the tickets arrive, Bill noticed that they are for the last flight into Pensacola, arriving about midnight. He discounted this as being a routine 'free ticket' and paid it no mind as 'first class' is something that they had never flown before. It would be a treat.

In reality, Phil made a clean decision that since both must be eliminated; he would need to offer something unlikely to be refused, a first class ticket. When they arrived, it would be late and dark and Veronica would offer them a cup of tea or coffee and a small snack on the way to the motel. Both would be tired from the trip and likely accept the generous offer. A short time after drinking the beverages, they would either be asleep or dead and then Veronica could finish the work and drive them to EverRest for cremation.

If that didn't work, they would be brought to the motel and offered the same. One way or the other, they could not and would not be brought to the home.

Unless someone was looking for them, no one would be investigating that they arrived in Pensacola and never went further. But if someone were looking for them, by the time the investigation started, he, May and Veronica would be long gone.

Chapter 28

As for Bill and Edna, the plan detailed by Phil worked perfectly; they took a taxi to the airport where they waited for about an hour before boarding the plane.

The first class seats were more comfortable than they can believe and they wondered why they hadn't flown that way before. The flight took off on time and even with the connecting flight in Philadelphia, they landed at just about midnight in Pensacola.

It's not more than 30 minutes until they can deplane and get to the arrivals area where they saw Veronica holding a sign reading 'Bill and Edna'. She greeted them with a practiced smile, took their two carry-on bags and said, "Follow me. It's just a short walk to the Transport. You must be tired after the long trip and it is late."

As they walked to the Transport, Veronica didn't hold any other small talk conversation, just walked with the couple following closely behind. She didn't bother to open the luggage carrier beneath the Transport, as the bags are small and will fit nicely into the overhead.

Bill and Edna are seated into the extremely comfortable reclining seats and once relaxed, Veronica offered them each either a cup of tea or coffee, both in either decaffeinated or regular. In addition, she offered them a snack of tea sandwiches made from small white or rye breads with a gruyere cheese, cream cheese, or sliced cheddar.

Bill and Edna are so content with the service that they both accept the offer of a beverage. Edna had a cup of tea and Bill asked for decaffeinated coffee. While Veronica is preparing the beverages, she provided a plate of the tea sandwiches.

Veronica had taken no chances with the sedatives. Just to be certain and to increase the possibility of their taking the sedatives, she had laced both the beverages and the sandwiches.

Shortly after they finished eating and drinking, Veronica began the long drive to the EverRest Funeral Parlor. She knew that both will be soundly asleep very soon and then she will finish the work by suffocating them. After the task is completed, she will drive to the loading dock at the rear of the building, unload the cargo and help mom with the delivery into the crematorium.

Her planning has worked well and the Timmins are resting comfortable in their reclining Transport seats, never to awaken again. Veronica called and told her mom that the motel was not needed so she is coming straight to the loading dock.

"I'll be there in one hour."

May understood without asking why and was waiting for her at the loading dock.

Bringing bodies to the crematorium was simple and well-practiced. She had helped mom with this for many years, bringing bodies from the storage area, new bodies that were to be cremated, not buried, and of course, these particular bodies, whom she sedated, suffocated and prepared. It was all the same to her.

May called Cap to let him know that when the personal items arrive, they should get them to her as soon as possible for disposal. In the meantime, she stored the ashes of Bill and Edna until the arrival of their belongings, likely tomorrow. She would cremate these items and the whole pile of ashes would be brought to the Gulf for disposal into the beautiful clear blue waters.

The following day, Cap called and told May that the Timmins shipment has arrived. May drove herself to the Sunshine Forever Home and picked up the shipment.

When she returned to EverRest, she asked Veronica to cremate the entire shipment and add it to the remains they boxed the previous night. Veronica completed her task and they both took a ride to the Gulf, the cremains in the rear seat. They parked at an overlook beach.

May got out of the car and without a word, emptied the large box of cremains into the waters.

"That finishes off Bill and Edna." She mutters under her breath, but with her concerns decreasing, knowing that the scheme is about to end.

"Veronica," she calls loudly to her daughter who is sitting in the passenger seat, staring out the window. "Let's get back and update the records. I'll call dad and tell him all is okay over here."

"Put on the calendar to send a Postcard to Decker Lake from Bill and Edna."

Veronica dutifully places a note on the calendar to send a Postcard in two weeks and another in four weeks, just as she has done with the previous non-existent residents.

Chapter 29

Two weeks pass quickly and the first postcard has arrived from Bill Timmins and was posted on the bulletin board. As was usual, it expressed how wonderful the home was, how beautiful the rooms and how great it was to have social activities.

George had taken a walk to the clubhouse and saw the postcard and quickly comes to the conclusion that it is not from Bill. Missing from the postcard was the Masonic symbol in the lower corner, or anywhere on the card. George had a cold, creeping feeling across his chest and the hair stood up on this arms.

He didn't want to think the worst and hoped that Bill just forgot about the symbol, but deep inside he knew that this card was NOT sent by Bill; but someone else sent the card.

That could only mean one thing to a person with George's experience. George thought out loud but with a whisper to himself as he needed to hear the sound of his thoughts,

"Bill was gone; maybe Edna also; but why? What's the purpose of moving them out and killing them?"

He decided to stop in at the tavern to say hello to Harvey, just to alleviate any suspicion by Harvey that he is avoiding anyone. When he entered the tavern, Barry is behind the bar and Harvey is seated at a table.

"Harvey," calls George, as he walks into the tavern, "How's it going? Haven't seen you for a while." George acts and sounds completely neutral and as he enters he notices Barry's body language which becomes tightened and Harvey's who tenses up when he sees him.

Both have been lost in their own thoughts as to how wrong everything is going. Seeing George catches them by surprise as George hasn't come to the tavern in a long time.

"Everything is good, George," Harvey reclaims his calm mannerisms and adds, "What brings you around? I haven't seen you in months."

George wanted to add just enough nervousness to their demeanor and just enough curiosity, since they knew that he knows the Timmins couple.

"Just looking for some contact with Bill, you know, Timmins; they went to the Sunshine Forever Home and I haven't heard anything from them. I saw they sent a postcard that their arrival was good and the place is nice. Maybe I'll make a call down there and try to reach them. I figured that while I was here, I'd stop in and say hello, maybe have a cup of coffee."

Harvey added, "Sounds like a good idea, giving them a call. How about we cook you up a famous tavern hamburger?"

"No thanks," answered George, "just a cup of coffee would be nice, maybe a slice of apple pie."

"Barry," Harvey calls from across the room, "bring George a cup of coffee and a slice of apple pie."

Barry nodded his head in agreement, prepares the coffee and pie and brought it to George, who sat at a table by himself, not where Harvey is seated. Barry returned to his prior position behind the bar.

All three remain in their positions and nothing more is said. George just stared out of the window into the woods but can also see the reflection of Barry behind the bar and Harvey from the corner of his eye.

Harvey just sat there and contemplated George's presence. Barry, on the other hand, was staring at George with a snarl on his lips, looking like a predator in heat that couldn't wait to get to his prey.

George waited just enough time, sipped his coffee in regular equally timed sips and ate the apple pie with small fork filled bits in regular equally timed bites, so Barry will notice.

The more he does this, the narrower Barry's eyes become. George believed he finished just before Barry decided to leap from behind the bar to attack him. Of course, Barry didn't, but George knew that he had baited him. It's all for effect and George had done this many times before to throw his enemies off kilter.

He knew these were his enemies.

"Harvey, the pie was great and the coffee perfect. How much do I owe you?"

Harvey responds, "It's on the house, George, don't be a stranger. Come on down for dinner sometime."

"Thanks," replies George "Maybe I'll take you up on that."

George went back to his house and into the 'workroom'. He needed to reset the satellite transceiver to the correct azimuth and connect to the secure Agency server.

Logging on to the Agency through the laptop, he realized that his movements would be tracked, but also realized that the nature of this particular investigation was just as dangerous as any he had done. The Agency would understand that if he, George, was working on something, then it was needed.

They would contact him within the next four weeks to gain some insight into the circumstance, but were unlikely to interfere, however, always likely to assist.

His first inquiry was directly into the secure servers of the New York State government agency that controlled real estate transactions.

This wasn't '**nys.gov**', but a dark server positioned by certain 'Information Technology employees' of New York State, who managed to build a covert back door link into the State Government servers. The 'covert dark server' existed in every State in every government agency, in most corporations and anywhere else the Agency felt it necessary to monitor activity.

Only a few knew of this secret network and only a few others knew how it began.

The first step was to gain access, which was a quick and simple command. He then scrolled to the 'real estate transactions' concerning Decker Lake, found and opened the file and reviewed the details of the Timmins' deal.

George used his access through the Agency to review all the details and the sales records for their house.

What George found was that Decker Lake made a first offer for the Timmins' house and for the same lowball rate that he was offered and he refused. He then learned that Harvey was the actual purchaser of the Timmins' house and for the rate that Decker Lake proposed. That could only mean that Harvey wanted the house and used his position as the President of the Decker Lake HOA to buy the place for himself.

He looked into the Timmins' finances and found that the Timmins took the deal because they were both on Social Security, and had about one year of savings to pay for the home. They certainly acted as if they were more self-sufficient. They took the deal because they were too old not to.

It was unlikely that they knew that Harvey was the purchaser and most likely that they thought they were selling to the Decker Lake Home Owners Association. Then it flashed into his mind, "Who was the realtor? Derik!"

"Who exactly is Derik?" he thought, but he put that inquiry to the side until he finished the current train of thought.

He knew that there was a connection between Barry and Harvey and would try to pose a few inane questions to Barry to determine their history. Considering Barry's outright hatred of him, it might be difficult to have a 'conversation'. Hopefully, he could do this without raising suspicion. He knew that this fellow Barry was more than just a giant of a man.

His size didn't mean that he was stupid. In fact, from the few conversations that he had overheard or from his limited direct contact with Barry, he recognized that he had some highly skilled intellectual qualities.

Then he looked into a small number of recent house sales from the lake, and the realtor and attorney was always Derik. The offerings were always low. And the actual purchaser was always Harvey, not the Homeowners Association. Harvey, being the President of the Decker Lake HOA might be directly involved with procuring homes for the Decker Lake Association, to be sold later, as an investment for the association, but in this case and he assumed that in every case since he took control of the tavern and became President of the HOA, it was Harvey himself who had bought these houses and the investments were for himself.

He investigated into the records for the past four years, just about the time that Harvey had bought Jesse's Tavern. What he learned astounded him. From the first house sold, which was the Mallory's, unlike all the later homes, the Gruenwelds were the actual purchasers; Derik was the realtor/attorney and Barry, the witness. For the next four years, Harvey was the actual purchaser, who resold the house as quickly as possible; Derik was the realtor/attorney and Barry was the witness.

That raised his eyebrows as the data pointed directly to the conspirators involved. In his mind he began coordinating the data surrounding the real estate deals with the incidents of postcards sent from those who moved to the Sunshine Forever Home.

For a little more than two years, the postcards were random and more numerous and then for the past eight months they became static at two weeks and four weeks. He instinctively knew that the next postcard from Bill would be in about two weeks' time, corroborating the pattern he had discovered.

"The first house," he repeated to himself, "after Harvey bought the tavern was sold to Phil and May Gruenweld, who moved in almost the next day."

Phil and May bought the first house at the lake using Derik as the realtor so it would not raise suspicion, in this case, Derik's suspicion.

It's not a coincidence that shortly after Harvey became the President of the HOA that he appointed both Phil and May to be on the Board of Directors.

"Who are Phil and May Gruenweld?" he thought, "and where did they come from."

A coincidence of their arrival and that first sale was a direct deterministic connection to what's happening now.

George was a master at deterministic logic, piecing together disparate bits of information that had some relationship to determine the inevitable outcome, particularly when the outcome was seemingly murder.

The Agency knew of his genius in this particular behavioral analysis and used it to their advantage. The fact that George was also a Master at Arms didn't deter them from using his mental abilities as well.

In fact both were mutually intertwined. George could work almost independently and reach the same conclusions in days that many others working in concert would arrive at in weeks or months. George could then affect the outcome swiftly, making deaths look accidental, or causing the 'disappearance' of subjects. Yes, George was a valued asset at the Agency.

"Phil and May, they deserve more attention." And he said this aloud to reinforce his thoughts. "But first, I must look into the direct recipient of the residents; The Sunshine Forever Home."

"Who owns the Sunshine Forever Home?"

He found the names Tim and Henrietta Folsom.

"Who are Tim and Henrietta Folsom?" he thought, as he placed them into the category of endgame conspirators, being that they owned the Sunshine Forever Home.

He knew that senior citizen facilities had arrangements with mortuaries, cemeteries and doctors and all provided finder's fees when introduced to the families of the deceased. "Finder's fees?" he scoffed at the term, "just another word for kickbacks and who knows how extensive these fees are or how many are involved."

Digging deeper in the Folsom's records, he found an arrest history of small time cons, embezzlement, fraud, and a few other white collar crimes, but no violent behavior to speak of. Most of the arrests did not lead to convictions and when they did, it was for a few months or just parole.

During the search, he found that they were arrested with Harvey Paul's parents and even spent a short time in a local jail together. The 'relationship' with Harvey Paul's parents ended when the Pauls were convicted for all the major embezzlement crimes they had committed and were now serving near life sentences in a federal minimum security prison. He found that neither of Harvey's parents had committed any violent crimes. Extrapolating Harvey Paul from this conglomeration of criminals was rather easy.

"Harvey was raised by crooked parents with crooked friends to be a life time con man and the lake was an ultimate con."

George learned that Phil and May Gruenweld own and operate the EverRest Funeral Home which is equipped with a large mortuary that is, coincidentally, just a short walk from the Sunshine Forever Home.

It didn't take much to link the two sets of people and Harvey together as the fundamental orchestrators of the scheme.

Likely, the Gruenwelds just participated with a kickback, finder fee arrangement with the home and it transformed into this money making scheme.

He believed that they were likely participants in the missing people. Looking more deeply into the mortuary's architecture and layout, he learned that that have sixty refrigerator shelves for body storage, more than the typical ten that smaller mortuaries have.

The large number of shelves was due to this building having originated as the morgue for the nearby police medical examiners. The building was later sold and converted into a mortuary and funeral home when the various police departments constructed new facilities which included their own morgues.

Phil and May were the original purchasers and he marveled at the fabulous deal they were able to sign with the city to purchase the building. He surmised that renovations were basically simple and the storage offered other opportunities to lease the extra space to other funeral homes when the need arose.

Coincidentally, the EverRest Cemetery was also available and even though it required State approval, the Gruenwelds were able to simultaneously purchase the controlling share, rename the mortuary to the EverRest Funeral Parlor and link the two to enhance their offerings.

His next thought was directed to the recipient of the victims. He now referred to everyone who went to the Sunshine Forever Home as victims, maybe not at first, but definitely now.

"I will get to the bottom of this hole," he thought, wringing his hands in a strangling manner, thinking about Mary, where she might be, and if she stumbled upon this scheme so long ago. "Whatever's going on, it will end."

Piecing together all the relative data, the postcards, Barry, Harvey, Derik, the Folsom's and the Gruenwelds, George began the deterministic logic necessary to understand the end game.

Purchasing and reselling homes at the lake meant profit for those selling at a better price. The next step in his investigation was to explore the resale price of the houses that Harvey surreptitiously purchased to correlate the sale and resale to determine the profit.

Also required were the backgrounds of those purchasing the lake homes from Harvey. Yes, there was profit to be made in reselling the homes for a better price and Derik was making commissions and additional fees on the resales, but he believed that Derik was just a necessary worker in the scheme, not a real participant. Since Harvey, who was the reseller of the homes, made very little on the resale, the object was not the homes themselves but those who did the purchasing or maybe those who were selling.

A second objective was the location to which a number of the sellers went, namely the Sunshine Forever Home. Derik was just a dotted line, not irrelevant, but just a dotted line.

As he began building the complete scenario, he determined that this was an elaborate scheme to make big money, otherwise why do it.

When you correlate old people, and senior facilities you head for one answer,

"Where's the money come from? After the old people's funds run out, who pays? Medicaid!"

"Medicaid pays about $4000.00 per month in Florida. That's a lot of money and if the quantities total up correctly, it is an enormous scheme. For the initial two years, the scheme was typical of non-violent offenders just scamming the government and the elderly. Happened many times before and will continue forever.

But the next year, something else was afoot. Greed turned into violence? An accident?"

"Derik? Derik! It's time to look into Derik's background."

Evidently he did not live in Deckersburg all his life, but moved in a number of years back. He is currently an attorney but has never presented himself as such. He owns the real estate office, not actually practicing law, but can, if the need arises, example: real estate transactions that require filings.

His investigation into Derik's background led him directly to the embezzlement cases of the two non-profit organizations, the facts of Derik's indictment as well as the other conspirators, the convictions of the others and the eventual dismissal of charges against Derik, due to two missing witnesses.

He delved into the American Bar Association servers and learned of Derik's suspension for two years and where he moved and registered as an attorney after the suspension was lifted. He found how often he moved and when he finally landed at Deckersburg, purchasing the small realty office. It was there that Derik registered as an attorney but did not overtly practice law.

"Missing witnesses, never found. Was this a sign of Derik's violent behavior or just co-conspirators that wanted to disappear? Which was more likely?" George considered all the circumstances surrounding the embezzlement cases and decided that this was a case of co-conspirators, not violent behavior.

Derik was probably a sociopath when it came to dealing with people and he wanted their money, not caring if it hurt, but was unlikely to commit the violent behavior himself. Derik's behavioral patterns indicated that he had no issue with others doing the violence.

It was obvious that Harvey enlisted Derik into the realtor resale scheme offering a kickback and unlikely that Derik was aware of anything else; with the additional thought that Derik's mercenary habits may cause him to look into Harvey more closely so he could either insert himself more directly or blackmail additional kickbacks.

George's second thought was, "Derik better watch himself as whatever violence is happening to the elderly can surely head his way if he pushes too hard."

"So," George theorized, "the initial scheme was to funnel the elderly from Decker Lake to the Sunshine Forever Home to get their Medicaid reimbursements and the EverRest Funeral Parlor received the bodies and the burials.

It can't just be Decker Lake sending the people to the place; it's likely that the home is running as a State recognized facility in order to receive Medicaid reimbursement so they must take others.

Also, The Sunshine Forever Home has more than 500 rooms that need to be filled to maximize the profit to Tim and Henrietta. Funneling the deceased to the funeral home and eventually to the EverRest cemetery did the same for the Gruenwelds."

A sudden thought came to George, "Whatever happened to the Mallorys?" Looking into the burial records in cemeteries near Pensacola, he finds that the Mallorys purchased two lots at the Everest cemetery and that, according to a small obituary in a local Foley newspaper, Mr. Mallory had passed away and was interred in Lot46-1, with -2 reserved for Mrs. Mallory who still resided at the home.

Of course, Mrs. Mallory employed the services of the Gruenweld's EverRest Funeral Parlor for the preparation of the body, preparing and signing of the death certificate, as well as the notification to Medicaid of the passing.

Corroborating the death records, he searched into the Medicaid records where he learned that Medicaid indeed had records of Mr. Mallory's death, but their records indicated that he died eighteen months later. Another search into the IRS records indicated that joint returns were filed for them during the two year period.

The returns were sent from the Sunshine Forever Home, signed and dated by both. The death certificate was signed by a doctor, but the handwriting was illegible.

Then he knew the story. Mrs. Mallory went to a funeral, but Mr. Mallory was not in the coffin. Mr. Mallory was in one of those sixty storage units at EverRest and obviously for eighteen months, so the home and the fellow conspirators could reap the Medicaid funding. What followed was strictly intuitive. Mrs. Mallory, being alone, would be asked to move to a single room rather than the duplex, to which she would agree, and the home could re-rent the duplex to another couple.

"Now that's what I call double dipping."

For George, it was all coming together, the scheme, the fraud, the players and the game. What he needed now was enough evidence to call in the outside authorities and he needed to find out how, why and where were the people who were totally missing for the past eight months. And he needed to find out what happened to Mary.

Chapter 30

They were taking more than $250,000 each month from Medicaid and Social Security but now the active storage units were nearing fifty and the home itself was at maximum occupancy.

They were dividing up the spoils among the individuals, Harvey, Barry, Phil and May and Cap and Henny each received a full share, and portions of the profit were used to pay off Ivan, Derik and purchase the homes at Decker Lake. That's a lot of cash but it also meant a lot of work and the more work the more chances of an error and eventual exposure.

Hiding all that money was also difficult. Harvey decided to use offshore storage units to place his cash. Barry was buying property in Italy and other parts of the Mediterranean, a place he always wanted to live. Cap and Henny could launder the money in their Sunshine Forever Home business and stash it in offshore banks and Phil and May could do the same with the EverRest Funeral Parlor and Cemetery.

Harvey, on the other hand, began feeling the pressure and wanted to convince the others that they must eliminate the risk associated with moving all these bodies from storage into their coffins, opening and reopening graves, moving older residents from duplex to single rooms, the murders and all the other complexities which this con included. He wanted them to come to the conclusion that it's time to get out.

Barry, Harvey and Phil were in the tavern lunch room just making some small talk when Harvey turned the conversation to the 'project'.

Harvey began the meeting and said as emphatically as possible. "If we keep sending more people to the home from Decker Lake, they can't arrive or they'll be looking for the people who aren't there. We know that and we have been systematically resolving that issue by continuing to use Veronica."

He and everyone knew that no one from the lake could go to the home after Veronica killed the Murphys, but it didn't deter them from continuing. He also knew that the plan couldn't just be shut down. It would take time undo the storage, rebury bodies, eliminate what needed to be eliminated and he thought to himself, "I have Barry for that."

He continued, "You don't need bodies to get their Medicaid. All you need are signatures; maybe a doctor to certify someone was getting regular checkups. The problem was that people expect others to be there when they know they're supposed to be there."

Harvey spoke to Barry and Phil from the point of view of earning more and risking less and as he spoke he realized that this entire scheme was mass murder and will collapse under its own weight. He could hardly believe that he was thinking or talking in a positive way about this. It was one thing to act with expediency in tough situations but he knew that it must end. Harvey knew that the best way was for the team to figure out that the plan needs to end and it should be their idea, not his.

He knew he must plan his exit and he meant his exit (emphasizing his), not anyone else's. He asked Barry to explain to Phil the Ivan situation, so Phil could become completely aware of everything that was happening. He advised them that Cap and Henny shouldn't be included in this conversation.

Barry did as Harvey asked and told Phil about Ivan. All agreed not to tell Cap and Henny.

Phil thought to himself, "This is Harvey's way of separating us before he plans his escape, so we get left holding the bag. Not going to happen the way he thinks."

"Okay, here it is," Harvey began his dialogue with his arms resting on the table at the tavern, his hands raised and his body leaning into the words for emphasis.

"The Jones situation was unavoidable but it taught us something valuable. We couldn't let anyone get in the way or uncover our operation. None of us want to be caught."

Barry and Phil both nodded in agreement and neither had any human feelings for what they had done to Jones.

Harvey continued, "Right now, we have reached 90% of the monthly profits we can possibly earn. May has a full time job maintaining the database, shoveling bodies back and forth, keeping track of timelines and Henny is extremely busy tracking the money, sending out new signatures when required and everything else she is doing to keep us from being investigated."

Phil added a quick comment, "There's no doubt that they can keep this up for some time, but I see this ending because of the Murphy situation. When Veronica accidentally killed them and we had them disposed of, it made sending others from Decker Lake to the home a risky proposition. Hence all the other disposals"

"I agree with Phil," Harvey added and demonstrated some deceptive reluctance in his voce, "It's enough, We can't have any more new people from Decker Lake asking to go to the home. Here it is in a nutshell. We've already gotten rid of two old widows, one old widower, the Murphys, the Hendersons, the Goodmans and the Timmins. That's eleven dead people we are currently data basing to bill Medicaid in the future. We had Ivan dispose of nine of them and the last two were cremated by May. We have Power of Attorney for all of them so we can drain their bank accounts monthly."

Barry decided he should join the conversation and not just listen. He didn't consider himself a hired lackey. "So that's it from Decker Lake. No more Sunshine Forever Home. And we have a number of loose ends, like Ivan."

Phil agreed with Barry by nodding his head and added, "The real question is whether we want to continue, if so, how long or just get out while we still can, because this scheme is now tenuous at best. I think ending it as soon as possible is the best way forward."

"Hey guys" Harvey interrupted, "The plan was good while it lasted and now, as far as I'm concerned, I agree with Phil and believe we all agree and decide it's over."

Harvey had an ambivalent look in his eye, one was sorry for the untimely end to a great scheme due to an inadvertent accident to Joe Murphy and the other was greedily looking and thinking of how they could continue on and reap these great rewards. Intellectually, he knew it was over. "We just need to decide when."

Barry and Phil agreed with the assessment. Barry, looking directly into Harvey's eyes asked him a direct question, "Knowing it's coming to an end and ending it are two different things, but every scheme eventually comes to an end. Sometimes it's better to end it early, take the money and move on. Unless you have an idea how long we can continue, maybe it's better we part ways now and you can end it when you want."

Phil just listened and didn't say anything. He and May were reluctant partners in this and never thought that their containment system would ever be filled. Now it was nearly filled, eleven people were murdered by their daughter and disposed of and Harvey was looking to end his scheme but didn't offer a timeframe.

Phil thought without making any facial expressions, "How the hell do we get out if this? Harvey sounds like a madman, declaring it coming to an end but talking about draining bank accounts."

Harvey basically agreed with Barry's assessment and he nodded his head as Barry spoke. He needed to add a plan to disengage.

"Barry, you're right about the end. But we need to clean the place up before we do. First, we all agree that we're not going to send or offer any more space to the local residents."

Barry and Phil nodded in agreement.

"Barry, can you disconnect the generator and the speakers from the woods. This equipment has to go."

Barry quickly agrees and says that he will do this as soon as it becomes practical and he can do it alone since hanging the stuff up is more difficult than taking it down.

Phil is appreciative that Barry can do this by himself as he wants to go back to Florida and make the arrangements with May to get the hell out, likely before Harvey makes his decision.

Harvey continues, "With no other residents being able to go to the home from here, we can plod along for the short term, slowly cleaning out the storage units and declaring the 'stored' actually dead to Medicaid.

We should try to 'kill' the eleven we already killed and get them 'buried' as soon as possible. That might take a couple of months. In the meantime we can continue billing and taking their funds. Phil can better describe the timing of this as he has the financial records."

Phil agrees with Harvey's assessment but in his thoughts he knows better. "There's no way that May and I will be hanging around the funeral parlor for the next two to four months while we clean out the storage units and bury those that were supposed to arrive but didn't. That's a recipe for disaster."

As he's contemplating the thoughts, his eyes look upwards into space.

"Harvey," Phil decides to comment on Harvey's last statement, "This sounds like a plan. I'll get down to Florida and work with May on the closeout phase. We'll get to work on the most critical short timers in storage and plan how to 'bury' the ones that were sent back to Decker. The two we disposed of, I think we'll do last as like most things 'last in, last out'."

"Next and not the least is," Harvey pauses in the midst of the statement and adds with finality to the conversation, "What do we do with Ivan?"

Barry looks at Harvey and Phil with a stare that could make concrete burn, "We'll cross that bridge when the time comes. Don't worry about Ivan."

Chapter 31

Interpol performed a routine check of their database and recent searches. This wasn't performed very often and usually it was due to a new supervisor taking over.

It seemed to be a standard procedure for a new supervisor to want to impress those who hired him or her and do something not obvious to many, which was the routine check for traces. In this particular case, it was nearly a year later that the routine check was made.

Unlike other agencies such as the FBI, or Police, where clandestine searches could be deleted, any search of Interpol would leave a trace behind indicating that a search was performed. The trace didn't always provide a statistical analysis of the search, but the search could be re-initiated providing the analyst with a complete record where only the trace existed.

Interpol didn't do this on a regular basis but could, with the proper analyst, re-initiate a trace of searches, when there was an incomplete record. There was no time limit associated with the re-initiation.

Interpol knew, due to the complexity of their agency and the many national boundaries that they crossed, that there might be clandestine searches of international criminals for personal reasons. Many times, these personal reasons conflicted with Interpol's, which were solely for the purpose of bringing criminals to justice.

With so many international criminals, there were plenty of regular examinations to complete and criminals to catch without worrying too often about the clandestine searches.

In this particular case, the search was a fingerprint match request for one 'Ivan Pochenko' and the results turned up a match to 'Karl Romanz'.

Mr. Romanz traveled to America many years before and his passport indicated that he had not returned. A further check on this file indicated that Mr. Romanz was wanted in Romania in conjunction with a number of murders of Russian messengers.

The Romanian government had a standing warrant with the Russian government to coordinate the extradition of Mr. Romanz, should he be found and the charges investigated further.

It was likely that the Americans also had his name on a list as a person who was an illegal and not registered.

This 'Ivan Pochenko' must be one and the same as Karl Romanz. Evidently Karl changed his name and ran off into America somewhere.

The Interpol analyst promptly informed his manager of the circumstance and situation and was told to contact the FBI counterparts concerning 'Karl Romanz' and 'Ivan Pochenko' being one and the same.

The fact of a trace being performed, even if it was nearly one year prior meant that the person in question was active and alive and was being investigated by someone, someone who was not the FBI or other overt agency looking for criminals.

Because of this and the year delay, the FBI was given an 'urgent' status and asked to find and detain the individual.

The FBI, with their usual efficiency, began the searching and investigating process. 'Ivan Pochenko' was well hidden in his Deckersburg market but not that well-hidden that the FBI wouldn't locate him eventually.

As the FBI search for 'Ivan Pochenko' began, George was immediately given a notification that the FBI was looking for Ivan.

George had set up the parameters for Deckersburg to include all the people in the community as well as who he believed might be participants in the illegal activities at Decker Lake. He didn't suspect Ivan, but there it was in lights, an FBI inquiry.

George began his work through the Agency contacts and to the source of the FBI's inquiry, which happened to be Interpol. A quick call to his contact in Interpol gave him access to the warrant produced by the Russians for 'Karl Romanz', the original name of Ivan, wanted for murder in Romania.

"Son of a bitch," exclaimed George, "son of a bitch. Ivan, the butcher, involved with murder in Russia. What are the odds?"

George updated his forensic white board with this new information. "It's more than coming together now. Mayhem, fraud and disappearing people and now a real and genuine wanted murderer."

George had to make some quick decisions. He needed to bring in the regular authorities into the mix, but he also needed to keep a number of things from them. Of course, he could never tell anyone who he was, nor could he explain much of what or how he had discovered it or his own personal involvement.

George also knew that the FBI bureaucracy would take about two to three weeks from the point of getting the information from Interpol before acting upon it. He didn't want the FBI inserted into this case until he had time to expose the other conspirators.

"I think the best first step is to talk to Bob. He may be only the sheriff but he has police skills and will recognize the situation once explained. I believe he'll also have certain insights to the information and how it's presented but won't ask any detailed questions of me."

George calls Bob at the sheriff's office, "Bob, you and I need to talk and I believe it will be worthwhile. I can get there in about 40 minutes."

"Okay George, I'll be here," Bob answers and wonders at the sense of urgency in George's voice.

George can't bring all the information he has with him as Bob might become overly suspicious and ask him things that he certainly wouldn't ask under most circumstances, but he does bring along enough to make certain that Bob is convinced about the seriousness of the allegations.

George is on his way quickly and decided to stop at the Post Office for his mail. Charlie is behind the counter and greeted George.

"I was just about to leave when I saw you drive up. You have one letter, no return address. Even holding it up to the light I couldn't tell who sent it," Charlie quipped.

"Thanks Charlie" responded George, reentering his car and driving down the road to the sheriff's office.

George parked right in front and quickly covered the short distance to the office. The door has a sign that read "enter, no need to knock" so George does just that.

Bob is sitting behind his desk to the right side of the office and he's shuffling papers to the right from a pile on the left. George can't imagine what these could be in such a quiet town but that isn't why he is here.

"George, have a seat" and Bob, always smiling when he sees George, waves his hand to the seat just across from him.

"Thanks, Bob, I believe I will"

"Bob," says George with a very straight and serious look in his eye and tone in his voice, "I'm going to tell you some things that you might find it hard to believe but please let me finish before you ask questions."

"There's been a, call it 'darkness'. up at Decker Lake for a number of years. It all began just about the time that Jesse sold the tavern to Harvey." George opens up the letter as he's speaking to Harvey and sees it's a message from Jesse. "Bob, I don't believe in coincidences, but this letter just came today and it's from Jesse. Let's just call it fate."

"What's it say?" asks Bob

"Dear George, I hope this letter finds you well. I am doing fine here in California with my son. I haven't included a return address because I'd rather no one knew where I was. Let me tell you a bit about the people who are running the tavern. It was Barry who approached me and made me an offer I couldn't refuse, which is why I sold. Barry is a felon and has been accused of murder, even though he was not convicted. It's likely he bought the tavern for some covert reason and for someone else. Whoever that person is, is likely to hurt you and the community. You would be wise to either get out or inform someone before people get hurt. That's all I have to say. My conscience is now clear. Good luck. Jesse"

"Well, that's a kicker," said George, "I wish I had this sooner".

"Okay, Bob, that being read, I need to tell you a few things and it's important that you don't ask how I came about the information. I couldn't tell you anyway. What I'm about to tell you is going to be shocking and eye opening and now that we've read Jesse's mail, it won't be much more than a finale to his opening statement. I'm going to give you some profiling on Decker Lake and some of the residents here in Deckersburg. You don't have to take notes, because it's all in the pad."

George holds up a small laser printed notepad.

"First, Harvey Paul is a long-time con-man who set up a plan using Barry as his muscle. He forced out Jesse and bought the tavern and now you know that's true, because Jesse corroborated the story."

"You know Phil and May Gruenweld?" Bob nods his head in agreement. "They're the ones who bought the first house in Decker Lake after Harvey bought the tavern. They are also appointed to the Decker Lake Board of Directors." Bob looked astonished as he heard this and even though he didn't ask, he wondered to himself, "How the hell did George get this information?"

"Phil and May own the EverRest Funeral Parlor and EverRest Cemetery just down the road from the Sunshine Forever Home. That's the same home that the Decker residents are being pressured to move to. The Sunshine Forever Home is owned by a Tim and Henrietta Folsom, close friends and associates of Harvey Paul's parents; parents I might add who are both in prison for fraud."

George paused to allow that to sink in until Bob asked him to continue.

"Remember the Mallorys?" Bob nods his head and doesn't say anything as this story is incredible. "Well, Mr. Mallory died sometime back and he had a funeral, but he was never declared dead to Medicaid or the Federal government. In fact, it wasn't until many months later that he actually was declared 'dead' and the Medicaid payments stopped. I believe this has been going on with a number of the residents of the Sunshine Forever Home."

Bob manages to blurt out, "You think this is all about Medicaid fraud?"

"I believe it started that way but now I believe there is murder involved as well." George describes the postcards and their random delivery in the first two years and then the symmetry of the change in the postcard delivery in the last year. He adds that it all started after the disappearance of the Jones woman and the first symmetrical postcards were the Murphys. Bob is just staring at George as to how he put this together. "Random postcards and then symmetrical postcards; who looks at this shit?"

"And Bob" George states for emphasis so Bob will listen and believe, "Ivan Pochenko, our butcher and owner of the market, has an outstanding warrant for murder from Interpol and the FBI is coming for him. It might not be more than a week or two before the FBI contacts Duggin, the DA, for police assistance with his capture. If there is a murderer in our midst, and you know he deals with Barry on a semi weekly basis to get meat and provisions for the Tavern, he may have some involvement."

"Also," George pauses after his last statement, "I believe the Timmins have disappeared as well, even though a Postcard has come to the clubhouse."

Bob looks at George for a long time before he says anything. He knows George is more than he seems and intuitively he knows better than to ask where he's gotten all this information or how he put it together. He believes that George is telling him the details of an extremely sensitive investigation.

"Okay" Bob says in a low voice, "Assuming this is all true, what's our first step? What can we do about it?"

George hasn't thought much about the "how do we get started', just the 'what's going on'. He hasn't really done much on-site Police work.

He decides that the best course of action right now is to let the DA, Izzy Duggin, know about Ivan before the FBI gets involved. This heads up might help Bob when he tells Izzy about the rest of the crap at Decker Lake, so maybe the useless sack of a DA might be encouraged to do something for a change.

It would certainly help his political chances at the next election, which is only one year away. He lays out the groundwork for Bob and some of the reasoning behind it. Although it sounds like a good idea, George's purpose and motives are conflicted. He wants to get these conspirators, not just for the murders he knows they have committed, but with some hope it might lead him to Mary. He recalls that she never sent the safe words, 'I found the earrings'.

When these events became clear, he lost some hope but he needed to know the truth. The thoughts about Mary he did not tell to Bob.

Bob agrees with the premise as laid out by George and decides to contact Duggin first thing in the morning. Bob adds that Duggin is so useless, it may not help.

George understands and predicts that Duggin will take some action, maybe not what they would like but he will do something.

Chapter 32

Ivan has come to the decision that he must get out of Deckerburg. He has more than enough money to buy the new identity and has found a nice little town in California for the relocation. He calls his old friend in Brighton Beach, Brooklyn; a Ukrainian national who is here on an expired work visa.

"Benny, it's Ivan, remember me?"

"Sure," says Benny" I'll call you right back."

Benny calls back from a different cell phone and says "Ivan, how you doing. Is all okay?"

"Not particularly," answers Ivan "I need something new. Can you get that for me and quickly?"

"Certainly," answers Benny, "a complete new or just a little bit?"

"Complete new, and quickly. Premium applies"

Benny understands and responds, "You'll get a package in two days. Just send overnight the airmail."

"Thanks" and both hang up.

Ivan understands the airmail reference and prepares forty thousand in cash for Benny, places the cash into an x-ray proof container, into a FedEx overnight box and sends it off immediately. He knows the workings of Benny and the others. They will prepare a new identity, social security number, everything he needs to move on and become someone else. Ivan will disappear just like Karl. He makes preparations to leave within the next few days.

The day after Ivan ordered his new paperwork, Bob called the DA's office to find out when Mr. Duggin will be in Vermontville. Learning that Duggin will be there Thursday, in the afternoon, Bob made an appointment, stating the urgency of the request and was on his way to meet the jerk.

George preferred strongly that his name must not be mentioned, to which Bob agreed, only that Ivan is wanted and the FBI will be coming for him within the next two weeks. The whole purpose of this visit is to get some action started before the conspirators get away or murder someone else.

George told Bob that under no circumstances, "No matter how much or what Duggin asks, the information came to you from an informed source, undisclosed and will remain so. You let him know that he can either act upon the information or not, his choice."

Bob understood the importance of this because as George was speaking, he was tapping his finger on the desk as to reinforce the words.

It's a long drive to Vermontville and Bob has a lot of time to think about the impending visit to the DA, but most of his thoughts are on what George told him about the Timmins, that they are likely dead.

"Who else is dead?" These thoughts were revolving themselves in his mind, including the uneasiness he felt about the lake residents and the fact that he went to Duggin and got nowhere.

As far as Bob was concerned, Duggin was partly responsible for this for not having acted upon anything back then.

"What an asshole!"

Bob arrived at the DA's office about 2:00PM. His appointment was at 2:30PM. During this half hour he practiced what he will say and attempted to not be sidetracked or distracted by too many questions or snotty comments.

It's nearing 3:00PM when the secretary announced that he can enter the king's chamber. Bob walked in briskly and sat down in the single chair across from Duggin, without waiting for an invitation. Duggin stared down at the random paperwork placed there as a display.

Duggin didn't even look up when he addressed Bob.

"What can I do for you, Bob? I understand it is urgent."

Duggin waved his hand in almost a dismissing manner, as if what could be so important to disturb his day.

Bob, not acknowledging this nasty display, any another distraction or the deliberate long wait outside the office to annoy him, leaned into and above the desk to get Izzy's attention and when he does, just stared straight into Izzy's eyes and told him point blank and not more than a foot from the fat man's face, "You have a wanted murderer in Deckersburg by the name of Ivan Pochenko. The FBI will be contacting you in the next week or so to provide police assistance with his capture."

Bob adds for effect, "It might be good for you to take an action prior to the FBIs arrival. You could get all the credit."

Bob loved that last sentence, condescending and right on the mark, the perfect insult to a useless politician.

Duggin was taken aback by the directness of the statement and his eyes opened wide, his lips began a sentence but not being formed yet, caused them to quiver and him to stammer.

"Fi,fi,fi First of all" replied Duggin moving backwards from Bob's face, "Why would I believe that story and where did you get the information?"

"Izzy" and Bob used his first name to show how little respect he had for him, "That's two questions in one sentence. You can believe it or not, it doesn't matter to me. I told you there was shit going on up at Decker Lake and you ignored it before, so ignore it again at your own peril."

"It comes from a trusted source who believes that the sooner Ivan is brought in, the better. The rest is up to you. You don't believe it, go ask him."

Bob didn't think that Izzy would do that but just wanted to emphasize how important this was.

Bob said "Thanks for the time. I hope I didn't make a long trip for nothing."

He rose from the chair, turned and left, closing the door behind him.

As Bob stood and just before he turned to leave his office and close the door, Izzy waved a hand with his finger pointing upward, dismissing not only Bob but his story as well.

He made sure that Bob saw the gesture. Izzy did this to demonstrate his disdain for Bob, but he also knew that Bob was a top cop from Philadelphia and didn't just come to see him to perpetrate a practical joke. Izzy knew that this had substance, just wasn't sure which direction to take.

Once Bob left the office, he took a deep breath to clear his head. "Man, I really hate that asshole. A year from now, he'll use this as an election issue to show how wonderful he is and get re-elected. Well, so what. This is the same crap that happens everywhere. I've got to let it go."

On the drive back to Deckersburg, Bob wondered what Izzy's next steps would be. He hoped he would take an action and not just wait. Bob never considered that Izzy might drive to Deckersburg to confront Ivan.

If he did, he might have stopped him and then again he might have not.

Izzy wasn't much of a DA and he knew it. He only won the last election because no one wanted to run but next time he would have an opponent. He needed to do something, something proving his bravery, his courage.

He needed to convince this guy Ivan, if he really was wanted, to turn himself in. He just could not believe that there was a murderer in Deckersburg running the butcher shop and for so many years. No, he needed to formulate a plan that would do him some good next year and maybe preempt either a big mistake by the FBI or the capture of an actual runaway murderer.

"I think it's time to take a ride to Deckersburg, maybe get some fresh hamburger, stop in the diner, shake a few hands and walk down the street. No, I'll go to Ivan's market and just ask him a direct question. I'll be able to tell by his demeanor and the response whether I've hit a sore point. If Ivan laughs it off, then I'll go to the diner, walk the street and shake some hands."

Izzy begins to form the conversation in his mind. He would go to the market and wait until no one was inside except for Ivan. He would tell him that his name had come up in an investigation by the FBI and that he should come into Vermontville on Friday to clear everything up. It would be best for all. After Ivan agrees, I can call the newspapers to be there and when Ivan is cleared it would demonstrate my integrity and how I look after people in the community. That's a sure winner. And then the FBI can be informed that their information was incorrect.

He told his secretary that he was leaving for the day and to take messages. He also explained that he would not be in the following day as well, that she should handle the place as she always has. Just to make her feel more comfortable, he told her that she could work on Saturday if she needed to finish up any paperwork or send out responses to inquiries.

The next day, Izzy took the long drive into Deckersburg. He didn't tell any of his staff where he was going, which wasn't unusual because he did that often.

He thought about the great place near the Canadian border that had the finest women. He could participate as much as he wanted and no one knew. And of course, this being Friday, he had a nice long weekend ahead of him.

When he arrived at the market, he decided to park in the rear, not to bring attention to his government vehicle. Parking just across at the cemetery, he walked to the front of the shop and entered, looking to the right and then to the left.

No one else was in there.

It was a nicely furnished store, meat section to the left and market area to the right; neatly appointed and professional looking.

He saw this very large fellow behind the meat counter, wearing a V-neck T-shirt, dungarees and covered by a body apron, slightly bloody from the meat he was carving. He casually and slowly approached the counter so as not to alarm this man, who he assumed was Ivan.

"I assume you are Ivan. Is that so?"

And Ivan nods his head in agreement, "Who are you?"

Izzy acknowledges that most don't recognize him and answers, "I'm the District Attorney for this area of New York."

Ivan shrugs and says "So?"

Izzy continues, "I figured we should have a talk."
"About what?" asks Ivan.

But now Ivan is already thinking about his next steps. Whoever this guy is, he thinks he knows something. If he does, I may be forced to leave sooner than expected.

Izzy doesn't recognize that the stress level in Ivan's voice has risen and he continued, "It's come to my attention that you are a person of interest in connection with illegitimate activity," Izzy deliberately does not say murder.

"I don't necessarily believe that since after looking into your history here in Deckersburg, you've always been an asset to the community. I would like you to come into Vermontville tomorrow morning so we can clear up any misunderstandings. I believe it would be in all of our best interests."

Ivan thinks about what this fellow has said and makes a quick decision. He smiles the best smile he can, without showing too much teeth and pulls out a prime roast from the counter.

"Mr. Duggin, I want to thank you for coming this long distance to talk to me. I'm sure it's just some wrong information or someone else they are looking for. It's a good idea. I'll get Charlie to watch the shop and come to your office in Vermontville first thing in the morning."

"Please accept this roast. It will be delicious. Oh, Yes, I have something for you for later. Please" and Ivan pauses in his sentence for effect, "come with me."

Duggin is obviously disarmed by the fellow's gentle smile and his generosity, so he follows Ivan into the backroom without thinking and just as he enters, Ivan grabs him by the shoulder and slashes his neck at the carotid and along the larynx.

Izzy is at once shocked by the massive trauma and in the milliseconds before the light goes out from his eyes, he wondered why he made this trip alone, but it's too late.

The last thing he sees as he falls to the floor is Ivan standing over him with a grisly smile on his face.

Ivan looked down at the body, the blood draining into the area under the floor he has built just for that purpose and contemplated his next move. He is tired of these people, the pushing, the threats, the questioning. This Duggin is just like the Russian Commander, thinking to take advantage of him, to use for his own purposes.

He doesn't know how the authorities finally discovered him but he was certain it had something to do with Barry.

"Cossack's, all of them!" he couldn't help but utter these words. His eyes narrowed, his mouth turned into a sneer and he thought, "this is the time when they will find our exactly who Ivan is."

"He is Karl, a name I have not thought of in a long time. He is Karl, the butcher of Neag, who understands how to take revenge and this Duggin will be a prime serving."

Ivan stood near his butcher block and pounding his fist as he speaks.

"Karl will come alive once more and Duggin will be like the messengers. Duggin will be the message and Karl will do the sending."

And then in a lower voice, sounding like a throaty whisper, "This Duggin will make a fine addition to the next shipment of meat to the tavern which is this Wednesday. But first, his car must disappear."

Ivan took the keys from Duggin's pocket and drove the car up into the hills where he knew there was a sheer cliff. There, he stopped and looked around to see if anyone is coming. He then pushed the car over the cliff into the woods below.

"This won't be found for a couple of weeks and I'll be long gone."

He knew that he has a long walk back to the town, but he feels he needed it to clear his head. He always felt more comfortable when he spoke his thoughts out loud, as if hearing the words made them more secure and real.

"I just killed the District Attorney," and it came to him of the severity of what has happened. "But I had no choice."

"What is done is done, but this is all Barry's fault, for exposing me. Now it's my turn." he spoke loudly.

"Barry and Harvey must pay for this. Everything was good until they came."

He had resentment in his voice that his years of solitude and peace were gone and he added,

"I will make a special preparation of Mr. Duggin, one that will be appetizing and will teach them the final lesson."

And his thoughts went to how the Russian commander's face must have looked when he discovered what he and his troops were eating.

"He is a fat person so I think he will make a good string of Italian sausage. I can add sweet flavors or spice for those who like a bit of heat. I can add Venison types of spice and flavor and call some of it Venison sausage for those who like deer meat."

And the rest of his plan begins to form in his mind; a truly shocking way of exposing the criminals, Barry and Harvey; and using the community to do it.

"The rest of anything usable I will make into beautiful, plump, lean meat patties, but with one addition." and the forming thought makes him smile.

"I will place one of his teeth flat into every patty and when they come to the tavern for those very best hamburgers in the area, they will get a big surprise."

He laughs at the thought and the surprise by the patrons as they take the teeth from their mouths but most of all he laughs at the revenge he will take upon Barry and Harvey.

It wasn't just the enjoyment he knew he would have by taking revenge on these murderers of the innocent; it was also an objective lesson which would live with Berry and Harvey forever.

In Ivan's mind, that the community is consuming the Duggin will just add fuel to the hatred and revenge against Barry and Harvey. They will be despised by all.

The collateral damage that others were also eating the Duggin did not occur to him. The others were to be used to bring these murdering criminals to justice. The rest of the community, even though innocent of these murders, was not so innocent. If any of them had human feelings about their neighbors, they would have known them, stayed in touch and could have stopped this scheme, maybe even prevented all of the murders from happening.

"Well, they are about to get to know their District Attorney."

Ivan whispers to himself with a small chuckle in his throat as he contemplates their eventual knowledge of what they are eating.

"Bon appetite."

Having returned to the market, he began the process of converting Duggin into the preparations he was considering on his walk. He added enough lean meat to the sausage to keep it solid after cooking and adjusted the spices so the residents would enjoy without complaining that they might be too spicy.

It's the hamburgers that need to be crafted just so, enough plumpness in the center to hide the tooth, placed horizontally in the middle of it. Since people tend to eat around the outside of a large burger before they get to the middle, they will have consumed much Duggin before finding the tooth.

He has plenty of time to put the rest of the DA into a plastic bag and bring his remains into the cemetery area where all of the other bodies are buried. Since there are only bones, skin, remnants and some internal organs, and of course, his head, he decided to place him into one of the previous graves.

"At least," he thinks, "this will be the last of Deckersburg for me."

Chapter 33

Just as Ivan is disposing of the District Attorney's remains in the cemetery, Phil has made his way to the airport for the return trip to Florida and his family. He's formulating a plan to extricate themselves from this morass of fraud and murder and he's certainly not waiting for Harvey or Barry to tie up all the loose ends so 'THEY' can get off while the rest of them disappear.

"Who is this guy Ivan? Just the name gives me the shivers. I've been running funerals and working with the dead for a long time. Handling bodies doesn't bother me and doesn't bother May. Now we've got Veronica involved and she doesn't even know what she's done. No! This is bad ….. Bad."

Phil arrives at the airport in Florida and gets a taxi back to the EverRest where he finds May and Veronica chatting idly and having lunch. He decides to join them.

Lunch being over, he asks Veronica to go to the morgue and clean up. Now he is alone with May. He describes Harvey's end game and how it may take weeks and months to complete. He also describes Harvey's demeanor and how he has asked Barry to tie up the loose ends at the lake and Ivan, who seems to be the ultimate murdering lunatic.

Barry even hints at finishing off Ivan to tie up the rest of the loose ends. Phil explains how he doesn't believe it would be over until all of them are tied up.

"It's easy for Harvey. All he's got to do is rid himself of Ivan and no one knows anything about the bodies. Then he can give instructions to Derik to sell his properties and the tavern, take a good helping for himself and deposit the rest into the off shore account he has. Harvey moves on, Barry disappears again and somehow we have all these missing people that we have Power of Attorney over in storage, empty graves and phony death certificates. It's all on us. Even Cap and Henny can come up with some lame excuse that they had no idea. Burials and handling are all done by the EverRest."

"They can claim sloppy bookkeeping if any monies come in from accounts that are supposed to be closed on account of death. Death certificates get lost, mislabeled, errors in dating, all due to having so many residents and they being so new at this."

"No, it all winds up on us so we need to get started now."

May is looking at Phil and the shock and dismay on his face and knows that he would only be having this anxiety if he knew how bad it was. She wasn't going to add an 'I told you so'.

"Phil," mumbled May, "anything you say. What do we do now?"

Phil was thankful that May was with him completely and also for not adding the 'I told you so', that he knew she was thinking about. He told her what he believed would be a good plan.

"First we need to bury the bodies that are supposed to be buried and cremate those that are supposed to be cremated. This is going to take time. We can't use the services of the caretakers at EverRest. This we've got to do ourselves. That means night work. Each night we rebury at least one body into the empty casket. That will take about thirty days. In the meantime, we can cremate the other ten as they were supposed to be cremated a while ago. We can do this each night or every other night during those thirty days. That means our plan is a month to get the hell out. I'd like to shorten that up."

"As for the death certificates, this is not our primary problem but if the authorities get Cap and Henny, you know they're coming our way next. We'll have the doctor back date them to the original dates and we'll file them as if they were always there. That puts the problem right back where it belongs, to the Sunshine Forever Home and errors in the Medicaid database.

After all, they're the ones who are doing the billing. Just make sure our database is not accessible to any outside warrants or searches.

The only two of the missing lake residents that we had were this Timmins couple but they and their stuff have been cremated and dumped into the gulf."

As Phil rethinks the whole situation, he realizes that he can't just pass blame on Cap and Henny, because it will come back to them as well. No, they're all in it together, down here in Florida.

"I changed my mind. We can't leave Cap in the dark and if we work together, maybe we can rebury two or more each night rather than one or maybe even three. All of us together can get this done and the quicker the better."

May agrees with the overall plan with the exception of including Cap and Henny.

"We don't need to include Cap and Henny because after we bury all the bodies, the only real evidence is the billing. That's all on them. Our end was keeping the dead in storage and the doctor. The doc is so old, he can hardly remember what he did yesterday much less over the last three years."

"Veronica needs to completely disappear before this breaks. We can handle the heat if they find us, but she's not capable of deception."

Phil adds another question. "Should we include Veronica with the burying?"

May thinks about this very carefully because she knows that objectively, Veronica will be a great help, but her condition makes it difficult should she be caught.

"I really would rather not, but I think we need her. We can't complete this on time without her."

Phil and May disagree about including Cap and Henny, but after another lengthy discussion they both understand that the only way out for all of them is to work together, on the burials, the database and the billing.

The next call is to Cap to organize a quick meeting. They maybe have two weeks to get away or at least rebury all the bodies.

"Cap, we need to meet, and meet now. Bring Henny." Cap knows that the plan is collapsing in Decker Lake and tells Phil that he and Henny will be right over.

The meeting with Cap and Henny is tense but all agree that they need to work to get these bodies in the ground. They can reissue the death certificates with original dates and resend them, causing the error to look like it was a Medicaid computer problem.

They'll work it so Medicaid will only expect a few months from eight or so dead as a refund. This will give them time to close up shop and activate their escape plans.

They all agree that telling Harvey about their plans will not be helpful. We don't need him sending Barry down here to tie up loose ends. And after commiserating with how this all began, they all think back to how it started, with Harvey having a good idea, which most of them decided not to do and then they were hooked.

"What the hell!," exclaimed Cap, "We had a good thing going with the Sunshine Forever Home and even if we limited the fraud to just the storage; even if we were only at twenty-three 'undead', we were still making a lot of money and we had almost no risk. What made us add this Decker Lake crap? What the hell!"

"We can't go back more than two years and change what we did" responded Phil. "We're no better than every other typical grafter… … greedy and at the end, stupid."

May couldn't help but insert, "Let's just try to get this over with and not dwell upon what we can't alter. Okay?"

Chapter 34

Ivan receives his package from his friends at Brighton Beach the following day, as he expected. Inside is a full identity change. He will become Alex Cosgrove, a person who lives in a small town in California, just as he requested.

He has a new social security number, new birth certificate and driver's license. The note inside gives him the new address and adds that a rental car is waiting for him in Vermontville under a third name.

Three credit cards are in a small leather pouch. One is under the third name. He has plenty of cash. He understands that when he picks up the rental car, he uses the third name and identity, will drive the car to the second location outside of Detroit, Michigan where a five year old Ford Explorer is waiting for him in his new identity.

There he will leave the rental and pick up the Explorer and finish the drive to California. He will disappear into California just the way he disappeared into Deckersburg so many years before. They add a single sentence in bold type.

"MAKE SURE YOU WEAR DRIVING GLOVES AT ALL TIMES. LEAVE NO FINGERPRINTS."

Ivan packs his bags as minimally as possible with only the personal items that he needs. Everything else he can purchase later. He will take his car and drive to Vermontville, park it behind some alley and walk to the auto rental where he will begin his journey.

But, before he leaves, he must give instructions to Charlie about the package in the freezer and the package of regular items just behind the counter for the tavern. Barry is expected on Wednesday to pick up the tavern's provisions for the next two weeks.

He will tell Charlie that he must go to Vermontville for the day and because it's a late appointment, he will be staying overnight on Monday. It's a medical thing and hopefully it won't be more than one day and he should be back by Wednesday afternoon. He will tell Charlie that if Barry doesn't come in by 10:00AM, he should call the tavern and tell Harvey that he will bring up the items, if Barry is busy.

Charlie is such a good guy that he will have more concern about Ivan's health than to ask any questions and be glad to help.

Monday morning Ivan sees Charlie and gives him the instructions for Barry. Ivan adds a sticky note in the meat package that he has made some beautiful fresh sausage. He knows that Harvey likes to post a 'new special and the sausage would be a perfect choice' for the Friday evening. Ivan also knows that the special for Saturday is always the Jesse Tavern Hamburgers, loaded with everthing you could want.

Ivan writes another note and leaves it in the freezer, under a bag marked 'look in here'. This way, the authorities will know where to look. He is certain that eventually they will come looking for him and discover the note. The note is simple and includes a map. And they will find his souvenirs.

Ivan leaves that evening as planned.

Barry drives to the market to pick up the bi-weekly provisions for the tavern. Charlie is working in the Post Office when he sees him drive up and quickly walks to the market to meet him. He has the spare key that Ivan gave him years ago.

"Barry, Ivan told me to meet you and get you the tavern's package. Come on in."

"How's it going, Charlie? Where's Ivan?"

"Ivan had to go to Vermontville, on a medical thing. He didn't say much else, other than today is when you typically came for the tavern's supplies and asked if I could make sure you got them. That's about it."

The only surprise that Barry felt was that this might have been the first time in all these years that Ivan wasn't in the market. It never crossed his mind that Ivan could have other plans, since Ivan didn't know all the details about the situation.

"Okay," Barry says with a smile on his face. "Thanks Charlie, where's the stuff?"

Charlie is rarely given the opportunity to feel important but having to help Ivan makes him feel useful for the first time in years. This added activity is kind of exciting, getting food and frozen stuff for Barry. He thinks, "Maybe when Ivan gets back, I can offer to work for him, part time, deliveries, packaging, and other things?"

Then he answers Barry. "Stay there and I'll get the box from the freezer. The bags of groceries are just behind the counter. Check out the items just to be sure you have everything."

Barry is looking through the groceries and speaks loudly so Charlie can hear him as he walks into the freezer, "All is okay."

Charlie retrieves the large box from the freezer and hands it to Barry. Barry rummages through the frozen packaging and sees the sausage, London broil, steaks and a large package of hamburgers.

"Perfect as usual," Barry exclaims with a big smile.

Charlie helps Barry bring the packages to his car. Barry waves at Charlie as he drives away and Charlie can hear him say, "Thanks Charlie, see you soon."

When Barry arrives back at the tavern, he restocks the hamburgers into the daily items as they have been running low, typically putting the new burgers to the rear of the older ones, adds the package of sausages, and puts the other stuff into the tavern freezer.

It's Friday and nearing the dinner hour at Jesse's Tavern. Harvey looks through the new cuts of beef that Ivan sent, finds the sticky note and sees the beautiful lengths and varieties of sausage.

"Three different types and quite a bit of it" he thinks, "Ivan certainly knows what people like to eat and his note makes perfect sense. Why not make sausage the special for the evening?" emphasizing the word 'not'.

He adds the sausage to the top of the specials board "Hot, Sweet and Venison," along with the typical Chicken selections, Marsala, Parmigiana, Jesse's famous hamburger smothered in onions and mushrooms. Soups are always the same.

He needs to act as if nothing is happening. Barry's serving tonight but tomorrow, when everyone is eating, he'll be in the woods, dismantling the generator and the speakers.

It's about 4:00PM and the residents begin to shuffle in. It's only Friday but his tavern is doing well and serving about forty dinners in the evening. He has more than enough sausage and will have it as a secondary item for the next day.

For some strange reason, even with the turmoil going on with the scheme, he just loves to cook and serve people. It makes his day when he sees everyone enjoying his offerings.

As expected, most are ordering the sausage, sweet and venison style. The hot doesn't sell as well but he knows it will keep in the freezer. The variety of standard chicken meals and a few hamburgers are ordered. The new burgers in the package are still way back in line.

"It's a good evening at the tavern" he thinks to himself, if he wasn't a schemer he could make a nice living just doing this."

He begins to understand why Jesse loved this place.

The evening goes well. Everyone just loves the sausage and even Bob, still in his sheriff's uniform, decided to come on up and sample some of this great one time sausage special. Bob decided to put the sausage into a pita pocket with mustard.

"Harvey, this is the best," Bob exclaimed loudly so the other patrons could hear.

Everyone laughed and agreed. "Harvey, where'd you get this great sausage combo? It's a perfect blend of hot and sweet. Another patron applauded the Venison sausage and exclaimed, "Haven't had anything this good in years."

Harvey didn't answer them directly and only made certain that they knew that the great taste was courtesy of one fine butcher and the added spices and blend of onions and mushrooms that the tavern always served.

Quite a bit of the sausage was gone, just a dozen links left in the freezer good for about six meals. Typically, when only a small amount of an item was left; either he or Barry would have it for lunch the following day.

Harvey thought about tomorrow's dinner. Ivan made some super-size plump burger patties. I believe that "tavern hamburger specials, made the classic way with a lot of toppings" will be the special for the day, just as they are every Saturday.

Friday dinner is over and the last of the customers leave, again thanking him for the excellent dinner and service. Harvey and Barry sit down at a table near the window to discuss tomorrow's activity.

"Barry, I guess you'll be out there in the early afternoon to turn off the generator and then when it gets darker, you'll begin dismantling the rest of the equipment and wiring."

Barry responds to Harvey's question, "Right, first, I'll turn it off. Anything I can get done without being noticed I will do and likely it will take me all evening to tear it down and remove everything. You'll have to make and serve dinner by yourself."

"I can handle it," replies Harvey. "It's more important that you get this done; one less risk for us."

Barry returns to his apartment and gets himself ready for the next day's activities. Harvey retreats to his quarters behind the tavern. Both are contemplating the end of this scheme, the end of their arrangement and all the loose ends that need tying up. Harvey's loose ends are just real estate and money. Barry's loose ends include a list of people, a list he will never disclose to Harvey.

The following day, just as Harvey and Barry planned, and as Harvey is preparing the Saturday dinner service at the tavern, Barry puts on the camouflage suit and walks into the woods to disconnect the generator and the speakers. It's just past 1:00PM, not late but he needs to get this done, at least turn it off. Maybe he can remove just a portion of the equipment and then get back to help Harvey with dinner. He can finish off the rest of the dismantling on Sunday.

The sun is high but the shadows of the forest are elongating to the sun's rays as it slowly moves across the afternoon sky. Barry works his way slowly into the woods, being careful not to be seen. At the same time, George was taking his daily early afternoon stroll along the path when he saw a shadow in the woods from the corner of his eye.

His training as well as the circumstances surrounding Mary, the Jones woman and the lake kept his senses in a state of alert. George quickly turns his head and directs his vision to the area where the shadow was and sees it again, but this time as a large dark figure literally skulking through the woods.

Didn't Mary say something about this? He tried to remember the exact words, but maybe this is what she said she saw so many months ago. George moved slowly into the woods and kept a low profile as he tracked the figure deeper into the woods. Evidently he wasn't seen, although it seemed that the person he was tracking was looking from side to side and behind him to make sure he wasn't followed.

George was being extremely careful as he followed and then the figure stopped and removed a pile of branches from around the base of a large tree.

George noticed that a small red light was blinking on some kind of equipment under the tree, or in the tree root. But as George was staring into the darkness he accidentally stepped on a dried twig, which snapped, and the large figure quickly turned and stared directly at him.

He was seen. The hulking figure quickly came at him and stopped about ten feet away. It was Barry in a camouflage suit.

Barry looked at George and said in a sardonic voice "Hello George, it's nice to see you out here," and Barry paused and deliberately slowed down the speaking of the following words, "all alone. You look kind of surprised."

Barry smiled and smirked at George at the same time with the most threatening look he could muster. He began to inch closer, so slowly that he believed that George wouldn't notice.

George responded, "What's going on Barry? What's that device in the tree?" George saw that Barry was slowly moving towards him but did not flinch or look as if he would be ready to run.

Not having to answer, but deciding that he would, "It's a low frequency generator attached to activators which make everyone out here feel anxious and depressed; Just like you must feel right now."

Barry, even though he was still more than six feet away, began to loom over him, menacing and intimidating. Barry began smiling more broadly and grinding his teeth at the same time; his jaw clenching and unclenching.

Barry didn't mind telling George exactly what the machine did, because in Barry's mind, George wouldn't be around much longer. He hated that smug face for a long time.

George didn't respond as quickly as Barry thought he might and he didn't look afraid.

Barry wanted to instill either fear or hatred in George, so he'd make a mistake, so Barry added, "How's Mary? Seen her lately?" He tried to insert a hint in his voice that he took care of Mary.

George didn't answer, knowing that enemies attempted to create anger, to gain an advantage.

But George did say, "What's the matter, you going to talk me to death, you big pussy?"

George's advantage was he could quickly understand another's character and what they would react to. Barry's mental weakness was evidently people slapping him in the face with words; not being afraid of his size and strength.

Barry became enraged and charged at George with the full ferocity of his 6'6" 260 pounds of muscle and bone. He wasn't afraid of anyone much less this puny old guy who decided to challenge him.

"I'll crush his head" Barry thought. "I'll smash his face and make him suffer."

In that split instant that George came within his reach and just about to latch those massive arms and hands onto George's neck, George crouched and sprang up with a stiff arm into Barry's nose with such speed and force that his nose was driven into his brain.

Barry died instantly, his massive arms flailing into the empty air and his bull rush landing him on the ground, face down, blood pouring from his face.

The irony of Barry's attack was that it didn't even rise to the level of causing adrenalin to flow into George; that's how confident he was that Barry was not actually a threat.

George actually felt good for the first time in many years. He knew from Barry's tone that he didn't kill Mary; it was just bait talk and bullshit. He looked down at Barry's body and at least for now, he would cover it up with leaves and dirt.

He left the body lying there, in a large camouflage suit heap. There would be no evidence of his attack since he wore gloves and would dispose of them when he returned home.

"There's nothing like a roaring fire to cleanse the soul. My, my, that felt good."

George makes a quick decision. He **will** call the Sheriff and let him know about Barry, what has occurred but caution him to keep this to himself until the entire scenario plays out.

George decides to go home, stay home and wait for the action he is certain is coming. But first, he will turn off the generator. "Not bad work for a Saturday afternoon."

Just before the Saturday dinner hour, when George returns to his home, he calls Bob. George tells Bob that Barry is gone, but hadn't given any specifics; that he'll give him more details later.

Bob, on the other hand, is actually enjoying some of this and decides to go to the tavern for dinner. He believes that Harvey is serving his special "Jesse's Hamburger", as he does every Saturday, and they are the best in the area.

George is interested in learning how Harvey handles the missing Barry, but he feels it would be better if he stays away. Bob, on the other hand, wants to see the action and tells George that he will take notes, and adds "Would you like me to bring you a burger and fries later?" to which George relies "No, thanks Bob, but thanks for the offer."

• * * * *

A week after Ivan disposes of Izzy Duggin's car, the FBI makes first contact with the local authorities in Vermontville to coordinate the required effort to detain one Ivan Pochenco, previously known to be Karl Romanz. The area State Police advise them to call the District Attorney, which they do, that same day.

The FBI makes the call to the District Attorney, Izzy Duggin. His secretary, not knowing where her boss is, but also knowing that he typically disappears somewhere for two to three days at a time, does her secretarial duty and informs the FBI that Mr. Duggin is out for the day and when he returns, she will be certain to have him return the call. Actually, she is considerably concerned because Izzy left last Friday and here it is, Friday, a week later, and he still hasn't returned or called. She can't tell this to anyone and as per his orders; she's not supposed to call him.

Agent Crosby tells her that this is an urgent matter and she should attempt to reach Mr. Duggin as soon as possible. They will be coming into Vermontville to meet with him tomorrow morning. It's imperative that she be there to meet them.

The secretary understands and agrees that she will be there.

The secretary calls his cell phone but it goes straight to voicemail. She tries a number of times with the same result. She decides that it's best that she just leave a message and finish the day as usual.

* * * * *

It's Saturday early afternoon and Harvey has been attempting to reach Barry, but his cell phone goes directly to his message and there haven't been any return calls. Harvey needs to get the dinner menu ready for the evening's patrons.

With the sausage being mostly eaten, he prepares the menu specials with those super plump Ivan special hamburger patties as the top item, just as he and Barry had discussed the prior afternoon.

Harvey wonders where Barry is and wouldn't be surprised if he ran off into the woods and disappeared rather than go through all the crap that they had to do to close shop.

Shrugging those thoughts off, Harvey concentrates on the evening's repast. "I'll pile those burgers high with sautéed onions and mushrooms, add some Canadian bacon and an assortment of melted cheeses."

Harvey loved serving the community even with all the trouble he knew was coming. He still had a firm belief that all would be okay and that they made their decision on time.

* * * * *

The FBI sent two agents early in the morning Saturday to Vermontville to meet with the District Attorney. One of them was Agent Crosby and the other Agent Harwood; both just stared at the secretary.

Agent Crosby, looking down to her desk, saw her name plate and inquired as to the location of Mr. Duggin.

"Ms. Randolf, do you know where he may be?"

The secretary again told them that he was not in and didn't know. But she didn't add that she was worried, likely more about herself than Izzy. It had been eight days. She became visibly upset and told them that sheriff Bob........

"Who is sheriff Bob?" said Agent Crosby interrupting her flow of words...... she stammered and added "Sheriff Bob Winkler from Deckersburg. I didn't mean to overhear but he told Mr. Duggin that this fellow Ivan was wanted for something and that Mr. Duggin should get ahead of this somehow."

"I know that Mr. Duggin seemed to dismiss Mr. Winkler and after the sheriff left, Mr. Duggin also left for the day."

Crosby continued his questioning. "Was that Ivan Pochenko they were talking about, the owner of the market in Deckersburg?"

"Yes, I believe so."

"And you haven't seen him since?"

"No." and by this time she was sobbing, because she knew something was wrong.

All three went into Duggin's office and the two agents searched through the desk drawers and a stack of papers on the desk while the secretary stood by the door, her chest heaving. Crosby's partner said "Bill, look at this." He said while pointing to a note left by Duggin to get quickly over to Ivan's; for a talk.

"You stay here where we can get in touch with you." Crosby directed her to back to her desk

The two agents conferred just out of her ability to hear what they were saying.

Agent Crosby added, "If you leave for the day, we'll need to have a contact name, telephone number and address. Is that okay?"

"Yes." And she wrote down her contact information on a sticky note and gave it to Agent Harwood. She was sobbing just a bit, knowing that something was wrong; first the sheriff and this Ivan fellow and Izzy leaving and now the FBI, and Izzy not coming back.

Agent Crosby called his office and explained the basic situation. He was told to take the ride to Deckersburg and stop by the market, say hello to Ivan. If necessary, they could call the State Police later, but in the meanwhile, they needed to assess the overall situation and circumstances.

* * * * *

Meanwhile, back at the tavern, it's nearing 12:00 noon and Harvey is contemplating the first dinner seating and preparing the rolling chalk board with the list of specials. Top of the list is the famous Tavern Hamburger Special, A half pounder smothered with a list of toppings. Barry has not shown up and still hasn't answered his cell phone. Harvey believes that Barry has fled but isn't particularly worried. They will all proceed as planned.

Harvey knows where the generator is and will go there on Sunday just to make sure that Barry took it with him or at least turned it off. If anything, it's well hidden and no one will find it.

Chapter 35

Ivan has taken his time driving from Vermontville to the location in Detroit, Michigan where he leaves the rental car and picks up the Explorer for the last leg of his trip to Southern California; a Ford Explorer, registered to his new name. He made sure he wore gloves during the entire time of his drive to Detroit so no one could track his fingerprints.

His new address is in a town near the Mexican border called Chula Vista. He plans to open a hamburger and juice bar on Paloma Street, close to a mobile home park. It is there that he can disappear into the low income wage earners and immigrant population.

He arrives in Detroit four days after he has disposed of this guy Duggin and his auto.

He thinks about what might be happening right now at the tavern and again chuckles about what everyone will soon discover.

He thought about the lake residents and the meal they would be eating. Even though his scheme was to get revenge upon Barry and Harvey for having exposed him, he also thought about these residents of the lake; these older people who didn't care enough about each other to stay in contact when they moved away.

"What was wrong with them?" he wondered, "that they thought so little about others to not even make a telephone call to say hello? Well, now they will get a 'taste' of what it's like when these sheep have so little caring that they let a wolf into their midst."

When he thought the word 'taste' he gave a little chuckle. "And people say I have no sense of humor."

As he sits behind the steering wheel of his Explorer, he marvels at how comfortable these American trucks can be. He thinks back to his last days in Romania and realizes that his good fortune was made from the tragedies of his past.

He hopes that he can live out the rest of his life in peace, in his new place in Chula Vista, California.

*　　*　　*　　*　　*

FBI Agent Crosby and his partner arrive at the market about 2:00PM. The door is locked but Charlie sees the two men in dark suits and comes quickly from his bait shop to ask if he can be of assistance.

Agent Crosby casually asks Charlie if he has seen Ivan. They need to ask him a few questions. Charlie is inquisitive and asks, “What about,” even though he knows it’s none of his business.

Of course, Agent Crosby explains that it is confidential and again asks if Charlie has seen Ivan. Charlie explains that Ivan left about last Monday evening and he hasn’t seen him since. Ivan told him he was going to Vermontville for a medical issue and asked him to take care of the market until his return, which he said would be Wednesday.

“He hasn’t come back yet and I haven’t heard anything from Ivan since. The only other person coming by was this guy Barry, who works at Jesse’s Tavern up at Decker Lake, picking up the provisions for the next couple of weeks. I have a key if you’d like to take a look inside.”

Agent Crosby agrees and Charlie opens the door. Crosby asks Charlie to remain outside and both agents draw their Glock19s and enter slowly. Crosby walks to the left and his partner, Jim, to the right and they meet at the rear of the market at a door that enters into the back room and shed area.

Crosby opens the door slowly, announcing himself and he and Jim enter the rear area and look around. No Ivan to be seen, just packages of boxes, bags and tape and a large walk in freezer. Crosby opens the freezer and half expects to see Duggin hanging from a hook, but the freezer just has meat products and large packages of frozen items stacked neatly along the sidewalls. They can’t look into the place any deeper than items that might be in plain sight without a warrant, so they decide to leave for now.

The two agents walk outside to where Charlie is standing and give him their cards, telling him "Please, if you hear anything, call either of us."

Jim wants to confer with Bill away from this Charlie character.

"Hey Bill. How about we go for a cup of coffee? There's a diner just down the road a bit."

"Sounds about right to me," replies Bill and the two agents walk down Main Street to the diner. Charlie stares at the two as they walk away, thinking, "Where the hell is Ivan? And what are these guys looking for?"

* * * * *

It's the first seating of the evening for the tavern. Typically, the oldest residents, who decide to come to the tavern for dinner, arrive for this seating, 'The senior citizen seating'.

Harvey thinks, "Sounds strange calling it the senior citizen seating when the whole place is senior citizens, but some are more senior than others."

He laughs at the thought.

He counts ten customers, seven of which order the burger special. As he's preparing the specials, another group arrives along with the sheriff, who always loved the burgers. They all take seats and as the first meals are cooking up on the grill, he takes orders for eight more and a double without the buns for the sheriff.

Using a serving cart, he brings all the meals out at once, seven burger specials, two chicken souvlakis and a ham sandwich and distributes them to the customers.

Just before he brings out the meals, he places the next set of burgers on the grill, preparing the next set of orders. He's no Barry, but he's pretty handy in the kitchen.

Ivan has carefully placed the teeth into the center of the large patty, so it would be the last part eaten, unless someone decided to cut the burgers in half.

This was not the case at Jesse's this night as all the patrons were dining and enjoying the great Tavern Special Burger plate when the next round of prepared foods were served to the sheriff and those that entered with him.

A third group had just arrived and was being seated. Harvey thought, “This is going to be a great night for the tavern. Too bad its’ got to end.”

* * * * *

The EverRest Funeral Parlor had been closed for four days, with a sign on the front door indicating that renovations were taking place and they would reopen shortly. Cap, Henny, Phil, May and Veronica were working each evening from dusk to dawn reburying bodies in the cemetery.

Fortunately, the cemetery only used part time grave diggers and didn’t have a staff. Visitors only came during daylight hours when the gates were open, 9:00AM to 4:00PM.

They had been able to rebury 20 bodies, using the trencher and digging equipment. Veronica, being agile, was able to hop into the grave, open the empty casket and maneuver the body into it, with the assistance of ropes and pulleys setup by the other four.

The effort to rebury the ‘undead’ was actually quicker than they thought it would be and only twenty or so bodies were left. At this rate they would be complete by the middle of next week.

At least all the physical evidence would be in the ground. Exhuming these bodies would take more court orders than the authorities would be able to get. And all they would find would be bodies, no foul play.

Phil thought “At least this part of the plan is going okay and ahead of schedule.”

He didn’t believe that they had months, but only weeks to get the hell out. He and May had the place mostly mortgaged, so the cash was theirs and now being well hidden off shore. When they left, they’d be leaving as rich people, likely never having to work again or do this bullshit any more.

Phil was mentally smacking himself in the head for not listening to May way at the beginning of this.

* * * * *

Danny was sitting with his wife Betty at a corner table. Both had ordered the burger special. He bit into the center of the Tavern burger and almost chipped a tooth.

“What the hell?” Danny yelled loudly, as he pulled a tooth from his mouth. He thought it was one of his own at first, but after feeling around in his mouth with his tongue, realized it wasn’t one of his own.

But the object he had bitten on is a tooth.

“What the hell? There’s a tooth in my burger. There’s a tooth in my burger.” He yelled for effect and in disgust and stood up.

The others turned to him as he yelled and then another bit into the burger’s center and bit down on a hard object and pulled it from his mouth.

“Shit, there’s a tooth in my burger, too.”

And then the third diner, an elderly woman, did the same and screamed “Oh, my God, oh my God!”

All the others stopped eating and began digging and they each found a single large tooth in the center of their burgers. The sheriff did the same and he immediately recognized that these teeth were human.

“Stop eating” sheriff Bob yelled to everyone,” Stop eating. It’s human teeth.”

The old people, who were able to, began screaming, leaping from their tables, pushing chairs over and others were vomiting. It was a puke and horror fest. Even those who ordered the chicken began vomiting and screaming.

The sheriff went from table to table collecting the teeth and looked directly at Harvey.

“Don’t you move.” he ordered Harvey, “Don’t you move.”

He pulled his gun and held Harvey, telling someone, anyone, to call 911.

“Get the State Police here. Make the call now.”

Bob handcuffed Harvey to the radiator, told some of the patrons who by this time had stopped screaming and vomiting and were still in the tavern, to watch him and he went into the back room.

He knew he should wait for the State Police, but he just ate there yesterday and even though he didn't take a bite of the burger, he had a strange feeling that whatever was in the meat today was in there before.

Bob opened the refrigerator and saw the pile of fresh burgers and the left over sausage. "Shit," he thought, "I hope this sausage wasn't somebody else."

The FBI had been monitoring the police band because of the circumstances surrounding the Deckersburg resident, Ivan Pochenko, so they heard on their radios when the State Police were called to go to Decker Lake, specifically Jesse's Tavern.

George was also monitoring from his office.

An elderly resident named Harry Hess, sounding mostly insane, made the call to 911 and was screaming and gagging at the same time "that human teeth were inside of the burgers at Jesse's Tavern and somebody better get up here and quick."

"This guy Harvey is cooking and serving human teeth in his burgers." Harry gagged and threw up again.

The operator who took the 911 call could hardly believe her ears and didn't think that questioning the caller would gain any other insight, so she relayed the call immediately for dispatch. Thirty minutes later, two State Police patrol cars rolled up in front of the tavern.

Guests were still outside; trying to clear their stomachs of anything they might have eaten, spitting and rinsing their mouths with carbonated water.

Some became so ill that the volunteer fire department was called to send ambulances to bring them to Vermontville and the nearest hospital.

Inside were three people, Harvey, the owner and evening's cook, Sheriff Winkler and Harry, the caller.

As the Police entered the tavern, the sheriff walked up to them and gave them a handful of teeth from the burgers that were already eaten. His police training was useful in this situation and he directed them to the uneaten burgers on the various plates that weren't overturned and to the refrigerator where a pile of uncooked burgers still remained.

The Police called a forensic team and within the hour they arrived as well, taking charge of the 'evidence'.

By this time the FBI agents had left the diner and took that drive up to Decker Lake. They arrived at the scene just about the same time that the forensic team arrived.

Agent Crosby was conferring with the lead forensic investigator and the Police sergeant, who seemed to be in charge.

"What's this about human teeth in the burgers?"

The sergeant replied, "They look human, but we'll need to get this whole place checked out. We're taking the cooked burgers, teeth, the uncooked burgers and all the meat to the lab for identification."

Agent Crosby told the sergeant that one Ivan Pochenko, the owner of Ivan's Market, seemed to be missing for about six days.

This fellow Charlie told him that he gave a meat package with sausage and burgers to a guy named Barry four days ago, just helping Ivan out while he had something to do in Vermontville.

"Coincidentally, the District Attorney, Izzy Duggin, is also missing." Agent Crosby continued, "I know this is a local matter and you guys are in charge, but we have a warrant for this Ivan character on an Interpol issue. Would you mind having one of your troopers accompany us back to Ivan's Market for another look around?"

The sergeant agreed and one patrol car, one patrolman and the two FBI agents in their own vehicle drove back to the market. The sergeant called his office to arrange for a search warrant and have someone bring it to them at the market.

Everything was wrapping up at the tavern. Harvey was taken into custody despite his protesting that he bought this stuff from the butcher. He didn't make it, just cooked it.

The forensic team and the State Police having taken as many statements as possible, and some of them visibly sickened by the picture in their minds, placed a 'crime scene' banner over the door of the tavern and left for their barracks.

The FBI said they should hold Harvey as a material witness for now and that he might be a flight risk. A number of people were missing. Ivan, Duggin and a big guy named Barry.

Bob called George and asked if he could come over. He had plenty to tell and he'd rather not do it over the phone. George didn't say that he knew about the 911 call and the teeth, but it sure sounded interesting, and he thought, grinning widely and happy he wasn't eating at the tavern, "was something he could sink his teeth into."

While the authorities were driving to the market, Bob was walking to George's, needing the long walk to clear his head and his digestion. Before Bob could knock, George opened the door. He saw him coming up the walk on his surveillance system.

"Come on in, Bob. We have a lot to talk about."

* * * * *

Agent Crosby, Harwood and a trooper parked at the entrance to the market and once again, Charlie saw the action happening and rushed out to meet them. A search warrant was waiting for them when they arrived, so there wouldn't be any legal hassling because of the search.

The judge who had the warrant request had to read it twice since it had 'eaten human remains' and 'human teeth' associated with a butcher shop.

Charlie had the key ready and was again prevented from entering.

It was a crime scene just as the tavern was up in Decker Lake.

This time, a forensics team met the agents and the trooper and began cataloguing everything. They took all the meat from the refrigerator, the shelves, and the freezer.

Agent Harwood noticed a paper bag in the freezer just sitting on top of a few packages. Written on it were the words 'look in here', not some ambiguous written note.

"Bill, take a look at this," shouted Jim from inside the freezer to his partner who was rummaging through the shelving section behind the butcher's counter.

Bill answered Jim and responded "Bring it over here."

Taking the bag to his partner, they opened it and found teeth, many more than from one person. And under the pile of teeth were a note and a map.

"You have found this bag of teeth. It is from many people but the only teeth in the hamburger are from this fat guy Duggin. Follow the path in the cemetery to a spot that you will find marked."

"In the graves are many people from the past as well as from Barry and Harvey. A girl brought them to me with a van with the words 'Sunshine Forever Home' on the side panel. They have forced me to take this action because they are criminals."

"They told me I must dispose of the bodies, so I did. I am sorry for Duggin. He was in the wrong place at the wrong time."

"I hope everyone enjoyed the sausage and hamburgers."

The two FBI Agents looked at each other with a sense of nausea, astonishment and incredulity in their eyes and when they called the trooper over to look at the note, he almost gagged and was forever thankful he never ate at Jesse's Tavern.

He placed a call to his barracks, gave them an indication of what they had found and told them to hold Harvey on suspicion of murder.

The forensics team had a lot of work to do.

* * * * *

Bob and George sat on either side of the dining room table, with the fire roaring and the wood crackling belying all the ills of the world that just came to light in Decker Lake.

George could not explain his position but needed Bob to understand and agree to that simple fact. Everything else would shed light on the terrible events and Bob was needed to bring all this information to the authorities without exposing him.

George told Bob where to find Barry's body and added.

"There are no forensics to lead anyone to his killer."

George told Bob about the low frequency generator and the activators still in the trees and how the unheard sound made people fearful and anxious.

George had previously told Bob the balance of the details about the Medicaid fraud deal going down with Harvey, Phil and May Gruenweld who owned the EverRest Funeral Parlor and EverRest Cemetery and the Sunshine Forever Home who happened to be owned by a fellow named Tim and his wife Henrietta, close friends of Harvey's parents.

He reiterated to Bob that if the FBI looked into the death certificates and the actual burials, deaths and cremations, they would find that Medicaid was paying for many dead people, still claimed as residing at the home.

They need to look for those who never arrived, like the Hendersons, the Murphys and the Timmins. They might even find signs of Evelyn Jones.

George told Bob, "You can bring all this information to them but you need to say it was left in a plain envelope and you don't know where it came from. I'll give you the printed version so when they ask you for it, you can hand it over. Don't worry, it can't be traced."

George felt he should add just one more detail. "Bob, let them know that there is a large crematorium at the EverRest Funeral Parlor. Even after cremation, some bits of bone and material may be left and possibly they can find some evidence of others that might be missing. Anyway, it's just a thought."

Bob had a lot of questions that George could not or would not answer. But George had previously provided the details of the plan and the people and this was just added information. Bob agreed and did exactly as George said.

* * * * *

The following day, after the forensics team left the butcher shop, another forensics team went into the cemetery to the location on the map provided by Ivan. There they found the old graves and when opened, they found the bodies of three unidentified couples and three elderly people, two women and one man. One of the couples was dismembered and had parts put into small bags.

All their teeth were missing. The Medical Examiner would be matching the teeth to the bodies and then begin the process if identification.

A black bag was included with the bodies. It contained the skin, bones, internal organs and a head, with all of its teeth missing. One of the forensics Police said it looked like the DA. The ME said that he had never seen or heard of anything like this nor would he want to again.

Subsequent to the identification it was remarked that the Timmins couple and Evelyn Jones were not located.

* * * * *

Sheriff Bob called the State Police and asked for the lead investigator on the case surrounding Jesse's Tavern. He explained that he received a package with details concerning the case and would like to bring it over.

Of course, they agreed and told him that they had set up a field office on Deckersburg at the rear of the bait shop. It seems this local guy Charlie had plenty of room and very little business and was happy to rent out the space.

Bob agreed to meet them there and on the third day after the puke fest at Jesse's, Bob sat across from the State Police investigators and the FBI agents who were also participating and gave them the large brown envelope with the paperwork inside, detailing the entire scheme and who were likely involved. It also had a location of Barry's body and the generator.

Bob asked if he could be written into the investigation as he was also involved with the investigation of the missing Jones woman and there may be others as well. All agreed that he could be, but parts of the investigation were interstate and were in the purview of the FBI.

The ME had already identified the remains of Duggin as this was a priority. DNA proved that the teeth as well as the hamburger itself were human remains, specifically Izzy Duggin. A DNA match to Duggin was also made from the sausage that was still in the freezer and refrigerator at the tavern. All the other meat products were actually products from animals.

Those that had the chicken rather than the sausage were relieved.

As this was being described, Bob turned slightly yellow as he remembered shouting how great the sausage was. He knew that he ate quite frequently at Jesse's Tavern, where the butcher's products were typically used.

Thinking back, he understood and expressed to the team what it meant that the community was well served by Harvey. Everyone around the conference table became nauseated by the thought.

And not being a queasy person, Bob added the next thought for effect, "I didn't like the fat bastard anyway, and he wasn't much on a sandwich either." What he thought was a joke didn't go over very well.

* * * * *

The group in Pensacola wasn't aware of the dinner time horror that happened that evening at Jesse's Tavern. They were working diligently to rebury all the bodies and actually only had a small number left before they would be done. Maybe they had four or five more days of work and then they're all not only dead, but buried as well.

The following day, Sunday, Cap tried to call Harvey and all he got was a ring and then the answering machine.

"Sorry we can't answer your call right now. Please leave a message and we'll get back to you as soon as we return."

Phil tried to call later on and received the same message and this went on for the balance of the day and the next day. Calls to Harvey's cell phone received the same result, ring no answer and only a number you have reached is, "Leave a message at the tone." The same result occurred with calls to Barry.

Neither Cap nor Phil left messages and since they had privacy on their phones, the Caller ID would not be captured.

Cap, Phil, Henny and May met for a lunch at the Sunshine Forever Home and talked about the lack of response at Decker Lake.

Phil began the conversation with a simple question "Where are Harvey and Barry? No one answers the phones, not local or cell."

Cap decided he would be the next to speak out "Okay. It's an unknown. They don't answer the phones and they don't call. So they must be gone, maybe got out quick leaving us holding the bag."

"I suppose so, but how can we be sure?" Phil responds

May was the next to speak out. "I don't know, but let's work as if they are and not worry about it, with the exception that we better get this done and quick."

Phil adds "No more calls, no more contact. Agreed?

"Agreed." all respond.

They would all work diligently to get the rest of the bodies in the ground but it was time for Veronica to disappear. She wouldn't be needed for the last of the bodies. Veronica had a passport and could make her way to Mexico, where she would travel down through Central America to an old friend living in Panama, just in site of the canal.

There she would stay and live and do the best she could until they could join her. Veronica knew that this might never happen but true to her nature, she felt no emotion about it, just the factual evidence of the circumstance. May gave her the car, an envelope filled with cash, told her a number associated with a private bank in the Cayman's and to get going and get into Mexico as soon as possible.

When asked at the border the purpose of her visit, she should respond that she was traveling for pleasure, just a short vacation. From there she knew exactly how to get to her mother's friends in Panama and never to mention their names to anyone.

Veronica knew how to follow instructions. She said good bye and left without turning around. The four watched as she drove away.

All that remained was to finish the work, close up the shop here at the EverRest and at the Sunshine Forever Home and disappear.

*　　*　　*　　*　　*

The following day, the ME declared that the DNA of the teeth from the bag matched that of the Murphy', the Hendersons, the Goodmans, Rae Magon, Sue Middleton, and Carl Peters, all of whom were supposedly residents of the Sunshine Forever Home in Pensacola.

The Timmins' bodies were not found even though they left for the Sunshine Forever Home. Airline tickets were found in their name, and they were seen boarding in Albany and then arriving at the Pensacola airport. A security camera at the airport verified that they met a young woman with a sign and followed her. No further security footage was available. The young woman was identified as Veronica Gruenweld. The Timmins never arrived at the home.

An inquiry to the Sunshine Forever Home was not made at that time to ensure the secrecy of the raid at the home and then at the EverRest Funeral Parlor.

Using the paperwork provided by Sheriff Winkler and armed with the DNA evidence, a search warrant was issued to the FBI for the Sunshine Forever Home and the EverRest Funeral Parlor and EverRest Cemetery.

*　　*　　*　　*　　*

Veronica drove to the nearest American - Mexican cross point and managed her way into Mexico. She then drove through Mexico and eventually to Panama where she met her mother's friend, Gustavo. Gustavo sold her car to some people in Columbia, so if anyone were able to trace its' progress, they would see it passing through a border checkpoint into Columbia and Veronica would be safe in Panama.

The day after Veronica left for her trip to Panama, the Pensacola police and FBI units raided the Sunshine Forever Home and rounded up Cap and Henrietta. They were both charged with Medicaid fraud and held without bail until the final details surrounding the murders of the elderly residents of Decker Lake were disclosed.

Phil and May Gruenweld only had four bodies left to bury when they received word that Cap and Henny were arrested. They both knew that attempting to flee would be ineffective since they were likely under surveillance. So they both sat quietly in their home in Foley when the police came, read them their rights and took them away.

They never found Veronica. The last trace of her location was traveling into Columbia and disappearing. First degree murder, embezzlement and fraud, were only a few of the charges in absentia against her.

* * * * *

Shortly after the remains of the District Attorney's body were found and the details surrounding the horrors of Jesse's Tavern and Harvey became public knowledge, George had another meeting with sheriff Bob. They met at the clubhouse so George could get a handle on the finality of the arrests, at least those that Bob knew about. Bob brought the coffee and donuts and both sat across from each other at one of the round tables.

It seemed that Ivan escaped into parts unknown and Derik couldn't be charged with anything concrete. Veronica Gruenweld also disappeared. The last known location for her was at a border crossing into Columbia. George thanked Bob for the information and added that he hoped that they could always meet under better circumstances.

Bob agreed with that assessment and added that from that point forward, they might just go to the diner in town for a cup of coffee. Neither could bring themselves to ever eat Jesse's again, which was closed and for sale.

After the meeting, George walked slowly along the lake path to return to his lake front home. As he walked to the left at the fork, he heard a familiar voice calling his name.

Turning slowly, he saw what he believed to be a ghost. It was Mary, looking a bit older but just as beautiful. She ran into his arms and began explaining why she wasn't able to contact him and why it was so difficult for the past year.

George was taken aback and in shock by the unexpected return of his beautiful Mary, someone he believed might have died the year before and someone he believed suffered the same fate as so many others at Decker Lake.

But his love for her overcame his despair, loneliness and shock and he hugged her tightly, vowing that they would never part again, "Until the next time," he thought to himself.

When they returned to their lake home she continued her explanation by telling the whole story, how her anxiety got the better of her and the shadows in the woods and whispers in her head made her more susceptible to depression and suggestion; also how their 'friend' at the Agency contacted her and told her that she was needed for an assignment, not George, and needed to disappear and quickly.

"Remember the day I left," she spoke softly and slowly, "They directed me to a drop off point where the typical transfer happened. The Volkswagen was driven by another Agent elsewhere and I was transferred to an SUV and taken to a secure location."

George took in her words like a dry sponge longing for moisture.

"Once I was 'placed', I was not allowed any external contacts due to the sensitivity of the assignment. It wasn't possible to send the follow-up message. You can't imagine how I worried about you. It's not like we were in our twenties or thirties or even in our forties."

George had tears of joy welling up in his eyes and knew exactly what she was talking about.

She couldn't tell him about the 'assignment', which George fully understood. At the time, she felt it was important for them to leave the lake; and didn't know that all of the anxiety and trepidation was caused by, as she found out later on, the low frequency assault. The day after she left, the feelings of uneasiness began to dissipate and she never understood why, until the Agency just told her about the low frequency noise generator.

No one else could ever know as it was classified information, even if in the public domain. There was much she could not tell George, with the exception that the 'assignment' was over and they could resume what was left of their happy lives. And she told George again, "I am so sorry that I could not get the second code words to you but I was isolated and it was just impossible. Forgive me."

Somewhere deep inside the recesses of George's analytical mind was the understanding that the Agency knew about the code words and they wouldn't allow the follow-up for a variety of reasons. One of which was certainly to keep the Agents separated and not dependent upon each other. He would keep this in mind and vowed to find another way, should this circumstance happen again.

"There's nothing to forgive. It's been our lives forever. My heart is so happy that we are together again." And he turned and kissed her gently on the forehead, cheek and lips.

"Let's go for a walk"

George and Mary walked hand in hand along the road. His love for her overwhelmed the feelings of loss he had for the last year. They would leave Decker Lake and never look back. And if the house never sold, they couldn't care less.

The evil at the lake would remain and the dead would never rest, even though most of the monsters were either caught or killed.

George said he found a very nice and secluded area in Southern California called Chula Vista. They could afford a spot in a mobile home park just off the main highway.

EPILOGUE

The FBI entered the mortuary with a search warrant and found the remains of some of the once residents of the Sunshine Forever Home, but all the deaths were from natural causes.

All of the debris in the crematorium was sent to a special FBI lab in Virginia for analysis. This, they all knew, would take considerable time and any answers secreted within the debris might never be found.

The data records compiled by May were recovered by FBI specialists and were pristine. It was easy to recompile the embezzlement from Medicaid by those that died locally and were not reported for a number of years. Exhumations were not required.

The database included the Timmins couple. Since they were not in the cemetery at Decker Lake, the Gruenwelds would be questioned as to their location. Hopefully, either one or the other would provide the answer.

Derik, although questioned by the FBI and the State Police, was not implicated in any of the schemes because all they could prove that he did was sell properties and make a nice commission.

After the news hit the tabloids, and seeing headlines that read "Eat your Neighbor at Decker Lake," and "DA becomes dinner for Decker Lake Residents," and "Duggin burgers are a special at Jesse's Tavern," sales of properties at the lake fell dramatically.

Derik decided it was time to move on but hadn't picked a location yet. "Maybe he'd go west. California had a lot to offer."

The residents of Decker Lake, who normally frequented the tavern, reacted with revulsion to ever eating meat products again and generally did not go out to eat.

Many became vegetarians.

One older couple, who were farmers in their youth, began raising and killing chickens on demand for the community.

The Decker Lake side of this horror for the last year was still mostly unknown and still being resolved. The State Police were satisfied that the FBI, working on an international warrant, would uncover all the horrors and share the information.

No one would ever find Evelyn Jones or the Timmins couple.

And as for Ivan; Ivan (now Alex) looked peaceful as he walked the streets of Chula Vista. The small eatery that he purchased was doing just fine and making just enough money to keep him comfortable. It was nice that after all these years he believed he found a place that he could call home.

"Grandpa, you would be proud."

ABOUT THE AUTHOR

Martin Zuckerman is a baby boomer (someone born after WWII) who has written and published a number of articles and technical papers for the Information Technology Industry. His first novel, “Going for the LAUGH”, was originally published in 2003. He is currently living nearby a peaceful and serene rural lake community. This is his first entry into the world of mystery.